PENGUIN BOOKS

HOW IT HAPPENED

Shazaf Fatima Haider was born in Islamabad in 1982 and received her master's degree in English Literature from the University of Karachi in 2006. She is a writer and teacher and is currently based in Karachi, Pakistan.

PRAISE FOR THE BOOK

'Full of charming irreverence and nail-biting suspense, this delightfully funny book by a fresh young author is a great read'—Bapsi Sidhwa

'A delectable, laugh-out-loud family tale about negotiating age-old marriage traditions in contemporary times. Shazaf Fatima Haider will delight you with the feisty, outrageous and witty women who people her world' —Chitra Banerjee Divakaruni

'Shazaf Fatima Haider's unfailing eye for drama, warm-hearted understanding of human foibles and her sparkling humour make her the person best-suited to tell this moving, dramatic tale. *How It Happened* is destined to become a classic, and its author one of the most important writers of her generation' —Musharraf Ali Farooqi, author of *Between Clay and Dust*

'Hilarious'—*Dawn*

'A delightfully funny book…readers will fall in love with the characters' —*The Express Tribune Magazine (Pakistan)*

…aracters, this book will …o lives with imperious

How *It* Happened

The Story of an Arranged Marriage
Based on Many, Many True Stories . . .

SHAZAF FATIMA HAIDER

PENGUIN BOOKS

PENGUIN BOOKS
Published by the Penguin Group
Penguin Books India Pvt. Ltd, 11 Community Centre, Panchsheel Park,
New Delhi 110 017, India
Penguin Group (USA) Inc., 375 Hudson Street, New York, New York 10014, USA
Penguin Group (Canada), 90 Eglinton Avenue East, Suite 700, Toronto, Ontario,
M4P 2Y3, Canada (a division of Pearson Penguin Canada Inc.)
Penguin Books Ltd, 80 Strand, London WC2R 0RL, England
Penguin Ireland, 25 St Stephen's Green, Dublin 2, Ireland (a division of Penguin
Books Ltd)
Penguin Group (Australia), 707 Collins Street, Melbourne, Victoria 3008, Australia
(a division of Pearson Australia Group Pty Ltd)
Penguin Group (NZ), 67 Apollo Drive, Rosedale, Auckland 0632, New Zealand
(a division of Pearson New Zealand Ltd)
Penguin Group (South Africa) (Pty) Ltd, 24 Sturdee Avenue, Rosebank, Johannesburg
2196, South Africa

Penguin Books Ltd, Registered Offices: 80 Strand, London WC2R 0RL, England

First published in Viking by Penguin Books India 2012
Published in Penguin Books 2013

ISBN 9780143421436

For sale in the Indian Subcontinent only

Typeset in GoudyOlSt BT by R. Ajith Kumar, New Delhi
Printed at Shri Krishna Printers, Noida

In memory of my father
Syed Wasi Haider
(1934–2009)
Here's to a hole-in-one in heaven, Abba!

Contents

Chapter One

How Dadi Got Carried Away

The history of arranged marriages in our family starts with a single white-robed Sufi who arrived one day in the village of Bhakuraj and saved the life of the local medicine man—Pir Jan—who was asleep under a banyan tree. Sufi Sahib saw a cobra undulating towards Pir Jan's conical head. Sufi Jee shouted, the cobra panicked, and Pir Jan woke up just in time to see the black creature slithering away. In a show of gratitude, he offered his daughter to the Sufi, who promptly married her and settled down in the village and became the first Bandian of Bhakuraj.

The Bandians of Bhakuraj, true to their ancestral heritage, married not for love but because it happened to be convenient. It was the same with my grandmother. Dadi was considered a veritable spinster in her day because her marriage had been arranged and then un-arranged three times. While most girls at sixteen had already blessed their husbands' families with at least two or three boys, she remained disgracefully single.

'And there I was, unmarried. Toba, those were terrible days, I can still remember. The local midwife, who also procured proposals for girls in our village, said it was because I wasn't fair like milk. My complexion was like old register paper: sometimes yellow, other times filled with spots, but never glowing or radiant. But my mother knew the real reason why I wasn't married yet. It was the evil eye! Hai, the number of spices she burnt to undo its evil effects! Always on a stove she was, burning one chilli pepper after another. I had many envious relatives, you know, because their daughters were not nearly as blessed as I was, despite my complexion. Some had blunt noses. Others had no lips. Masooma Khala's daughter had hair that looked like rat-tails sewn up together! Now who would marry them, just tell me? So people used to ask for my hand in marriage. But then these same ugly girls and their mothers would do black magic and then whoosh, the engagement would be broken.'

I listened, lying on my stomach with my face in my palms, eagerly awaiting another Bhakurajian tale—one of many my grandmother told every night before dinner, firing up my imagination and taking me into the world of her past, where she had been a teenager.

My great-grandmother had taken great pains to ward off the evil looks that envious relatives had aimed at her precious daughter to safeguard her remarkable beauty, colour notwithstanding. And don't you forget: she *had* been beautiful! Eyes as round as the moon that glistened as if full of tears. In those days, the moisture of unshed tears in a girl's eyes was a sign of beauty. It proved that she was too delicate for the roughness of the tough and wicked world and therefore quite useless and overwhelmed when it came to accomplishing practical matters at hand. This, in turn, proved that they were true nobility. Dadi had attracted many a lustful gaze with her full lips and small nose that resembled a button of her future husband's coat—the very one he had worn the day he had swept her off her feet. She had been petite, with a waist so narrow that it had been easy for my grandfather to circle it with just one hand. And indeed, it was this particular characteristic of my grandmother that, she said, was so influential in her kismet.

One day, her story goes, after having been refused by yet another family who wanted someone younger for their son, Dadi had fled into the garden to look at some jasmine flowers blooming at the time of sunset.

'It was almost Maghrib, and the moon had come out early. I think it was the twelfth of Rajab. My mother had burnt some spices around my head, since she was sure that some evil influence had resulted in the break-up of my proposal. I picked each little flower and dropped it into my palloo. I was wearing a pink shalwar-kurta . . . no, no, I don't care if I said yellow before—it was pink, now stop interrupting me. Where was I? Haan, I was in the garden, full of motia. Hai, the smell of those flowers was so heady! Even now, I cannot say my prayers without some of those little pearly flowers on my prayer mat. All of a sudden, there was the sound of hooves and your Dada rode into our garden. On a big black horse he was. What do you mean brown—were *you* there or was I? Do you want me to continue or not? He took one look at me and let out a loud yell. I was so shocked! I took a few steps back, almost falling into the motia bush. But he kept riding and upon reaching the spot where I was standing, he scooped me up in his arms! I fell into a dead faint! Your Dada, Allah send peace to his soul, told me later that he had come to meet my father but when he saw me, he fell in love with my eyelashes because they were so long and my lips so moist and full!'

'And then what happened, Dadi?' I asked, anticipating scandalous details of passion consummated at the inappropriately holy hour.

'What else? He marched straight into my house and asked my father for my hand in marriage!'

'But Dadi, what did he do with you in the meantime?'

'Hush! Don't be badmaash! What does it matter? There were more important matters to consider! He might have left me on his horse. I don't remember. I was unconscious, as I have told you before. My father, Abba Huzoor, insisted that he meet with your paternal great-grandfather—as is the way in all good families—it is the parents who discuss issues of marriage, not the young people. My marriage was arranged within a week. So you see Saleha, it was only after the spices had been burnt that my marriage was set up. The Bandian line was started with an arranged marriage, which is the only Islamic way to get married. May Allah always guard us from the evil eye!'

Dadi swore by spice burning. She believed that the Bandians have been, are and always will be infinitely superior to everyone else. This made us likely targets of

envy and jealousy of other families. Spices, therefore, offered
protection and enabled the procurement of proposals all in
one go. The minute Dadi suspected the workings of the evil
eye, she marched into the kitchen, took out the longest, most
menacing red chillies, burnt them on the stove and twirled
them around the head of She Who Was Being Harmed (in
most cases this was my elder sister, Zeba Baji, who Dadi
was convinced was the recipient of envious looks due to
her beauty). If the burning resulted in an acrid odour that
caused one's phlegm to rise up in one's throat, then it was
a false alarm: no evil eye—for the time being. However,
if there was no smell, then it was an ominous but certain
sign that a black spell of jealousy had indeed been cast,
but which the searing magic of the spices had kindly done
away with. As a safeguard against the routine envious looks
that naturally came in our direction, Dadi practised this
exercise at least once a week. Anything less frequent was
considered careless.

I had several reasons to doubt the account of how Dada
chose my grandmother. Though shrunken and frail in her old
age, Dadi had once been of robust physique and disposition.
She was a woman of steely resolve and, no doubt, had a
uterus made of the same material, having given birth to six
daughters and three sons. Therefore, the brown-and-white
pictures encapsulating her past showed her to be a short,
somewhat plump woman with a waist resembling a barrel
rather than a bedpost. Also, since she had survived two
wars and the death of two of her three sons, I had grave
doubts that even as a sixteen-year-old she could faint under

any circumstances or let herself be picked up by any horse rider. A tight slap would have been a likelier course of action considering her personality. But apparently, picking up women was not an anomaly in the village of Bhakuraj at that time. Dadi would answer my objections with an 'Arey Baba! How was I supposed to know that he wasn't like Raja Takhur Majhu?'

The Raja in question was a frequently cited example of the evil impetuosity of love marriage. He had come riding into Bhakuraj one day and seen a young widow in a white sari, sitting on the porch of her in-laws' house, in front of a little coal stove, making chappatis for her mother-in-law who treated her like a slave, no doubt blaming her for her son's untimely demise; since it is well known that the wife's fortune affects that of her husband. Seized by passion, he had ridden up to her and scooped her up, just as she sat, squatting with her knees drawn up against her chest. It was reported by my grandmother, in a low whisper befitting the telling of most horror stories, that he had disappeared with her for six months, and when she had returned, her belly had been round with his child.

Another reason I objected to the veracity of Dadi's story was because my Dada had been a frail, asthmatic man. I found it unlikely that he would have followed the Raja's example of scooping a woman up and then dumping her on his horse while he dealt with matters more practical. He would more likely have gingerly stepped into the house with a handkerchief on his nose to ward off the dust and let his father do all the talking while my grandmother illicitly listened from the women's quarters. However, she was fond of the dashing tale of her romantic-but-arranged marriage and I knew better than to challenge her.

Dadi believed in a few basic things: spices, prayers and arranged marriages. She repeated the tale of her marriage often because it illustrated a philosophy she had ingrained in her daughter and her daughter's daughters: there was greater romance in arranged marriages than in the irrational immorality of love marriages. We were therefore to rely on the elders of our family for the management of all proposals, never taking matters into our own hands. We were to remain in a state of feminine helplessness, much like Dadi in pink—or yellow—as she remained unconscious on her future husband's horse, while her almost-captor had the good sense to consult her father before almost-kidnapping her.

'Dadi, *surely* someone in our family must have married for love?' my sister Zeba asked her.

'All good girls marry boys of their mothers' choice,' was the predictable reply. Her starched white sari rustled like the pages of a book as she straightened up from her normally hunchbacked frame to make this Sacred Proclamation like Yoda from Star Wars. Zeba instantly nodded her head in agreement and Dadi recoiled back into her shrivelled-up eighty-year-old self, satisfied that she had been heard. But after some grunting and betel chewing, she revealed rather reluctantly that there was an exception.

'There was a girl by the name of Iraj. But she was a cousin twice removed, who wasn't really a cousin at all but a distant relative of my sister's husband's aunt's daughter's niece, so she doesn't really count. She love-married. Shameless creature she was. Born and bred in a respectable family, nearly as well off as us. But what did she do? She ran away! Eloped! And with whom? That's the final nail in the coffin. Ran away with the haveli chowkidar's son! A gardener! Of all people I tell you, a gardener!'

Dadi rolled up a betel leaf and thrust it into her mouth and chomped with firm resolve as my mind flew to this mysterious Iraj whose name was Never To Be Mentioned. I imagined a girl like me, only prettier, gazing down from her balcony at the man she loved, his shalwar sticking to his sweaty legs, the epitome of virile masculinity. He would stop at his work in the garden to rest, wipe the sweat off his forehead and look up, his black eyes gleaming in the scorching sun. His gaze would meet hers. Then he would pluck a rose and look at her, kissing it sensually with his lips, and smile as she blushed. And then she . . .

'Her mother tried to commit suicide and her father couldn't show his face in public again! Such shame she brought to her family. I know I haven't raised *my* girls like that, no Baba! My girls will trust my judgement when a proposal comes their way, not run off in lust like wanton prostitutes with the first man who catches their fancy!'

My daydream ended as Dadi, in her white sari, once again dominated my thoughts. Of course, we would never shame Dadi in the way Iraj had shamed her parents. We were no ordinary folk! Our last name was Bandian, and it was respected wherever we went. We hailed from an ancient village called Bhakuraj in India, a village that had become famous for its female population's singular trait of unquestioningly deferring to their mothers' wishes when it came to matters of matrimony—just as Pir Jan's daughter had willingly married the Sufi whose hair had been just as white as his robes once he had taken his turban off. Through the use of guile, blackmail and several subtle and not-so-subtle pressure tactics, our great-grandmothers, grandmothers and mothers had managed to avoid the stigma of love marriage blackening the name of our prodigiously chaste family tree. Not one of our female relatives had been exempt from the Sacred Tradition: each saw her husband and Representative of God on Earth through a silver mirror placed on her lap during the ceremonial Ar-see-masaf with only a discreet glimpse of the face that was to dominate the rest of her life. Before I proceed to tell you about the event that shook the foundations of our household and deep-rooted regard for all things arranged, I think it prudent to explain how holy the halo of prearranged nuptiality that hovered around our family honour was.

Chapter Two

How the Bandians Were Married

My grandparents had been married off very quickly, lest my grandfather change his mind and back out of the arrangement in the style of his predecessors. As was done in most respectable families, the couple did not talk to each other before the marriage, but spoke for the first time on their wedding night.

'What did you talk about, Dadi?' I asked, hoping for a story that would infuse some personality into the dour-faced black-and-white portrait that hung in Dadi's room. Dada had died before my eldest brother had been born; hence I knew nothing about him and was always looking for some information about the man who had managed to stay married to my strong-willed grandmother.

'What a question to ask! Why, you girls these days know no shame! Asking your grandmother what she talked about on her wedding night! I can tell you, though, Saleha—there were no love poems! Sensible Bandian women know that this love-shove business is all nonsense. We must do our duty to please God and our husbands. That's it!'

This reply disturbed me because I thought my duty to God was quite different from my duty to my husband. Surely the latter had *some* enjoyment in it? But it seemed to be close to the truth, because Abbu told me that Dada and Dadi had maintained separate bedrooms and rarely talked to each other except on matters regarding finance and the procurement of suitable sons-in-law. Nevertheless, I suppose they managed to garner enough enthusiasm for each other off and on to produce my six aunts and my three uncles, all of whom were born within the space of fifteen years. After that, my grandmother took upon herself the role of the matriarch, the mother of three eligible sons, who more than made up for the disadvantage of six daughters who would need to be married off one day. Moreover, she was unusually savvy about procuring suitable husbands for her female offspring. Needless to say, they were all arranged marriages.

Sakina Phuppo: She was the eldest daughter and was married to Hussain Alam, the renowned poet who was not able to earn a decent amount of money from his poetry alone. He came from a respectable Shia family, and Sakina Phuppo never saw or talked to him until her wedding night. On that fateful occasion, he recited a number of verses on the wisdom of economy in the household in sophisticated Urdu that she didn't understand, so she started crying. He retreated to a separate bedroom. She was therefore miserable for the first half of her marriage. They had a son and made several sacrifices to send him to a good college. He earned a degree in accounting and got a job in the city. Soon, he called his parents and asked them to leave the village and come live with him so that he could take care of them in their old age. Phuppo was delighted and moved in immediately. She was therefore able to live the next half of her life in luxury in Calcutta. Her husband, to her secret joy, remained in Bhakuraj where he died writing a ghazal lauding the beauty of the cow that provided him with his daily milk for breakfast. It was then that she discovered with horror that he had actually been a communist.

Fatima Phuppo: She was otherwise known as Fati Phupps and was my father's favourite sister because it was she who had really brought him up, since Dadi was already quite old by the time he was born. Fati Phupps was married off to a businessman who owned a shoe factory. Every day for the ten months of their marriage, he returned home smelling of rotting skins and processed leather and therefore, she never allowed him to touch her. Of course, this made for an uncomfortable arrangement, which lasted until his death from asphyxiation after having inhaled a lifetime of fumes in his tannery. She is fifty now and has no children and is very relieved that this is the case. She looks at the lives of her other sisters and brother and proudly proclaims herself free and a feminist. She is an editor of a women's fashion magazine in Lahore and has taken to wearing sleeveless sari blouses and has the best figure I have ever seen in any fifty-year-old woman.

Zainab Phuppo: She is the most prolific family member to date. Proudly boasting five sons and no daughter, she is constantly on the look-out for an eligible girl. Her sons are all short and fat and Canadian citizens, like her husband Kareem. Fati Phupps says that when Kareem first came to see Zainab Phuppo, he had parted his hair in the middle and worn a safari suit. Zainab Phuppo had been quite dismayed at seeing her fashion-disaster of a fiancé. But since he was a stockbroker and from a good family, his proposal was accepted and Zainab Phuppo, like an obedient daughter, relented. But I'm told she did manage to persuade him to abandon the safari suit for trousers, which he wears so high that he resembles a grey waddling penguin with two arms moving valiantly with every step he takes. However, compared to his safari suits, his new style is generally considered a positive step in fashion.

Rania Phuppo: She was selected by her husband at a wedding when he saw her reflection through his glass of champagne. At that time, the Bandians had moved to Pakistan while her future husband, Suleman the Third, was still a resident of Bombay. His numerical epithet was merely an attempt by his incredibly rich family to make him feel more important and boost his self-esteem, which had taken quite a blow when he stopped growing once he reached five feet three inches. Dadi first refused the match, but he threatened that he would never marry and went on a protest fast so that his desperate father had to travel to Karachi to beg my Dada to accept the proposal. My grandfather was alarmed that the continuity of Suleman the Second's line depended on his assent and therefore consented to the match, much to the ire of my Dadi. She feigned the Second Faint of her life, but to no avail. In the end, they were married, and Rania Phuppo is very happy and manages to flit across the Line of Control to visit Dadi annually. She has two daughters who are extremely snooty.

Abbas Chaccha: He died before Dadi could arrange his marriage. 'He was such a frail child,' my Dadi remembers tearfully on every twenty-seventh of Shabaan, which is his death anniversary. He was twelve years old when he died. It was his habit to play all day in a field behind the house. It was suspected that he was accustomed to periodically quenching his thirst from the lota in the bathroom, because the kitchen had to be accessed by crossing the courtyard, which was too much of an exertion. Due to this unfortunate habit, he contracted dysentery, and the fever affected his brain. He remained unintelligible but conscious for a few months before Dada Jan found him dead with flies buzzing around his open mouth.

Fareed Chaccha: He also died before his marriage could be arranged. Dadi maintains that he died because he was about to love-marry. I don't believe her. Fati Phupps says that he was quite the ladies' man, the Casanova of the university where he studied English literature. He frequently fell in love and out of it and it was all considered a great joke, except by my Dadi who informed him that he could do as much of this 'love-shove' business while he was single, but when the time came, she would choose for him a nice Shia, Syed girl. Despite her warnings, he hurtled into a romance with a Sunni named Ayesha whose parents had Wahabi leanings —they wanted my uncle to 'convert' before he could marry their daughter. Dadi was outraged and declared that it was the girl who should convert to Shiaism and change her name to Fatima or Zainab. In the midst of this, the 1971 war broke out and Dada thought it prudent to move to Karachi. Fareed Chaccha was heartbroken because he was forced to move, too. He enlisted in the Pakistan army and went to East Pakistan to be with his true love. Nothing was heard of him again. Dadi was notified by the army that he had been killed in battle by the Mukti Bahini but his body was never discovered. Dadi was heartbroken and to this day, she wakes up at Fajr and prays to Allah that her Fareed will return. Now, having lost most of her senses, she harbours the belief that he has been snared by his Sunni girlfriend named Ayesha and that he is still angry with her. She sometimes suffers bouts of fury at his Wahabi in-laws who have made him a ghar-damaad, and since it is better to be angry than depressed, we think this delusion is healthy for her.

Haseena Phuppo: She is a sour woman who has never been able to live down her name, especially because it doesn't ring true. Many a proposal was reeled in on the basis of her name, only to be spat out on the basis of her face. She remained unmarried until the age of twenty-seven, which was considered the point of no return in those days. Dadi had to work extra hard, but she managed to arrange a meeting with a divorced man who had no hair and no sense of humour. These handicaps were not considered too crippling, so he was approved, and Haseena Phuppo was married off to Uncle, whose name to this day we do not know, in a small, rushed and embarrassed ceremony. She has a son, Hassan, who is loved by all because of the affable ease with which he is able to interact with those around him. He is living proof that two negatives make a positive.

Malaika Phuppo: She has two passions: her husband and her shoes. Her marriage had an inauspicious beginning. It is reported that when she first met Raheel Phuppa in Dada and Dadi's drawing room, she declared, in a dramatic fashion, '*Ye Shadi Nahi Hogee!*' Dadi slapped her and Dada Jan apologized. Phuppo ran out of the room and Raheel Phuppa fell in love with her instantly. A Harvard graduate, he thought everyone was beneath him, and he found it a huge turn-on that *he* was beneath someone else. Although his parents left the house in a huff, deploring the impertinence of modern girls, he resolved to woo her and win her, which he did, after a year's courtship. So once more the parents met in the same drawing room and Malaika Phuppo was brought in, eyes downcast and grinning ridiculously. To this day, she and Phuppa glance dreamily at one another, and are, according to my mother, a little too touchy-feely in front of everyone else. I think it's rather romantic, actually.

Hussain Bandian (Abbu): He, needless to say, is my father. Being the youngest and the only surviving son, he is the sun, the moon, the maghrib and mashriq of my grandmother. He wanted to join the army, but Dadi had horrific recollections of 1971 and forbade him from doing so. So he became a doctor and always smells of antiseptic, even on weekends. My mother tells me she almost died of shock when Dada, Dadi and Abbu came to see her for a match.

'I came in, carrying a tray of Rooh Afza which I gave to

your father. When I bent to serve your Dadi, she took the glass and said, "Yes, yes, she's very fair. We'll have her." Just like that! Can you imagine? As if I were a goat they were buying for Baqra Eid! Of course, I almost refused, but when I saw your father looking embarrassed and mortified, I decided to give the family a chance. And I'm glad, otherwise I wouldn't have you!' she said, drawing me in for a hug.

My parents had three children—my eldest brother, Haroon Bhai; my sister, Zeba Baji; and of course, me, Saleha Bandian. My brother is the second apple of my Dadi's eye, because he apparently looks remarkably like Fareed Chaccha. Therefore, when he finished his master's from New York University and came back with a degree in business administration, she took on the business of arranging a match for him with zealous enthusiasm.

Chapter Three

How Haroon Was Tied to the Knot

The male Bandians of the family historically have tended to be less hardy and more temporal than their female counterparts. Dada Jan was the only frail and wheezing remnant of the six heirs of my Par Dada, each of whom died either in bed or in street fights or while attempting to swallow a fistful of sewing needles. Be it genetics, machismo or pure stupidity, men died fairly early in prior generations, without having sired future Bandians. Therefore, those who managed to survive were held in great esteem and affection. Accordingly Haroon Bhai, who was good-looking by normal standards and long-lasting by our family's, was awarded the status of a brown-skinned Adonis by Dadi. My grandmother, who usually went overboard in all aspects of life and also in her love for her grandson, suffered palpitations—real and imagined—whenever he was away.

Dadi's inordinate love for her grandson manifested itself in a small library of pictures kept in a huge chest of drawers.

The first drawer was filled with Baby Haroon Baba shown as a shrivelled infant; as a crawling blob of fat on her carpet; and as a toddler sitting naked on the baby-commode while being potty-trained. Dadi wanted to frame this last flattering photograph, but Haroon Bhai declared he would never talk to her again if she did, so she desisted. The second drawer contained snapshots of the adolescent and teenager: Haroon posing for the camera with a posture emulating that of Hulk Hogan, who had been his favourite WWF wrestler when he was growing up; Haroon smiling shyly at my cousin Naureen, a distant older cousin who grinned at the camera, well aware of his fourteen-year-old affection; Haroon grinning proudly at having won the science exhibition at school; Haroon with a new haircut; Haroon wearing a brand-new kurta, lovingly stitched by Dadi; Haroon with his first car; Haroon on his first day at college; the list went on and on. We estimated that Dadi had about three thousand pictures of our brother. The last two drawers of the dresser were reserved for pictures of Haroon Bhai's wedding and his future offspring. Dadi had great hopes for her beloved grandson. When I asked her where Zeba Baji's and my chests of drawers were, she replied, 'Don't I have framed photographs of both my chandas on the wall?' Since her two chandas were lost amidst the sea of faces of her other grand-offspring, it was clear that furniture storage space was to be reserved exclusively for Haroonmania.

Apart from arranged marriages, Haroon Bhai was Dadi's favourite subject. 'Doesn't my Haroon look like a prince in this photograph? I still have this shirt he's wearing; *your*

mother wanted to throw all his old clothes away but only a
grandmother knows how precious these memories can be!
Hai, I still remember when Haroon was born . . .'

And then we would hear the story of how Dadi had had
a dream that she'd have a grandson a day before my mum
went into labour. She had made herself a jubilant presence
in the delivery room and almost danced a triumphant
bhangra when he was born.

It was not unusual for my grandmother to be present in
the delivery room with my mum. In those days, except for
a famous Parsi gynaecologist who was very Western in her
methods and therefore not visited by respectable families
like the Bandians, the only option was to go to a Ms Zubaida
Malik, a spinster who had strict rules about chastity. She
was a stickler for segregation, having forbidden the entry of
all husbands into the delivery room—deemed by her to be
a women-only domain. Once, a mother brought her child
and complained that it was suffering from colic. The straight-
laced doctor undid the baby's diapers and her chaste eyes,
which strictly observed the purdah, were offended with the
spectacle of a tiny masculine member aimed straight at her
face. So flustered was she at this violation of her See-No-Evil
policy that she immediately put the diaper straight back on
and forbade the woman from ever entering her clinic again.

In any case, Ms Zubaida Malik believed that the joint
attendance of both sexes at such an occasion was disgusting
and offensive, thus the birth of a child was for female eyes
only. My mother's mother was a weak-willed individual
who gave way to my Dadi's strident demands that only the

paternal grandmother of the incipient infant be present at the time of birth to ensure that it would be a boy. Dadi had therefore stood next to my screaming mother as Ammi gave birth to Haroon Bhai. If my mother resented the absence of her mother, she never mentioned it. Although Dadi reported that once, when the going got tough, my mother turned around and sank her teeth into her palm. I suppose Ammi figured that this was the only time that Dadi wouldn't be able to hold it against her.

As time went by, one more set of photographs was added to the collection in the chest of drawers: that of Haroon Bhai graduating from IBA with a bachelor's degree in business administration. It was generally believed that he would do his master's from the same university, but one night, while we were watching a drama on the NTM channel and Dadi was dozing off on the sofa, we heard a whoop and a holler. Our brother burst into the room saying, 'I've been accepted by New York University!'

My father jumped off the sofa with an 'Acha?' and went to the computer room to confirm if this proclamation was based on credible evidence. My mother was taken aback, but then she looked at us and started laughing. I remember only registering that my brother was happy, so I did a little jig that I had seen Scooby Doo doing on Kid's Hour. Zeba Baji, more perceptive and wiser than all of us, glanced warily at Dadi who was blinking away tears and preparing herself for the tantrum of the century.

'What if he gets married to a gori? My handsome young grandson married to a huge cow with hair like a broomstick who eats McDonalds-Shuck Donnels and all manners of haram meat all the time? No Baba, no! I won't let that happen! Bahu, how can you allow this?'

'But Dadi, I've received a huge scholarship from New York University! My tuition will almost be free!'

'You can continue to do your MBA from where you are. That way I will have you with me. Why do you want to leave me? Don't you love me any more?'

'Oh-ho Dadi! Don't be so infuriating!'

'Haan haan, call me infuriating! I, who changed your diapers and woke up in the middle of the night to sing you to sleep! *I'm* infuriating.' By this time her shoulders were beginning to shake and Dadi's frail form started to sway with emotion. 'Okay Beta, I'm used to it. This was my fate, raising you, slaving away for you and then having you call me . . . How do you youngsters say it? A pain in the buttocks!'

Since all of this was blatantly untrue, Haroon Bhai was momentarily silent. He stole a look at my mother and saw her rolling her eyes.

Dadi had a great fondness for telling everyone how she had helped her daughter-in-law bring up her children, when all she had done was issue instructions from her chair and expect them to be followed. Those included edicts like: 'The milk is too sour, get another bottle' or 'Change her clothes she looks like a parrot in that dress.' And none of us ever slept with Dadi in her bedroom at night for her to sing us to sleep, so there were no lullabies. Ever. There was a very good reason for this.

Dadi was mortifying to sleep with at night. I suppose

it is so with most old women. She had prayed five times a day from the moment she had hit puberty, but after I was born she made an occupation out of her religion. Her worship schedule would commence in the middle of the night, when she would switch on all the lights in her room, thereby jolting the unsuspecting sleeper out of his slumber. Then began the elaborate ritual of her ablutions. Off came her precious gold bangles with a loud series of thuds on her dressing table. Then she waddled into the bathroom without closing the door, distressing the sleeper who was no longer asleep with sounds that should, under all circumstances, be kept to oneself. After a mortifying forty-five minutes in the bathroom, she would emerge and sink down on her prayer mat with a loud and slow 'Allllaaaaaaaah' that was both a call to God and complaint against her stiff joints. Then began the long-winded process of the Tahajjud prayers, after which she would say her Fajr prayers. Out came her prayer beads and she said a prayer and then blew it on everyone's face. The habit disconcerted us at first, but we became immune to it later. When I was much older, Dadi took her 'phoonkification' or blowing to a whole new level. She blew at everything that she deemed needed protection. When my hair turned silky in winter, she blew on it, so that it would never revert to the stringy, curly mess it formerly was. When my father developed a paunch—a sign of prosperity—she blew on it. When I turned twelve, she blew on all of me and the candles on my birthday cake for good measure. When Haroon Bhai received his bachelor's degree, she blew on the degree. When my mother purchased an expensive new console for the entrance of our house, she blew on it. She soon spent all her time praying and blowing and then sitting down in a huff proclaiming she was growing old because she was dizzy and out of breath. Nothing could distract Dadi from her self-appointed duty as the family's protector against the invisible forces that she was convinced would harm us, if it were not for her prayers and burnt chillies. I remember one day there were no chillies to be found in the kitchen. Dadi was convinced that Zeba Baji's flu was the work of an evil eye. Unfazed, she decreed that the prayers to God were an excellent alternative. She blew so hard and so frequently on the patient's head that she nearly fell on top of Zeba Baji. Thereafter Ammi appointed it my duty to keep a glass of water handy at all times in order to avoid a real faint.

The process of morning prayers took about three hours. Exhausted, she would collapse on her bed, beginning a whole new cycle of prayer and puffing, this time to protect the house from the evil spirits of the early morning. Throughout this time, the unfortunate sharer of her bed suffered in resentful silence and with a firm resolution never to spend the night in Dadi's room again. If we happened to fall asleep despite the disturbance, the periodic jet streams of air inevitably directed our way would awaken us repeatedly, as we were specifically included in her prayers for protection. Hence, any assertion of having 'raised' us was a falsehood. Dadi was too busy fending off the evil eye to have actually done anything of the sort.

But to get back to Haroon Bhai who, with a petulant pout, was proclaiming: 'Come on Dadi, what can I do to convince you that I will be fine? I'm only going for two years, and then I'll be back and with you all over again.'

'You say you'll come back. All boys say they'll come back. But look at what happened to Qurrat-ul-Aine's son? He went away and stayed away. And he married an Amreekan! Not even a white one, that would have been bad enough, but a kali! Oh, how my heart goes out to my poor cousin!'

The cousin in question was hardly a kindred spirit as the matrimonial conquests of her children equalled those of Dadi's children. Therefore when we discovered Salman had married a rather buxom African American woman with a voice like a trombone and a laugh like a tuba, we were amused. Dadi, however, had been careful to hide her secret ecstasy at having involuntarily bested her cousin by marrying all her children to pure-bred Indo-Pak Shias. That Dadi was also racist and had a well-developed paranoia of all dark-skinned individuals was also well known to all who knew her. Therefore, this false proclamation of sincere sympathy was wisely ignored by my brother.

'I won't marry anyone you don't approve of. Okay?' reassured Haroon Bhai.

Since that was exactly the promise Dadi had been working towards all along, she suddenly stood up. Slowly, she took her dupatta off her shoulders and bid my brother: 'Come here!'

Mystified, Haroon Bhai complied.

She tied one end of the dupatta around his hand and put the other end against her heart.

'Now hear this: you've said that I will choose the girl you will marry. I will never approve of anyone Amreekan, unless, of course, she is Pakistani, Shia, Syed, Urdu-speaking and has lived most of her life in a respectable neighbourhood in a proper Pakistani city. If you do not, then I pray to Allah in front of witnesses that He take my life: let my soul slip away from this body and may this heart beat no more.'

Shocked at this uncalled-for theatricality, Haroon Bhai nodded and looked warily at the knot, affirming his promise to marry only as and when my Dadi approved. She nodded and blew on it for good measure.

'Dadi, you're being very unfair!' Zeba Baji protested while Haroon Bhai continued to blink at the knot. 'Haroon should have the freedom to marry someone he likes!'

'You be quiet! Listen to you! *He should marry someone he likes* . . . Hussain! Look at what your daughter is saying! Good sons let their elders choose their wives for them. Do you hear what I am saying, Zeba?'

Zeba bristled but Haroon Bhai gave her a pleading look not to rile Dadi, whose assent he required to proceed with his foreign plans without guilt. She sighed and retreated behind her copy of *Lolita*.

Zeba Baji and Dadi didn't get along. I thought it was because Zeba Baji had once bitten Dadi's hand when she had been trying to feed her some karela and roti. Dadi used to make little ships of roti which contained her concoctions of gravy that were little more than a combination of oil, soya and meat or vegetable. She used to make up a story each time she made a little bite for us to eat—'In this bite I'm putting your father . . . you want to eat your father?'—to which the gullible child was expected to reply in the affirmative with great alacrity and chomp on its predecessor while Dadi went on and on about how good children should never eat their parent. It was an exercise in guilt that reaffirmed respect for our elders in the most unusual way: while we chomped on Abbu, we were reminded of all the great things he had done for us so that by the time we had swallowed him, we felt very bad for the crime we had committed and made it up to him by being extra nice to him when he returned home in the evening. We sometimes ate people who Dadi didn't like very much: such as Qurrat-ul-Aine Dadi. We were never given a guilt trip for *her*! 'Oh, you can eat Qurrat, but remember to chomp extra hard—her meat might be tough and rotten.' While Haroon Bhai and I enjoyed this game immensely and were easily manipulated into remorse at having consumed our forefathers, Zeba Baji used to chomp on her ancestors with great gusto and never felt guilty for her crime. Once, Dadi made a ship of food which supposedly contained her own person and Zeba Baji opened her mouth extra wide to take in this special treat.

'Badmaash, you'll eat your Dadi so eagerly?'

Nodding, Zeba Baji smiled and refused to feel contrite. In fact, to prove that she would indeed eat the real thing if ever given a chance, she bit Dadi's wrist with great zest, wringing a scream and drawing blood from her prey. That was the last time Dadi fed Zeba Baji. The responsibility henceforth was delegated to Ammi.

Their prickly relationship wasn't helped by the fact that they were too much alike. Dadi was a dominating woman who had assumed the role of matriarch with natural

ease. Having plenty of backbone herself, she didn't like
individuals who demonstrated too much spine, and Zeba
Baji had enough of that particular body part to construct
the structure of a brontosaurus in any world-class museum.
Dadi was on the side of tradition. Zeba, it became very
clear, was subversive. In one of her bitter moments, Dadi
wondered aloud what black magic had been performed to
make Zeba so disobedient.

But it was not Zeba Baji that Dadi was focusing on now;
her grandson was the sole focus of her undivided attention.
'You listen to me Haroon: you may be in Amreeka but your
roots are in Pakistan. You may meet all sorts of women there
who want to trap handsome men like you into marriage, but
remember . . . remember the promise you made to me and
keep girls at arm's length. Remember, my Beta, that while
you are there, I will be here, on the prayer mat, waiting for
your safe return. Don't disappoint me like Fareed did. He
disappeared with that Ayesha but he will come back one
day, I know it in my heart! But you, you promise this instant
that you won't make me wait too long!' said Dadi, clasping
Haroon Bhai's head to her bosom.

Haroon Bhai promised and two weeks later, he flew off to
New York. If he had looked back, he would have seen my
mother crying silently into her dupatta. When Dadi saw
him disappear from behind the glass doors of International
Departures, she wailed loudly, beat her chest and asked
God why He insisted on taking her babies away from her.
Her theatrics earned some shocked and then amused looks
from other spectators who momentarily forgot to say goodbye

to their loved ones. One elderly woman, about Dadi's age, patted her on her shoulder and told her to be patient in her time of adversity.

The time Haroon Bhai was away was a time of tremendous turmoil for my tremulous grandparent who had nightmares of him riding off into the sunset on a horse with a gori in a white wedding dress. She imagined him cavorting with all manner of multicoloured damsels-not-in-distress and worked herself into an anxious state so that she started blowing in the general direction of the USA with renewed fervour, while I followed her with a glass of water in my hand, telling her to rest.

Her palpitations increased when, upon the completion of his master's, Haroon Bhai said he might gain some work experience 'for a little while'. My mother was in agreement that this might be a sensible option for him to take, but Dadi was quick to grab the phone and whine: 'But you promised to return immediately!' Haroon Bhai explained that he had not forgotten, but he thought the work experience might be good for his resumé.

'Fine, whatever you say. I know you will come in time for my funeral, if that won't mess up your resume, I presume?' Dadi said. After the telephone conversation she proceeded to her prayer mat and fervently asked God not to let Haroon Bhai find any work.

So disconsolate was my grandmother that we had to recruit Fati Phupps, my father's favourite sister, to talk some sense into Dadi. Fati Phupps took a week's leave from her job as a magazine editor in Lahore and flew in to give Dadi a big bear hug followed by an admonishment: 'Don't be silly. The boy needs to work and improve his prospects! One should be glad that he is adventurous enough to be on his own and able to conduct his own affairs with efficiency.'

'Hai, what affairs-shaffairs are you talking about?' moaned Dadi while burying her face in Fati Phupps's embroidered, chiffon-bloused shoulder. 'When I think of all the girls he must be dating, my blood pressure rises! My head has already started spinning . . .'

'Oh ho, Amma, you should be glad if he is going after girls,' commented Fati Phupps with a wicked smile on her lips as she winked conspiratorially at Zeba Baji. 'Ask me. I work closely with fashion designers and the elite. You know what? They're all gay! Every one of them. Some are bisexual but the rest—total homosexuals I tell you. What would you do if Haroon comes not with a daughter-in-law but a son-in-law? Wouldn't *that* give the relatives something to talk about!'

'You hold your tongue you shameless girl! Look at what you're talking about in front of my granddaughters?'

'Oh, we already know!' I chimed in.

'Hain? What do you know?' demanded Dadi.

'About gay people. Don't you remember, Dadi? Fati Phupps wrote an article about it in her magazine!'

Dadi glared at her daughter who stared back with an arched brow of impunity.

'You're writing articles about that? What has got into you Fatima? Haven't I raised you better than to write about obscene things? What haram living are you earning, just answer me? And then suggesting that my Haroon is a . . . a . . . Hai Allah! Forgive us all!'

Fati Phupps put her feet up on Dadi's bed and said, 'Amma, I didn't suggest anything of the sort. But the next time you call Haroon and cry on the phone and tell him your end is near, just remember, better a girl than a boy!'

Despite Fati Phupps's less-than-comforting words, Dadi continued to bawl on the phone to Haroon Bhai once a week, using every technique of emotional blackmail to get him to return to Karachi.

My determined brother was becoming an inveterate New Yorker. In the end, US Immigration succeeded where Dadi failed. A year later it decided not to renew his work visa. Therefore, he had to come back, although not too reluctantly since he had a job lined up for him at Procter & Gamble. Dadi and Mum were proud of their son and ecstatic at the prospect of his triumphant return.

Dadi undertook the mission of arranging Haroon Bhai's marriage with the resolve of a wrinkled iguana I had once seen on National Geographic. It had stood still on the branch of a eucalyptus tree and locked its protuberant eyes on to an unsuspecting dragonfly basking in the sun. With steady deliberation it had unfurled its tongue and then flung it out, capturing the flailing prey. The colourful little thing was masticated with slow relish as the eyes rolled around to seek out the next victim. By the time Haroon Bhai arrived in Karachi there were several colourful insects flitting in front of Dadi, some quite coincidentally and others not so coincidentally. Several women flung their daughters at my

grandmother, hoping that she would notice and consider
them for Haroon Bhai. Appointments for visitation were
made over the phone and Dadi, by the end of four weeks,
had drawn up a formidable list of potential candidates for
Haroon Bhai's viewing pleasure. There was a checklist by
which Dadi made her choice. It was a series of rules and
conditions that the potential candidate had to fulfil in order
to be considered suitable:

- She *must* be fully female. I thought Dadi was pointing
  out the obvious, but was informed that in these days
  of confusion, even gender and sexuality must be
  clarified. The end of the world was coming and this
  needed to be mentioned at the very outset.
- She must not be what Dadi called 'The Lesbian'.
- She absolutely MUST be a Syedda. We Bandians are
  Syeds and therefore we will not despoil our blessed
  blood with the offspring of anyone less exalted.
- She must be a 'full virgin'. Girls who have been
  kissed or have had boyfriends are only half or quarter
  virgins depending on the enthusiasm with which they
  partook of these scandalous pursuits.
- She must be qualified to get a good job.
- She must not want to get a job. What are men for?
- She must be from a decent family. The word 'decent'
  opens up a vast subcategory that can be summarized
  thus: her parents should be professionals like my
  parents. Doctors, lawyers, engineers are best.
  Businessmen, under some circumstances, can be
  allowed. Contractors are in nebulous territory. We

haven't decided if they're respectable or not because they work too closely with the labourers. Pilots are totally unacceptable because we all know that when they are not flying planes, they are despoiling air hostesses.

- She should have studied in an all girls' school since this would mitigate the chances of her having had any boyfriends-shoyfriends.
- She must be shorter than Haroon Bhai.
- She must have long, silky, thick hair as opposed to the curls that Haroon Bhai has—we don't want the Bandian offspring to sport Afros, thank you very much.
- She must not, under any circumstance, be fat. She may be well-endowed. But being well-endowed is not the same as fatness.
- She must dress well. She should not cover her head or wear a burqa like a fundo. Neither should she be so liberal that we are forced to stare at her cleavage all day long. A balance between modesty and modernity is a must.
- Needless to say, she mustn't be anything but dazzlingly fair.

Dadi bemoaned the lack of suitable girls for her Haroon Baba, a complaint that irritated my sister no end, so much so that she was drawn into countless disputes with Dadi despite her better judgement. One day she accused Dadi of being picky.

'Haw hai! Picky? *Me?*' asked my grandmother in

wide-eyed innocence. 'What demands have I made, just tell me?'

'Okay,' my sister challenged, 'what if Haroon Bhai married someone dark?'

'My Haroon has good taste, so he would never pick someone who wasn't pretty. And if, God forbid, he does, there's an excellent paste of turmeric and yogurt that can make the blackest girl shine white like the moon!'

This time, even I could not resist.

'But Dadi, what if Haroon Bhai's future wife is taller than him? Or what if he falls in love with a divorcee?'

'That will never happen! Tall women are unnatural. Even men think so. And why would Haroon want someone used? Let me tell you girls—take advantage of my experience. In their youth men can be as "liberal" as they like, kissing-shissing dating-shating half-undressed women. But when it is time to choose a wife, they want someone as pure as snow! All this "beautiful inside" is fine in books-shooks, but this is practical life. I ask you, what will people look for in the two of you when they come to see you for their sons? Exactly all of this! Am I being unfair then? No! I'm just ensuring a good future for your family! Who else am I doing all this if not for you? What's it to me? I shall die soon and then you will realize what a blessing it is to have standards!'

Dadi believed that she was a woman of the world, one who could move ahead with the times. While my mum and dad actually got an opportunity to see each other before they wed, they were not allowed to meet, even under the supervision of an elderly chaperone. At that time, even allowing one meeting was considered quite 'mordren'. Dadi never let us forget that although Dada Jan had supposedly swept her off her feet, there had been no romance-shomance. The initial encounter had been enough-shenuf. She often gave us the example of her sister, who had been the model of obedience when it came to having her marriage arranged.

'My poor sister, Khanum, may she rest in peace. Abba Huzoor came home one day and told her she would marry a young lecturer who taught with him at Patna University. She bowed her head and said, "Jee acha, Abba Huzoor." Did you hear that, Zeba? That's how good girls respond to their parents. They trust their elders to do what is best.'

Zeba Baji had been displaying disconcerting signs of independence. She had committed a crime in my grandmother's books by wearing a sleeveless kameez and then going out to a restaurant for dinner with a group of friends. That these apocalyptic occurrences took place on one night was too much for my Dadi's nerves, who insisted that my sister was acting like a loose woman. Zeba Baji had merely rolled her eyes, just as she was doing now at Dadi's lecture.

In April we learnt of Haroon Bhai's imminent return. By June, Dadi had drawn up a list in her diary of twenty eligible prospects. By July, the number of girls who had been shortlisted for the interview stage had been reduced to ten and, much later, seven, after Ammi eliminated all those who were still currently in school. Dadi complained that good girls were hard to come by and it was very difficult to find full virgins who had graduated from high school.

'Arey Bhai, the younger they are, the more malleable!

They will be able to learn and adapt to our way of life!'

'Dadi,' Zeba Baji inquired, 'are we talking about women or plasticine?'

'Oh, you be quiet! You and your ideas will get you nowhere! Just wait till you get married and your mother-in-law asks you to cook a dish of her choice. What will you do then? Tell her you are not plasticine?'

The process of the arranged marriage has become more and more flexible with the passage of time. My ancestors were betrothed even before birth. Dadi's aunt was betrothed to her first cousin when he was in the womb and was a full five years younger than her. The reason for this unconventional match was that the aunt had been born with buck teeth and a squint eye and the prospect of ever receiving a proposal was paltry. So her uncle, Ashfaq Mian, took pity on her and promised that if he ever had a son, she would be married to him. This promise, of course, was made with the best intentions because his wife, Nameera Khala, was sickly and unlikely to bear any more offspring. But fate is a cruel trickster; rumour had it that Nameera Khala was soon with child. Nine months later, she let out blood-curdling cries during delivery; not due to labour pains but because of the visions of the rabbit-toothed daughter-in-law who was waiting patiently outside for the birth of her future husband. She lived most of her remaining life blaming Ashfaq Mian for such an aesthetically incongruent match. Had she lived long enough, Nameera Khala would have seen that despite being dentally and optically challenged, Dadi's aunt proved a good wife for her son, who loved her deeply. In Dadi's case, it was the parents who arranged their marriage. But with Haroon Bhai, a more liberal policy would obviously have to be devised.

The list of acceptable-girls-to-show-to-Haroon had been drawn up on the basis of, among other things, their readiness to meet with the boy in private so that he could decide which one he wanted. The new process would entail three or four meetings. Haroon Bhai would not go to the first meeting between the families. It would be attended only by my parents and Dadi. Of course, on the girls' side, the prospective candidate was expected to present herself before Dadi's unwavering scrutiny. If the first session was successful, then the second meeting would be arranged for Haroon Bhai to see and approve. If he approved, then the third and final meeting would take place for discussion on other matters of dowry, date and dress. This was the plan my 'mordren' Dadi had in mind.

Haroon Bhai had different ideas.

'We will go only once as a family. Then I and the girl will meet alone, wherever the girl's family wishes. If things look good, then you can take over.'

Dadi's bosom started heaving.

'Oh, and there will be no dowry-showry, Dadi Jan. We live in the twentieth century.'

Palpitations, protests and shrill opposition pursued my brother as he walked down the corridor to his room.

'Who does he think he is? What kind of loose woman would want to meet her husband before marriage? Unchaperoned! And talk! And have coffee-shoffee? Bahu—this is all your fault! I told you we should not have let him to go to Man-hate-un! He's come back with mordren ideas. What about our culture? Our family has done things the same way for generations upon generations. It is part of what makes us respectable!'

I remember trying to placate Dadi with an offer of a back rub.

'What has happened to this girl's brains? Offering a back rub when my grandson has told me he wants to meet-sheet the girls? And no dowry! What respectable girl comes to her in-laws without a dowry? She might as well parade naked in the streets!'

'But Dadi, would you like men and their families to constantly come to see us? Wouldn't it be annoying?' I asked.

'Annoying? It would be a compliment to you! It is a blessing and an honour to be viewed for a proposal! If you were ugly or from a bad family or had a bad character, would people come to see you? No. Oh ho Baba, stop stroking my back! I'm not a child! But Haroon is acting childishly. Are these the manners that Amreeka has taught him? Walking out on his grandmother while I am still talking to him—I tell you the Day of Judgement is coming.'

As Dadi worked herself up into a fever pitch of indignation, I silently pleaded with my mother to do something. I wasn't terribly concerned about Dadi's health; she routinely overreacted to everything. No, I was more concerned about the fact that after an hour of working herself up she would have a headache and instruct me to press her head, which was a depressingly tedious affair. I'd rather play games on my cell phone.

But Ammi knew how to deal with her peevish mother-in-law. It was an expertise that had come after years of watchful practice. Argument was useless. Opposition was futile. But distraction always worked. As Dadi glared at Haroon Bhai's closed door, Ammi switched on the television to Dadi's favourite Indian soap. Within five minutes, they were both sitting together amicably watching *Kyunke Saas Bhi Kabhi Bahu Thi*, a family soap concerning relationships between mothers- and daughters-in-law. On occasion, when the daughter-in-law (in the serial, of course) was treated unfairly, my mother's eyes shone with vicarious indignation. She bristled and darted dirty looks at Dadi. My grandmother, on the other hand, found every opportunity to use this programme to turn this situation to her advantage. After one particularly painful episode when the painted mother-in-law banishes her teary-eyed daughter-in-law to the basement and goes to a party with her son, Dadi looked sweetly at Ammi and said, 'Aren't you glad that you have an angel for a saas, Beti?'

Since my mother had no choice but to agree, she would nod her head and roll her eyes in an impressive feat of facial flexibility. However, my mother had learnt a few tricks of the trade living with Dadi and when on one occasion the television story's daughter-in-law launched a stinging slap on the shocked cheek of the mother of her husband, she promptly retaliated: 'Aren't you glad you have a saint for a daughter-in-law, Amma Jee?'

And so the familial wars, dramatic and latent, continued with all their cathartic charm and Haroon Bhai's rebellious dissent was momentarily forgotten.

Chapter Four

How We Searched for Girls

Although the process of the arranged proposal system can be harrowing for girls, it is no less traumatic for men. Haroon Bhai was the epitome of nervousness before every visit despite his efforts to show sophisticated nonchalance about the whole affair. His apparent casualness was belied by his multiple trips to the bathroom, after which he would promptly become dehydrated and Dadi would ply him with ORS and water. Then he would gell his hair frantically and ask Zeba Baji to inspect it, which wasn't the wisest of ideas. She told him, on two occasions, that his head resembled a pineapple and a tepee. I would have been kinder in my comments had he ever bothered to ask me but who takes the advice of a younger sibling seriously? After his hair was less spiky than before, he would spray himself with a liberal amount of cologne that would overpower our nostrils and trigger my sinuses. This is why we usually drove to the girls' houses with the car windows rolled down and hoped that his initial olfactory impact would not be as overwhelming for the girls as it had been for us.

So we interviewed six girls for Haroon Bhai. It turned out to be quite an adventure. Every visit started similarly with a warm welcome by the girl's parents and an invitation to sit in their drawing room. Small talk was followed by the entrance of each candidate. And that's where the excitement started.

Girl # 1: Madam Unibrow

Me: Did you see that thick line of hair across her forehead? Honestly, she should have taken *some* pains to fix her face on an occasion as momentous as our visit. Maybe she has a boyfriend and doesn't want us to propose?

Dadi: Unremarkable. Too hairy. Not good for the genes of the grandchildren. Barely up to par, physically—why, she was quite dark! Did you see her flat nose? Lag raha tha that someone has run a rolling pin down it. No chest, and hips like watermelons: a most unattractive combination. Shia: check. Syed: check. Quite stylish when it came to shoes-woos. And then she starts talking to Haroon about politics when she should have sat silently and respectfully in our presence! Aaj kal toh people have lost their values! What is the world coming to?

Haroon Bhai: I liked her, quite, but kind of tuned out of the conversation when she said that the City Nazim was the heartbeat of all Karachiites and all multinational companies are imperialistic whores and those who work for them are mentally colonized ants. I mean, do you think she'll respect what I do if I remind her of a cheenti all the time?

Zeba Baji: Whatever.

Ammi and Abbu: The parents were quite nice, except they were overly obsessed with trying to find out if we could sponsor them for the Golf Club.

What happened in the end: Haroon Bhai was rejected because she didn't like how Zeba Baji was dressed. Don't ask me to explain: my theory is that this candidate was already interested in someone else and needed an excuse. That the excuse was in no way ingenious or creative made her fall in my estimation.

Girl # 2: The Infant

Dadi: Hai hai! She was simply gorgeous! Looked like me when I was young. Petite. Good breasts and hips. Even her eyes glistened when she talked! Exactly how a young Eastern girl should carry herself. Very good, very good! Shia, Syed, although one grandparent may have been a Sunni, but everyone can't be perfect. I'm not an entirely picky woman.

Me: She's just sixteen—a year older than me! Eww!

Haroon Bhai: She's a toddler!

Zeba Baji: Marauders of the cradle! Paedophiliac freaks! Violation of human rights!

Ammi and Abbu: Oh dear, this will be awkward.

What happened in the end: Dadi vociferously claimed that she was The One. We ignored her as politely as possible. Haroon Bhai shut himself up in his room because Zeba Baji finally overcame her outrage and suggested that he could have the girl give him a lap dance because that's the only place she would fit. Ammi thought Zeba Baji was unusually coarse. I agreed, though when I secretly looked up what a lap dance was, I admired her wit.

Girl # 3: The Well-Toned Zealot

Dadi: A good, solid Shia family. Good values—a full ten days of majalis at home. The girl must be good at organizing events and accommodating guests, a useful skill for Haroon's career. Not as pretty as the last one, but that's okay. No one can compare to my Haroon Baba. Not much personality, so that's good. Has studied in a co-educational school for some years, though; wonder if she has had any boyfriends? Does she still have one? Toba, toba. She's fair so will look good in black. A little monstrously tall. Perhaps she could stand next to Haroon so I can make sure she's not taller than him?

Me: She could carry a dozen alams—what muscles she has!

Zeba Baji: She wishes she had been alive to serve Imam Hussain at Karbala. She says 'Ya Ali Madad' instead of 'As-Salaam-u-alaikum'. She walks on coals on the tenth of Moharram and doesn't believe in trimming her hair at all. Does she mean on her head or everywhere?

Haroon Bhai: Help!

Ammi and Abbu: Abbu visited the bathroom and couldn't get over the clogged toilet. Ammi had to distract him so that he wouldn't gag.

What happened in the end: The girl couldn't get over the fact that Haroon Bhai didn't know what Chelum was and why we don't stop mourning on the tenth of Moharram. She mentioned that if she were to marry, she would spend the two months or so after Moharram sleeping on the floor, not listening to music and not applying perfume. Since Haroon Bhai was a Nirvana fanatic, he didn't want to spend two months of his life every year practising an enforced austere celibacy. Since she had made it clear that she would be abstaining from *all* pleasures of the flesh, he decided that they wouldn't match. Therefore, my mother called her mother and delivered the clichéd phrase: 'Our stars did not meet,' to which the girl's mother responded: 'If you make them meet, they will meet.' My mother laughed uncomfortably and commented on how wonderful a girl Batool (name of candidate) was, but there were personality differences to which the mum-in-law-who-never-was-thank-God responded that her daughter would make a true Shia out of any man. My mother said if Haroon Bhai would say his prayers regularly, she would be happy. To this the forceful-parent-eager-to-foist-off-religious-offspring said that although namaz was obviously important, it had no bearing on being a true Shia. My mother was irritated, and she ended the telephone conversation with, 'May she find a husband like Hazrat Ali,' to which the latter responded: 'Ilahi Ameen.' Dadi pointed out after this conversation that this was exactly why it was best not to call to say 'no'.

'If you ignore them, they'll get the message,' she said.

Girl # 4: Miss Proactive

Dadi: Too forward. She just walked in and sat down next to Haroon! She said 'salaam' to me and then turned her back on me and just talked to him. She will keep him under her spell and leave us out! No. No matter if everyone likes her. No. No. Absolutely not. Over my dead body. Allah save us from this sheesh-naagan!

Me: Well, I felt a little ignored too but am used to it, considering I'm the youngest and all.

Zeba Baji: Hmm . . . is independent, has gumption. I like the word gumption.

Haroon Bhai: I LIKE her!!

Ammi and Abbu: A little attention our way would have been nice. But perhaps the poor girl was tense?

What happened in the end: With Ambreen (name of candidate) it actually did seem that it might happen. Amid much gasping and spluttering on Dadi's part of course, the situation proceeded to meeting number two with brunch at the Marriott, where she informed my brother that she did not want to live in a joint family system and that he would have to move out. He thought about it and suggested they have chocolate mousse. He dropped her off, came home, and much to Dadi's delight, suggested that we keep the search on.

Girl # 5: The Oppressed One

Dadi: Forget about the girl, did you see the mother? Wearing a big yellow flower in her hair! And a sari! What is happening to today's mothers that they have to compete with their daughters on such important occasions? What were those painted talons? Toba toba, her nails? How is her ablution valid? Does she even pray? Allah save us all!

Me: Okay, now Shireen, visually speaking, was definitely outshone by her mother. While she wore a white kurta with a red dupatta and green bangles—very reminiscent of an MQM candidate on Altaf Hussain's birthday—her mother sauntered in wearing a bright green sari with a yellow frangipani in her hair. Her eyes were smoky and green, mascara expertly applied. She dominated the conversation: didn't let anyone, including Dadi, speak (an impressive feat!) Can't comment on the girl, except she is quite pretty. But very thin.

Haroon Bhai: Okay . . . I'm confused . . . So who am I supposed to look at . . . ?

Zeba Baji (admiringly): I want to look that way when I turn fifty.

Ammi to Abbu: Take that grin off your face and stop staring at her—you look like an idiot.

What happened in the end: There was a second meeting. It was too bad Shireen was inordinately shy. I should know because I was there. The mother insisted on her and Haroon Bhai having a chaperone and Zeba Baji had to go to a Strings concert so I eagerly tagged along for a free meal. It was quite sad because she was trembling and nervous. The plan was for her mother to drop her off and leave her for an hour so that Shireen and Haroon could talk properly. Instead, she joined us twenty minutes later. I believe she circled the block and came back. In those twenty minutes, the poor girl found it very difficult to formulate any comprehensible sentences. She allowed me to order sandwiches for her. She answered every question that Haroon Bhai asked her with a 'yes' or a 'no' or a 'haven't thought about it'. It wasn't like my brother was grilling her. In fact, he was being very gentle and understanding. I was too busy guzzling down all the food I had piled on my plate from the buffet to notice it then, but he was very disturbed by something. Now I realize that he had immediately intuited what took me some time to guess: the girl was terrified of saying anything for which her mother might later berate her. So when her mother walked in unexpectedly, wearing a bright orange sari and announcing to everyone in general, 'How *are* my darlings doing?' I saw Shireen wince. The way her mother looked at her, with a slight widening of the eyes so that her eyeballs bulged out threateningly as if to say, 'You'd better not have made a muck of it' was intimidating. Shireen looked down at her dainty pink fingernails and let her mother take over, telling Haroon Bhai of all her daughter's tastes and distastes. She even contradicted her daughter when she said that Shireen loved Nirvana when Shireen had managed to gasp out that she didn't particularly like English music. Haroon Bhai took a week to think about it and was ready to marry her except Abbu intervened and said that one should never marry someone one felt sorry for. Haroon Bhai nevertheless wanted to go ahead with it. So my mother called Flowered-Hair-Crouching-Dragon to

Me: Erm . . . she can't speak English. I mean, I'm not a snob or anything, but she did say she skewered the fust pozeetion in English Leet-ray-ture. I hope Haroon Bhai doesn't pick this time to be enlightened. She has a brother who is looking at me in the oddest fashion, though. Freak.

Haroon Bhai: She won't even look at me! Is she shy or is she rude?

Zeba Baji: Why *is* her brother looking at Saleha in that manner? Oh, oh . . . this is going to be vastly entertaining: Gulawat coming up!!!

Me: What *is* Gulawat?

Zeba Baji: It's when the bride's brother marries the sister of the groom. It happened in Bhakuraj quite a bit, actually.

Ammi to Abbu: Our baby!!! What can they be thinking of, a Gulawat in this day and age! But it would be fun to goad Saleha into a response.

Dadi (overcoming her initial resolve to say nothing): My Saleha's future will be set as well! Why is everyone shocked? Why, I remember Bhai Jaffaruddin married his brother-in-law's sister to ensure a good match for his sister. His bride didn't even talk to him because she was ten years his senior. But did that stop him? No Baba, they had *ten* children, no less! Killing two birds with one stone! No one listens to me. There's no respect for us elders in this world any more!

Me: He's no Sean Connery and those pimples look like his face is trying to grow udders. If Haroon Bhai goes through with this, I'm committing suicide.

What happened in the end: The girl didn't like Haroon Bhai. Her brother liked me. His mother called my mother

Chapter Five

How Haroon Convinced Dadi

After a few weeks of girl searching, we were all exhausted. Even the prospect of tasting trolley yummies did not seem to be an incentive for continuing the confounded search. Zeba Baji declared that the entire process was stupid, and she was not going to poke her head into people's houses any more.

'It's so mercantile! It's like we're going shopping for girls!'

'Acha? And what will you do when people come to look at you? Put a NOT FOR SALE sign on your head?' demanded Dadi.

'You know, that's not a bad idea!'

'Haan, haan. Then you can merrily go around dating-shating, bringing shame on the family. This process is the *only* way respectable Muslim girls can get married. Stop behaving like you are above it!'

But for all her bluster, Dadi had also despaired of finding a suitable girl for Haroon Bhai. Several fake faints and half swoons later, which didn't bring her any attention from anyone since we were pretty near giving up ourselves and hadn't the energy to comfort her, she commissioned me to give her a back rub. Reluctantly, I complied. When I was younger, giving Dadi a massage was fun. I literally got to walk all over her. I balanced myself on her back and pretended I was a tightrope walker in Mr Galliano's Circus. But since I was now fifteen years old and too heavy, I was required to go the conventional route, with my hands. Dadi complained that I was too rough and my enthusiastic ministrations were insultingly compared to a kat-a-kat-maker gone berserk. She wanted me to pretend to grind flour on her back. Since I had no idea how to grind flour, I continued my karate massage, as Zeba Baji had once called it. Dadi couldn't complain since I was the only one who could be induced to administer the massage, the others being either too busy or even worse at it than I was. Try as I might, I could never please Dadi even though my arms ached with exhaustion. Dreading the massage, I sat down next to her and received a moan even before I touched her back. I gnashed my teeth and clawed my hands to strangle the back of her neck when Haroon Bhai walked in, whistling. He sat down with an odd expression on his face and opened his mouth as if to say something to Dadi. Having thought better of it, he said nothing and turned to my mother who was busy doing the crossword.

'What's a six-letter word for "fake"?' asked my mother.

'Ersatz,' Zeba Baji drawled.

'That's pretty impressive!' Haroon Bhai exclaimed as Zeba Baji's head jerked up with a suspicious expression, since it was very unusual for him to praise her.

Zeba Baji's sarcastic sense of humour and Haroon Bhai's distaste for anything even remotely acerbic frequently put them at odds with each other. Haroon Bhai often wished he were as witty as Zeba Baji. Their squabbles usually ended with Zeba Baji throwing an outrageous comment Bhai's way. He was left gasping and spluttering. He then turned as red as a tomato because he couldn't think of a witty retort fast enough. Their relationship had been especially strained during the girl hunt because Zeba Baji constantly harassed him on the subject of his appearance and his nausea, generally proclaiming him a lalloo for readily being subjected to the arranged-marriage process at all. This was a less-than-gentle reference to my ancestor whose wife regularly beat him and chucked him out of the house, thus implying that Haroon Bhai was acting like a henpecked grandson. Therefore, Haroon Bhai complimenting Zeba Baji on anything meant two things: either he'd lost his mind or he needed a huge favour from her.

Zeba Baji shot him a 'what are you up to?' look. Haroon Bhai grimaced, scratched his head, pulled at his collar and decided to confess. 'So there's a girl who works at my office . . . who . . . I mean whom . . . I mean who . . . I really think it's worthwhile going to her house, meeting with her, her parents . . . you know, for the sake of . . . asking for her hand in marriage.'

Dadi, who had just proclaimed extreme weakness and made a dire prediction of her imminent demise, slapped my hands away from her body and sprang up to look at my brother. My mother looked up calmly and put aside the newspaper and pen, waiting patiently for the storm to come. Understanding dawned as Zeba Baji sat back and crossed her arms and her legs. My father cocked his eyebrow and asked the first question:

'Is she Shia?'

'Yes.'

'Syed?'

'Yes.'

'How long have you known her?'

'Since I joined P&G.'

'And how long have you *known* known her?' interjected Dadi.

'Dadi Jan!! What is that supposed to mean? She works in my department, we've chatted and . . .'

'Just listen to him now!' she exclaimed. 'Here we are trying to find a girl for him and he's had one in his mind all along!!'

'I haven't had her in my mind, Dadi! Be reasonable. She's there, she's sensible, I've talked to her a couple of times about work. We've had lunch with a group of friends and she's unmarried. She comes from a good family, so what's the harm? It just occurred to me, so I'm mentioning it. I haven't talked to her about it or anything.'

'Do you love her? Have you dated?' came the high-pitched interrogation from my increasingly hysterical grandmother, who was beginning to sense that our traditions were about to be blemished by none other than the apple of her eye.

'And what if he does love her?' interjected Zeba Baji in a very low voice, which meant that Dadi, once more, had begun to irritate her.

'What do you mean "what if he does"? What kind of girl goes around having lunch with an innocent boy, trying to trap him into marriage? I may be old but I'm not senile just yet! I know the ways of the world much better than you young people. Girls who work alongside men in these companies are all the same. They have no sense of shame. Hai hai, working with men half turns them INTO men! Yesterday I saw this career woman on a talk show and she was wearing a SUIT!! They don't care about housework or childbearing, they have no time for Moharram! Loud and aggressive they are! And a girl who competes with other men in the office will have no maslas telling off her in-laws whenever something she doesn't like happens. Look at Sabeeha's daughter-in-law! A lawyer! Toba toba! Didn't take very long for her to persuade Sabeeha's only son to move out into a separate house, leaving his parents to fend for themselves!! Is that what you want for your brother?'

'Dadi, "to generalize is to be an idiot",' my sister said.

'Zeba!!' admonished my mother.

'I didn't say it; Blake did! And Dadi's jumping ahead of herself. What if this girl is not trapping him into anything? Maybe her innocent aankhon-ka-tara has an opinion of his own?'

Haroon Bhai threw Zeba Baji a pleading look, and I realized that the favour that he seemed to beg of her was to shut up and not to rile Dadi and complicate matters.

'Dadi Jan, just relax! Saima, that's her name, doesn't even know I'm thinking about this!'

'Well, there's no harm done then. We don't have to

approach her parents,' snorted Dadi while preparing to lie down to resume her massage.

'But Dadi,' I interjected, kneading below her neck, 'what's wrong with just meeting her family? She might be the one! Obviously, Haroon Bhai likes her . . . and . . .'

'Saleha, shut up!' groaned Haroon Bhai.

'Arey, why are you telling her to be quiet! You can't fool her or me. You're already in love with her. You've probably already dated her and now are coming to us for approval for her immoral behaviour.'

'Dadi,' I continued valiantly, 'even if Haroon Bhai . . . kind of likes her, is that so different from Dada Jan? Didn't Dada Jan fall in love with you and sweep you off your feet? But he went to your parents, so it was still through respectable channels. "A romantic arranged marriage", that's how you described it, right?'

'I didn't invite your Dada Jan's attentions.'

'Saima hasn't either!' exclaimed Haroon Bhai, catching on. 'I just like the look of her and think we should meet her parents. In a way, Saleha is right. I'm like Dada Jan, except that I don't have a horse to carry her off on. I'm not in love with her. But I am interested. Come on, Dado, don't be angry. I won't marry her if you don't like her!' And with this Haroon Bhai got up and lay beside Dadi, offering his head for her fingers to run through his hair. He was pulling out all stops to achieve his goal, which made me think that maybe he really did like this Saima a whole lot.

Silence prevailed as we all looked at Dadi. She grunted, looked left and right, as if consulting the angels on her shoulders who were recording her deeds for the Day of Judgement. The munkar-nakeer were particularly good friends of Dadi's. They had evolved from being a metaphor for Allah's omniscience to spirits to two little pixie-like creatures in her mind who she sometimes talked to, much like I used to talk to my imaginary friend when I was four. When I studied Islamiat I learnt that the munkar-nakeer were only supposed to record the deeds of the person whose shoulders they were ensconced on. So when I demanded to know from Dadi what *her* munkar-nakeer were doing writing down *my* business in *her* book, Dadi merely replied that my Islamiat teacher was a Sunni and didn't know her religion very well. At this moment she debated with both of them, looking right, then left, then right again. She snorted and cleared her throat as if about to deliver her oration, but instead called for her silver paan-dan, took out a leaf and inspected it carefully, running her fingers over it to make sure it was smooth and green all over. She lathered it with white, wet choona; sprinkled some sonf and chalia and folded it daintily so that it resembled a triangular pocket which she slowly stuffed into the corner of her mouth. Her eyes looked ahead into the distance as she carefully considered her options. Slowly, her hand approached Haroon Bhai's hair and massaged it. Haroon Bhai and I exchanged triumphant looks. Dadi was softening to the idea.

'Where do her parents come from?'

'Somewhere in India. UP I think.'

'That's good in any case. Is she thin?'

'Yes.'

'Fair?'

'Very.'

'Will she want to continue working?'

'Probably.'

'Well, she might change her mind after marriage.'

'Dadi, I have no problems with Saima working.'

'Yes, but *I* do. You might not recognize this now but a woman who works has no time to be a wife and a daughter-in-law. You leave this up to me.'

'Dadi, this is all for much later. Tell me you are willing to at least see her!'

'It depends. Does she attend all the majalis in Moharram?'

'Well, she goes for the first ten days very regularly.'

'Does she pray?'

'No idea.'

'Why not?'

'Haven't asked her.'

'Can she cook?'

'No idea.'

'Doesn't pray, doesn't cook, doesn't even observe the full forty days of Moharram. I don't like the sound of her already.'

Haroon Bhai got up and wrapped her in a giant bear hug.

'Come on, moti Dado Jano Mano. Just see her at least na!'

'Acha? And what if I don't agree to it? What will you do?'

'I will leave the decision totally in your hands.'

'It already *is* in my hands!' objected Dadi.

'Acha na. I'll leave it *more* in your hands. And . . .' And here Haroon Bhai launched his final stratagem. 'I'll take you on a ziarat to Iran. Personally. You, me and whoever else wants to accompany us.'

Dadi let out a delighted gasp. But she instantly sobered up and rolled another betel leaf for consumption. Without looking up, she said, 'Chalo, I suppose we will have to pay Saima Mohtarma a visit to get more of an idea, then.'

Haroon Bhai sighed and gave Dadi a squeeze. Ammi and Abbu smiled, relieved that they would not have to spend any time and effort convincing Dadi to see the girl who had so enchanted Haroon Bhai. Dadi Jan looked very pleased with herself as she rolled over on to her stomach and bade me to continue with the back rub.

Chapter Six

How Haroon Got Engaged

Our visit to Saima Apa's house was different from the other scouting expeditions we had made. Haroon Bhai's nervousness reached new heights. Ammi gave him an Imodium to control his tremulous bowels. He then proceeded to throw up in the bathroom. Zeba Baji laughed and commented on how big a moron he was. I was telling her to be more sympathetic when Haroon Bhai emerged from his room, less sick but still anxious.

Dadi dressed to make an impression; she needed to make sure that the girl's family was awed by us. Fortified with ten gold bangles on each arm and heavy gold earrings, which stretched her ear lobes to her shoulders, she donned a white cotton gharara as a tribute to her widowed status. Her silver hair was parted in the middle and a long, thin braid hung limply down her back, as shrivelled as her wrinkled skin that now glowed because she had slathered it with Pond's cream. The strategy was Intimidation by Force of Appearance. I thought it more likely that they would probably be induced into a dead faint due to the sheer pungency of the ittar that she had liberally applied. She was, indeed, a sight to behold and an aroma to withstand. With her ittar and Haroon Bhai's cologne, the ride to Saima Apa's house was rather suffocating for the rest of us.

But if Saima Apa's family was overwhelmed by Dadi, they made no show of it. The door was opened by Saima Apa's sister who Dadi thought was Saima Apa herself and nudged Haroon Bhai and whispered to her that good girls did not have the audacity to open the doors to their prospective in-laws—they waited patiently in their rooms before being summoned by their parents. However, Fauzia, Saima Apa's sister, welcomed us all warmly and introduced herself, quelling Dadi's objections. An apology was made for the absence of the parents. Both mother and father had had a busy day because there had been a death in the distant family and they had just returned home. We were settled into the drawing room. There was a tense, awkward silence as we waited to be greeted by our hosts. All sorts of apprehensions swirled in my head: What if they made us wait too long? What if Saima Apa really was militant and aggressive? What if the food they served was oily and inedible?

As I worked myself into a near frenzy, more at the prospect of culinary disappointment than Haroon Bhai's future, the drawing room door opened and Saima Apa's mother walked in, smiling. She was followed by Saima Apa's father, a handsome man with a serious expression on his face, which changed into a smile and a wink as if empathizing with my nervousness. I liked him immediately. Apologies were repeated all over again and both parents said 'Adaab' to Dadi in a manner so reminiscent of the old Nawabs of Lucknow that she immediately broke into a wide smile and acknowledged them with a dignified 'Jeetay raho'. There was something open and honest about this couple that immediately put all of us at ease. My mother politely offered her condolences at the demise of a family member and the conversation took off smoothly.

Routine questions were asked—who hailed from what part of India, when our ancestors migrated to Pakistan, what prompted the move and so on. The political situation was discussed: the merits of Benazir versus Nawaz Sharif were debated and ended with the general question of why we were not able to create a leader for our country. I began to wonder when Saima Apa would appear. Usually, the other girls brought in a trolley or a tea tray, but about twenty minutes into the conversation, Fauzia entered and, with her, Saima Apa. Her entrance, I believe, would have earned Dadi Jan's approval. She entered demurely, said a quiet 'Salaam' to everyone, smiled at me and sat down quietly next to her mother. I cast a quick look at Haroon Bhai who by this time was sitting straight up in his chair, looking distinctly queasy. I would have been afraid that he would throw up all over their lovely golden carpet had he not already emptied the contents of his stomach earlier.

She was beautiful, but not in the conventional way. Hers was not a plastic, insipid beauty —there was a certain vitality that matched the liveliness of her parents. A smiling face, oval eyes and lovely cherry lips. Her nose, I noticed with envy, was distinctly aquiline, very unlike my huge snout. I hoped in my heart that everything would work out this time.

Much later I was to learn from Saima Apa that Haroon Bhai had told her exactly how to behave in order to make a good impression on Dadi. Consequently, she was mostly reticent and only answered questions put before her. She never looked at Haroon Bhai; Dadi predictably took this to be an indication of the modesty of her person. Tea was served and I was delighted to see chocolate cake and chicken patties from a bakery. Dadi observed all this with a frown. She believed that tea was an opportunity for a girl to demonstrate her culinary talents; cakes and patties from a bakery were nothing short of sacrilege. She also thought that the way a girl held the tea tray would reveal her personality. Delicate hands were a plus. If she had a strong grip, she was probably adept at working and this could mean that she had been trained well by her mother. Either that or that she had a will of steel, which wasn't so desirable. If she kept the tray straight, she would be easy to live with. If the tray tilted to the right, she would have no spine. If it tilted to the left, she would have too much. If she spilt milk on the tray, she would bring bad luck to the family. The list went on and on. Sometimes, the meanings of each omen changed, but then that was because many of Dadi's superstitions were completely random. Of course, since tea was served by their cook and the plates distributed by Fauzia Baji, she was unable to observe Saima Apa's hands and felt deprived of that opportunity as well.

Eventually, sitting positions were rearranged to facilitate

think there's anything wrong with her. She's pretty. Not beautiful. A little too thin. Haroon, you should tell her to gain some weight. Men like women with a little more flesh on them. The way she is right now, she will prick you like a thorn, which won't make your nights at all comfortable, let me tell you!'

With this embarrassing response, that was that. Haroon Bhai drove on silently, but I could see the smile on his face in the rear-view mirror.

Ammi called Auntie Shehla the next day to deliver a formal proposal. Auntie Shehla responded appropriately, saying how wonderful she thought our family and Haroon Bhai were and asked for some time to think about it. Dadi Jan said it was part of UP culture for the girl's family to wait a few days before saying 'yes' so that they didn't seem desperate. However, four days later we still had no response from them and her approval turned to grave displeasure

'What kind of people are they? Why, anyone would jump at the opportunity of marrying my Haroon Baba! What's missing in him? Good job, good looks, good EVERYTHING! And they are making us wait! What impertinence!'

'But Amma Jan,' my mother coyly observed, 'weren't you the one who said that there was no need to get back to someone if you didn't want to say "yes" to a proposal?'

'Oh ho, that's for girls' families! I still don't understand why you called all those girls' mothers and told them it wasn't going to work. Let them figure it out when we don't call back! Otherwise they will stick to you like blood-sucking mosquitoes!'

'But then they'd be waiting impatiently just like you are!'

'The rules are different for girls' families! It is their destiny to wait, wait and wait! But for the boy's family to wait like this is ridiculous! I tell you, I have half a mind to call them and tell them to keep their stupid answer to themselves!'

Ammi ignored Dadi's petulance and asked her if she wanted some paan.

A week later, the phone rang and Ammi rushed to get it. The immediate relief on her face told us who it was. She smiled and said, 'Thank you,' and then said, 'Congratulations to you, too! Yes, yes, we will come over today with some mithai! Uff, Shehla you've made me so happy! Give my love to Saima and salaam to Tanveer Bhai!'

She put down the receiver and yelled out, 'They said "yes!!"' I immediately jumped up, hugged her, and sang *Congratulations* by Cliff Richards with plenty of enthusiasm and also a jarring lack of melody. Zeba Baji called up Haroon Bhai at the office.

'They said yes!! Don't know what they saw in you, but they said yes! Oh and Ammi says order a basket of sweetmeats; we're going to go to their house in the evening! Haroon? Are you there? Say something! Are you crying? God help me, Haroon, you're so sentimental! Right, I believe you have a cold! And by the way, big brother, I want a treat at the most expensive restaurant in town!!'

Dadi insisted on talking to Haroon Bhai and cried on the phone and declared that she could now die in peace. Haroon Bhai asked her who would conduct the wedding ceremonies if she did and forbade her to say that again and asked her to please stop crying.

Shehla Auntie had explained on the phone that it had taken some time for Uncle Tanveer to find out about Haroon Bhai professionally. He had even lunched with the head of the department to find out about his future in the company. After that, they had done an istikhara. They were waiting for their maulana to give them the go-ahead before saying 'yes' and had called as soon as he had.

Dadi snorted in contempt at their pitiful explanation; what was the need for so many background checkups-sheckups? A family like ours doesn't come by girls' doorsteps every day.

'But Dadi! You do an istikhara on everything!' I protested.

'Ek toh I don't understand this obsession with contradicting everything I say. Good girls should be seen and not heard. That is how their in-laws like them!'

'But it's true Dadi! Yesterday you did an istikhara about whether to go to visit Qurrat Dadi or not!'

'Well, I needed to know whether Qurrat would give me the evil eye or not. And in my dreams I saw black. Black, I tell you! So I decided not to go. Why would I expose myself to that woman's envy?'

'Amma,' Abbu interjected, not being able to withstand the temptation, 'a patient came to me today. I asked him what his problem was. He said he had diarrhoea. So I said, "Just go to the bathroom!" and he said, "I would like to sir, but the istikhara keeps telling me not to."'

Dadi, who was listening earnestly, blinked a couple of times and then realized that Abbu was joking.

'Hussain! That's not funny! The istikhara is God's way of telling you whether something is ill-omened or not! How can you make fun of that?'

'Why would God give us brains and the ability to make our own decisions if we could just do an istikhara on everything?' drawled my father, helping himself to some chalia from Dadi's paan-dan.

'Oh! And what if I had not done an istikhara when it was time to choose your wife? Answer me that!'

'Hai, that's where all my problems started!' Abbu declared dramatically, holding his heart and giving my mother a goofy look who glared at him in return.

'Don't be silly! Istikharas are a must!' announced Dadi, banging the lid on her paan-dan shut.

'So then why do you object to Saima Apa's parents doing one?' I asked.

'You be quiet and give me a back rub!'

Haroon Bhai arrived from the office with a big grin and a basketful of fruits and boxes of sweetmeats. Before I knew it, we were once again sitting in the same drawing room that we had sat in one week earlier, jubilant and delighted. I wanted to dance at the mehndi but was not able to choose a song. I knew that I wanted to wear an electric blue gharara on any one of the functions. These thoughts ran through my head as my mother hugged Auntie Shehla and Abbu shook hands with Uncle Tanveer while Dadi demanded to see Saima Apa. The latter was brought in wearing a yellow shalwar-kameez with a dupatta on her head, shyly smiling at Haroon Bhai who gave her a huge grin. Zeba Baji surprised all of us by marching forward and giving Saima Apa a tight hug and welcoming her to the family. I was told to call Saima Apa 'Bhabhi' but I couldn't because I'd already begun to think of her as 'Apa'. I tried a few times before she put her hand on my shoulder and ended my misery by saying, 'A*pa* will do just fine!'

Dadi was keen to initiate Saima Apa into the family. She made her sit on the sofa next to Haroon Bhai and began by reading a never-ending prayer to bless the couple. The dua was rendered even longer because Dadi often paused to blow on them. She then took out a 500-rupee note and waved it in circles above their heads seven times each to ward off any evil spirits or influences. She then kissed Saima Apa on the forehead and bid her to take excellent care of her precious grandson and then clasped Haroon Bhai and started weeping again, saying that she would have done this to her Fareed if he had not been tricked into becoming a son-in-law of that horrible Indian Sunni family. Auntie Shehla prudently intervened and hugged Dadi and said something to the effect of thanking God that He had blessed her eldest daughter with such a loving grandmother. Uncle Tanveer broke up the emotional outburst by proclaiming to Haroon Bhai that this was the day his life sentence of rigorous spousal imprisonment had begun. Haroon Bhai smiled and said, 'Jee, Uncle,' and Zeba Baji rolled her eyes at the lameness of his response.

Tea was served. Gulab jamuns and ras malai were distributed and I helped myself to five before Ammi gave me a look telling me to stop. Haroon Bhai looked extremely pleased with himself and was even more delighted when, urged by all of us, Saima Apa stuffed his face with an exceptionally large gulab jamun. All in all, he looked considerably happy with his eyes and cheeks bulging as he attempted to swallow all those sweetmeats.

Shehla Auntie said solemnly to Ammi and Dadi, 'Saima is my daughter and I love her very much. But you have daughters, too, and I'm sure they have their flaws as well as their good qualities.'

Dadi and Ammi looked at Zeba Baji and me knowingly.

'Saima cannot cook, her room is clean when she is not working on any major projects and she tends to eat less when stressed. I'm telling you all of this because she is going to become your daughter and you have seen how she is. Haroon Beta knows her well. But sometimes families tend to have certain expectations of their daughters-in-law, and I'm afraid my daughter is far from perfect. I just want you to know that she is very precious to me. In accepting your proposal I am handing over the dearest person in my world to you. Please give her respect and love and I assure you she will return all that you give her ten times over.'

Dadi Jan was horrified while Ammi seemed to understand. She patted Shehla Auntie's hand. 'Shehla Behan, don't worry. We shall treat her like we treat our own daughters! In fact, better! Rest assured that she is infinitely precious to us as well!'

Dadi remained quiet for the remainder of the visit, but she burst out at Ammi in the car. 'What did she mean, far from perfect? Arey wah! Telling us not to expect perfection! My Haroon deserves no less than perfect. And did you hear?

She can't cook! A woman is incomplete if she doesn't know her way around the kitchen! What kind of training are today's mothers giving their daughters? Just giving a general disclaimer like that and thinking their duty is over? What did she want us to say? It's downright deceitful, I tell you, making her daughter appear perfect and then when all is said and done and no one can go back on their word, they spring this on us! And you Bahu, you kept nodding and agreeing? These larkiwalas will walk all over you if you let them! Now, if you ask Saima to cook you a chicken karhai she will just say, "Oh, I don't know how to make it, my mother told you," and go to work from morning till night! I told you this was going to be a mistake! In my time, things were different! The boy's family used to send the girl a ball of knotted wool and the faster she unknotted it, the worthier she was! That's how it was done, when they knew the value of a good boy. But here! And Haroon had to insist that we visit!! I think we should reconsider this . . .'

'Amma Jan, girls these days are different,' explained my mother.

'And THAT's the problem with them. My girls on the other hand could cook for a hundred people in two hours and sew their entire wardrobes before they were nineteen! Back then, mothers knew how to raise their daughters with the *right* values.'

Dadi's jibes at my mother's parenting skills were a frequent occurrence, and Ammi had learnt to ignore them. However, this time, I saw her turn red.

'Your daughters, Amma Jan?' she asked my Dadi. 'What

about Fati? She hasn't cooked in twenty years!'

This was true. Fati Phupps had sworn in her magazine and to us in person that she would never set foot in the kitchen until women all over the world achieve equal rights and treatment in all societies. It was a clever oath because there was no chance in hell of that ever happening. Which suited my aunt fine because she had no intention of cooking if she could help it. She had hired a cook, male of course, to cook for her on the weekends. That was just one of the many stands for womankind that Fati Phupps had so unselfishly taken.

'Oh ho, don't talk to me about Fatima. The devil possessed her the day her husband died,' said Dadi with a shudder.

Zeba Baji had told me that when Fati Phupps's husband, a tannery owner, passed away, there had been hell to pay. Dadi had suggested that since Fati Phupps was a young widow, she should leave off all work and colourful clothes to observe the customary seclusion for four months and ten days. Then she had proceeded to forbid Fati Phupps from bathing for the next four days—as this seemed an appropriate show of grief. My aunt exploded in front of the entire family and her own in-laws, declaring that there was no need for any mourning period because she was happy she was free and that she was in no danger of being pregnant. She had kicked him out of the bedroom after his ungainly attempts to consummate the marriage. Moreover, she was *not* willing to smell like a men's locker room just because her husband had done her the favour of dying and leaving her free to live her life the way she wanted to. Apparently Fati Phupps had caused a scandal by not waiting for the body of her husband to be presented before her. She drove herself home, bathed, put on a bright red sari to goad Dadi and her in-laws and refused to allow any condolences at the house. When asked if she had lost her mind, she replied she had lost it when she agreed to marry a man who smelt of rotting carcasses merely because he hailed from the same sect as she did. Ever since that day, Fati Phupps spoke her mind and gave free rein to her temper on whichever unfortunate individual dared to talk to her about propriety or the Established Order. She said that a widow had a chance at a much more liberated life than a married or single woman, if she were brave enough to embrace it. She refused to accept that there was anything such as sacred tradition because those who believed in it were like mental patients who routinely bashed their heads against a brick wall, cracked open their skulls and spilled their brains out, only to pick their cerebral matter up again, put it back in their heads and go on ramming.

'Fatima, she is mad. But my *other* daughters . . .' continued Dadi.

'Are happily married and I'm happy for them,' Ammi interrupted, 'but I cannot put different standards on my daughter-in-law just because she is not my own daughter. Shehla did not say anything that I would not have said about my own daughters. Are Saleha and Zeba perfect? Can they cook? Zeba cannot even sew! And Saima has not learnt to cook yet because she doesn't have to. That does not mean she will never cook. I don't know what will happen in the future, but I know that the more love we give her the more she will

Chapter Seven

How a Phone Call Created Complications

Dadi was livid. She paced her room with prayer beads in her hand and a bad-dua on her tongue. 'That *witch* Qurrat! I can always rely on her to ruin everything!'

It all started with a phone call to Qurrat-ul-Aine, her arch-rival on matrimonial matters of their offspring and their offspring's offspring. Thus, when Saima Apa's family accepted our proposal, Qurrat was the first person that Dadi decided to call and boast to. When I asked her whether she wasn't being just the teeniest bit petty, she instantly denied it.

'Arey? What is petty-shetty about this? My Haroon Baba is getting married and she is my closest living relative. We've gone through a lot together. She would be upset if anyone found out before her.'

Now Qurrat was hardly Dadi's closest living relative, being only a second or third cousin. But she was the only woman of Dadi's age and she lived in the same city. For this reason, she was the bane of my grandmother's existence.

When it came to extended family, Qurrat's presence made Dadi's position as matriarch on the basis of age and wisdom precarious. She was as old as Dadi. On Eid dinners and occasions where the whole Bandian clan reunited, people showed Qurrat the same degree of deference as they did my grandmother. Dadi, who couldn't share the best betel leaf in her paan-dan much less public attention, resented Qurrat-ul-Aine immensely for her existence, age and geographical proximity. Still, both women pretended to be bosom buddies to present a united front to the collective 'youth' of the Bandian clan because they didn't want to compromise the dignity and grace of old age by submitting to crass fighting and unnecessary arguments. But that is not to say they did not wage a war of influence. No, fight they did—but like two bees buzzing over the same rose, they fought a honeyed battle. So saccharine were they in their attitude to one another that one could get diabetes by being in their presence.

I have often wondered why we have to pretend to get along with relatives whose company is hard for us to stomach. I think it is because to openly detest each other would be to acknowledge the competition that fuels the hatred. To acknowledge competition would be to acknowledge one's status as competitor with those below us. Since our belief in our natural superiority over all other families is sacrosanct and indisputable, we naturally cannot behave in a way that puts us in any way on an equal footing with those who are obviously inferior. That is why we often maintain Canderel relations with family: sugary but fake. An incredibly cynical reason provided by my sister is that we will need those relatives for the occasional blood donation, to fill up seats at a wedding function or to finish the Quran when someone dies. So, to make sure our stock is never depleted, we are forced to be nice to them.

I dialled Qurrat Dadi's number for my grandmother. Actually, I telephoned her at her daughter's house, where Qurrat Dadi lived. Qurrat Dadi had witnessed the tragedy of her only son marrying a heavyset African American woman originally named Desireè, but renamed Mariam. We were told that Desireè had converted to Islam on paper because that made it easier to find a maulana to do the nikkah after the church wedding. This was necessary, of course, because otherwise, by Islamic standards, they would be living in sin. After this blow to the family honour, Qurrat Dadi had turned all her attentions and hopes on her daughter, Perveen. Perveen had not disappointed because hers was a perfectly arranged marriage to a successful barrister that produced one daughter of her own, who was poetically named Naureen to rhyme with her mother's name and who imitated her not only phonetically but also in the realms of obedience and submissiveness. Therefore, Naureen was the subject of her family's abundant adoration. She was actually Zeba Baji's age but they didn't get along, primarily because Zeba Baji found Naureen totally insipid and dull with all her 'yeses' and 'of courses'.

It was Naureen who picked up the phone, said 'salaam', asked about all of us and the condition of Dadi's arthritis before asking her to hold so that she could give the phone to Qurrat. Dadi told me to put it on speakerphone: she wanted us to hear Qurrat gasp and splutter while she hid her envy and congratulated my grandmother on making *yet* another matrimonial conquest.

'Hello Gulbahar Bibi! How are you?'

'What took you so long to get to the phone? Don't be so slow, warna old age will catch you as a wolf catches a tortoise!'

'Na Baba, I was upstairs saying my namaz. Naureen brought the phone to me. Such a good girl she is. I'm very proud of her! Did you know . . . ?'

Not willing to let the conversation become about Naureen when it was meant to be about something much more interesting, Dadi immediately interrupted:

'Haan, haan, acha listen, I have the most wonderful news! My Haroon Baba is getting married! I've arranged a match for him!'

There was no gasping, no spluttering. There was a moment's silence before Qurrat Dadi responded by congratulating us with tremendous enthusiasm, which made Dadi arch one snowy white eyebrow in suspicion.

'What miracles Allah is heaping on both of us sisters! I was just about to tell you that we've found a boy for Naureen as well! He and his family came with the proposal yesterday and Perveen is going to say "yes" tomorrow! We were introduced to the family by Shabana; you know Shabana? My khala's brother-in-law's aunt? Anyhow, doesn't matter if you don't. The boy's family is very rich, I tell you: his father owns a factory. They're in packaging or something like that! The boy is a businessman, too! They have a pool-shool in their house! Who would have thought? I was going to phone you tomorrow after we had accepted! But now we can celebrate together. Hello, Gulbahar Bibi? Are you there? Hello?'

Dadi's face turned a multitude of colours that ranged from red to green to pale white. She gulped, cleared her throat and then said with smiley voice and sour face.

'Mashallah, that is very good! Congratulations to all of you! Imagine: my Haroon and your Naureen getting married at the same time! I feel so old! And I miss my Fareed. Haroon looks so much like him!'

This was yet another clever tactic to tilt the balance in Dadi's favour so that she would not have to pretend to be happy for much longer.

'Oh ho, Gulbahar, don't be upset, though I know that you are a mother and only a mother's heart knows what it's like to lose a son.' Qurrat meant the marriage to an African American woman but for Dadi it also applied to death. For the two women, such a marriage and death weren't terribly different fates. 'But tell me, who is the girl? How did you find her? What does she do? Is she pretty enough for our prince?'

'She is, she is. It was an arranged marriage, of course. I found out that there was a Shia, Syed girl who worked with Haroon in his office. Her mother and my bahu are friends. So I suggested why not have a look-shook? So we went and Haroon agreed to marry her. She liked Haroon too, of course. What's not to like? Such a star like Haroon falling at her doorstep!'

My mind reeled at how inaccurate yet technically correct

this account was. Dadi had found out that there was a Shia, Syed girl at Haroon Bhai's office. Ammi and Auntie Shehla were now friends, and it was at Dadi's suggestion that we went to their house. It was a masterpiece of manipulation: the facts fit to form a perfectly accurate lie.

The telephone conversation lasted for more than forty-five minutes, with the who-shoos, what-shots, when-shens and where-shares were discussed in great detail, each woman battling to get the other to listen about *her* grandchild, resulting in several interruptions so that neither was able to hear what the other was saying.

But the conversation ended with Qurrat on a high, making grand plans for her granddaughter's wedding and telling Dadi to take heart because her granddaughters would probably get married soon. Dadi slammed the receiver down and let out a few ugly-sounding expletives, cursing Qurrat-ul-Aine and her spiteful scheme to snatch the limelight by getting Naureen hitched precisely at the same time as Haroon.

'Nagori churail! That clever little witch says she was going to call me tomorrow to tell me about Naureen's match! As if I was born yesterday! As if I don't know she only told me today because she couldn't bear it that Haroon didn't give a proposal for Naureen! Is my Haroon less than a businessman? And they run a packaging factory. Wah wah! What do they package? Toilet rolls? Haramzada, joining daddy's business and then getting a pool—my Haroon is a self-made man, not a leech like Naureen's fiancé! Saleha Beta, always remember that people like Qurrat who were born in poor households always have an inferiority complex. One whiff of money and they lose control. A frog from a small pond always splashes around ridiculously when put in an ocean. And Qurrat is practically doing a bhangra in a pool! I feel sorry for her, acting so greedy! We've always been reasonably off—my father used to give money to her father so that they could run the household. And now she's throwing a pool at my face. What do you call them in English? Nirala reeches?'

'Nirala reech' was Dadi's interpreted pronunciation of 'nouveau riche'. Her version converted it to mean 'New Bear'—an unkind lampoon of Qurrat's hairy upper lip and corpulent figure. The virulence of Dadi's response was caused by Qurrat Dadi's swift achievement of grand-maternal nirvana. She would be in the enviable position of having all her female descendants married off while Dadi still had Zeba Baji, me and Rania Phupp's two daughters to deal with. It took one telephone conversation to make us go from being her pride and joy to unfinished business that, if not dealt with, would soon become a mark of her shame.

Dadi was not about to go down without a fight. She hollered for my mother and then proclaimed gravely, 'We need to get Zeba married. Soon.'

Dadi thought that if Zeba Baji was also arrange-marriaged, it would take the attention away from Naureen. A girl getting engaged was a much bigger deal in our family. The assumption was that because girls generally had no control over who brought a proposal and when and how, it was a much more mysterious and magical process involving fate and God and had a direct correlation not just with luck but morality, for who would want to propose to a girl without

looks, virginity and luck? Therefore, to proclaim that a girl
was engaged was to announce to the world that she had all
three. Since there were more women than men in the world,
it wasn't terribly hard for men to find a wife for themselves.
Therefore, Naureen's news would overshadow Haroon's.
But if we managed to get Haroon and Zeba engaged at the
same time, Dadi would earn a place in the hall of fame of
The Matrimonially Fortunate.

'We need to get Zeba married. She's twenty-five years
old and already done with university. It's time we started
looking for a good boy for her. I've been so busy focusing on
Haroon that I forgot we have a young girl sitting under our
very noses!'

My mother had heard most of the conversation with
Qurrat Dadi on the phone from the kitchen and therefore
was well aware of what had prompted her resolve. She
asked how she was expected to search for a boy for Zeba.
She couldn't go looking around in people's houses the way
she had for Haroon. Besides, Zeba was young yet and had
plenty of time.

'Plenty of time? PLENTY OF TIME? Zeba is going to
turn twenty-six next year! Why, when I was twenty-three I
was the proud mother of five children! Even now, so many
girls get married when they are eighteen! But I wanted my
granddaughters to be educated and I have given them an
education. But that is only half of my responsibility to them.
How will Zeba feel when she's attending Naureen's rukhsati?
She'll be the laughing stock of the family and I will NOT
allow that to happen! Qurrat told me Naureen's wedding is

a year from now. We must at least get her engaged before then! I'll spread the word around that we're looking for a boy and I tell you, they will come down in droves! Zeba is much prettier than Naureen—fairer, thinner; we're better off than Qurrat's family. And what good luck to have a wedding coming up so soon! People will see her dressed up and will want her for their sons. If that doesn't happen, we have Moharram yet. She looks good in black and there will be lots of opportunities to show her off. You tell her to get her nose out of her books and start meeting people. And tell her not to speak her mind. People cannot stomach it. She scares them off. I'll tell the maid to get some ubtan for Zeba to rub all over her face and arms so that her complexion starts glowing. As long as her Dadi is alive, Zeba will find a good match!'

With that proclamation, Dadi decided to get to work, but her determination soon gave way to helpless despair. As the grandmother of a boy, she was all-powerful. She was on the prowl and knew when to pounce.

Dadi approached all things with the subtlety of a charging rhinoceros, but a gentler approach was needed to lure an eligible suitor for Zeba Baji. If she left everything to fate, fate would not necessarily respect a year's deadline to produce a match for Zeba. If she took matters into her own hands and spread the word around that she was looking for a boy, she ran the risk of making everyone think that we were desperate because no one was proposing to Zeba Baji. This would give rise to speculations as to *why* there were no suitors. The virtues of chastity, beauty and fortune would be called into

Chapter Eight

How the Wedding Was Planned

A firstborn's first birthday and first wedding are similar because they have nothing to do with him and everything to do with the parents. When Haroon Bhai turned one, Ammi and Abbu celebrated in style. A grand function for a hundred people was organized. A Polka ice cream stand was hired. A clown sang and juggled with a cigarette in his mouth. A magician made a bouquet of roses appear from his assistant's mouth. Balloons popped everywhere. Hassan Bhai, Haseena's son and my favourite male cousin, got his hands on a needle and had a merry time scaring the living daylights out of everyone. A jumping castle was inflated for toddlers to jump on. It was another matter that Uncle Wajid, Dadi's cousin who had shown up a bit tipsy, also decided to have a go. He was asked to desist when he almost fell on top of a three-year-old who screamed in terror at the sight of a rotund belly descending upon her. Moreover, a donkey-wallah led a depressed-looking creature around the lawn, giving rides to small children and even to Uncle Wajid, who had been forcibly evicted from the jumping castle.

All these festivities took place while baby Haroon took an extended nap. He was awakened only when it came time to cut the cake. The only picture of his first birthday party with him in it shows him perched on Ammi's hip, his head thrown back and his mouth gaping open in a loud wail while a harassed-looking Abbu is blowing out the candles on his behalf. Dadi said that soon after, Haroon Bhai resumed his nap and remained oblivious to the family and children partying around him. Now that Haroon Bhai had turned twenty-seven, Ammi and Abbu planned his wedding with similar gusto. Very soon, his contributions mattered less and less. Once again, my excited parents planned to spare no expense in celebrating another major event in their only son's life.

My brother and his fiancée wanted a simple wedding: a nikkah and a joint reception, period.

But neither my parents nor Saima Apa's parents were ready to hear of it. They sat together with Dadi, who kept a jantri open and attempted to assign auspicious dates to all the functions. I was allowed to sit in and quietly observe the event.

'No, no, how can we have a function on the twenty-first?' protested Dadi. 'It is the martyrdom of the seventh Imam! How will you show your face to God, just tell me?'

'Well,' Abbu pitched in, 'how about the twenty-fifth? It says in here that on this date Halakoo Khan died and Hitler disappeared. Do you think God would approve of this day?'

Saima Apa's parents burst out laughing but stopped prudently when Dadi shot them a dirty look.

'Go on, make fun of me. Look what it says here in your horoscope. It says, "Not listening to your elders will land you in trouble." Go ahead, look for yourself. Do you think I am joking?'

After many arguments and much deliberation, a suitable date was agreed upon. Added to my parents' joy was Dadi's sense of competition. No matter how much money Qurrat's granddaughter was going to marry into, ours had to be the grander event. Saima had to have not one but five designer joras. Our functions had to be grander than grand. We had to have the best wedding planners. We had to have the greatest variety of eatables ever served in a wedding in Bandian history!

Since Saima Apa's and my parents were jointly financing the affair, they decided to cut the costs in ways that would not show that they were cutting costs. Ammi and Auntie Shehla agreed to have a joint mehndi, much to Dadi's ire. She felt that there should be two of them, one at the boy's house, one at the girl's. This would be followed by a small, private nikkah ceremony in the morning and a rukhsati in the evening. The valima would take place the next day. Dadi was supremely dissatisfied. There were technically only four functions, which were certainly not enough-shenuf. She added to the list a milad and mayun, which Haroon Bhai violently insisted were not for men.

'They *can* be for men! Why can't you wear a yellow kurta and put some henna in your hair? Your head will feel cool!'

'My head already feels cool Dadi. And I look like I have jaundice in yellow.'

'Uff, it's no fun getting a boy married!' complained Dadi. 'Now, if my Zeba were getting married, what fun we would have getting her mayun done! We'd rub ubtan on her so that she would glow. And she wouldn't be allowed to go out into the sun for at least three months!'

'That would give her a vitamin D deficiency.'

'Oh ho! I sat mayun for a whole year! I didn't have any deficiency. And my mother made me bathe in rose water every day. And my hair was oiled and brushed and I ate only fruits and vegetables. And sometimes my maid rubbed yogurt and egg yolk on my scalp and ubtan and turmeric paste on my arms! Did you know that I wasn't allowed to look at my face in the mirror during the mayun? And I also wasn't allowed to apply perfume. It was the custom in those days. These days all the fashion you girls do makes you vain and then you scoff at decent proposals.'

'But didn't you get bored staying indoors for a year?' I asked. 'It would drive me insane!'

'Because you are spoilt, that's why!'

'But Dadi, how will we make Haroon Bhai do a mayun? He needs to go to the office.'

'A boy observes mayun by not visiting or talking to his future wife until the wedding day. Absence breeds fondness.'

Finally, a grand total of six functions were decided upon and Ammi and Abbu had only four months to come up with the money to finance the extravaganza. Abbu took up extra hours at the clinic, calculated his savings and decided to sell off a plot of land so that we could afford Saima Apa's wedding dresses and her jewellery sets as well as the nine customary clothes that the groom's family provides for the girl, as well as the clothes provided for the girl's family. Dadi discovered that Qurrat planned to provide jewellery for Naureen's mother and sister-in-law and wondered for a moment if we should do the same. Abbu put his foot down and said absolutely not. Dadi said that this was precisely why it was unwise for the boy's family to tell the girl's parents not to provide a dowry. 'After all, we're spending so much money on them, the least we can get is a bedroom set, a television, an air conditioner and a fridge in return.'

Despite Dadi's opinion that my parents were being foolishly 'mordren', Saima Apa's mother was told to provide no dowry. Saima Apa, Dadi and Ammi went to see options for a wedding dress and Ammi and Dadi came back upset with each other.

'I'm telling you it's a bad idea to give your daughter-in-law too much of a choice in the matter. What was this idea of inviting her along anyway?' A good Eastern bride didn't participate in the wedding with the eagerness that Saima was exhibiting. What kind of girl brazenly went with her in-laws to choose her own wedding dress? 'And what about tradition? Hain? She doesn't want red! What kind of a bride doesn't want to wear red for her wedding? Did you see how she kept making a face at that beautiful fabric that *I* liked? She has no respect for me—how will she have any respect for you?'

'Amma, you kept showing her combinations of gold and red when she wants maroon with green, and you flat-out rejected her choice of blue and golden, which I thought was very attractive, not to mention cheaper than the one you liked,' retorted my mother. 'And I *wish* you hadn't told her she needed to lose weight! The poor thing! How rude she must think us!'

'Rude! Ruude! *RUDE*! I knew this would happen! You daughters-in-law think you can gang up on me! She should be prostrating herself before us, thanking us that we are giving her such a handsome and accomplished husband. If we give her advice, she should take it! After all, it's for her own good! With hips like those, she'll look like one of those red-bottomed baboons in her wedding dress. Which, Bahu, will be *red*!' Dadi banged her fist on the dining table where the heated debate had ensued.

'Amma! Please, let her choose for herself! And she looks perfectly good as she is! And now she's unhappy with a red dress that is outside our budget!'

'Ay hai, so why don't you just say that I'm a drain on your resources? I know you are waiting for me to die so that you can save on your groceries! Well, you just listen to me carefully Bahu—I'm going to have a say in this wedding. If I hadn't given birth to Hussain, you would not have married him and had Haroon. So it's because of my existence that your life is possible and I'm not going to keep quiet when I see that the control of this household is slowly transferring from m . . . you . . . I mean us, to an insolent young girl who has a mind of her own and who has no respect for her in-laws' wishes.'

'Amma, you can think whatever you want to think. But the order of the blue dress has been given. I gave it when you were getting in the car. Saima and I are going tomorrow to look at jewellery sets. This is not our wedding, it is hers and she should have a say in how she wants to look on her wedding day! All brides should be able to make decisions about their weddings!'

'*All brides should have . . .*' Dadi mimicked Ammi. 'What do you think of me, that I have the IQ of an egg? Why don't you say right now that you didn't like the wedding dress I selected for you? Haan? Say it! Say it right now! Ha-ray Baap!' These three syllables indicated that Dadi was about to go into a hysterical tirade of the helpless victim. 'After all that I did for your wedding and your husband, practically raising your children, this is the thanks I get! Being told I should have let you choose your own wedding dress! I should have let you choose your own husband! Let's see who you'd have ended up with!'

Ultimately, Haroon Bhai had to interject and relax Dadi's frayed nerves with requests for a hair massage while Ammi stomped off angrily to the kitchen to get a glass of cold water. I followed suit and got a glass of lemonade for Dadi.

Ammi suggested that Haroon Bhai and Saima choose a jewellery set for the rukhsati. Into this conversation Dadi jumped, unwelcome and uninvited, but determined to have her say.

'Why are you buying her jewellery? Gold is so expensive these days! Why don't you give her the choker and set that I gave you, Bahu?'

'Because it will not match with blue and golden. Plus it's too heavy. I remember I had a backache after I wore it.'

'Chalo sun lo! The set that I wore and my mother wore is too heavy for you! I didn't hear you say anything then!'

'I was too polite to do so.'

'So what has changed now? Where have your manners gone now?' Dadi baited.

'They are still there. I don't want to put Saima in the awkward position of saying she doesn't want to wear something she doesn't like. I want to give her a choice in what she wears. Amma, we have to take Saima's opinion into consideration or else we run the risk of alienating her. I hope you understand. But you must be so tired! I'll make you some tea. Haroon, stop bothering your grandmother and fetch her paan-dan. I'm in the mood for some chalia and betel leaves!'

Temporarily distracted by my mother's placating tone, Dadi submitted to assembling a paan for her.

But this was only one example of the disagreements that inevitably ensued whenever Dadi habitually countered Ammi's decisions. A second took place not two days later when Dadi learnt that Haroon Bhai had been given money by his parents-in-law to have his suits stitched for the rukhsati and valima.

'Suits? What do you mean suits? You will wear a sherwani with a turban on your head. And let me tell you now before you protest, you will wear a sehra of roses when you come in, I don't care what you say!'

'Dadi Jan! No!' protested my shocked sibling. 'No one wears a sehra! A curtain of roses covering my face . . . what will I look like? An Indian princess? I've heard stories of grooms stumbling and falling because they couldn't see where their feet were going because they were too busy inhaling rose petals! It's so horribly gay! And I don't want to wear those abominable shoes: the saleem shahees that are curled at the end? I'll look like a relic from the past!'

'What is this gay-shay business Bhai? And what is this I'm seeing—you all are scoffing at everything that is traditional! You are from the village of Bhakuraj and you will follow its traditions! You are going to wear a sherwani with a turban! And I'm not hearing any no-shos! It seems like everything I do is ridiculous and stupid! I raised your father and I raised you and if I'm so stupid then just lock me up in my room and declare me a madwoman!'

Dadi's tears this time seemed real enough and she seemed genuinely indignant. Haroon Bhai kissed her, I hugged her and Ammi told Haroon Bhai that he would wear whatever Dadi said he should wear. When Dadi went off to rest, Haroon Bhai protested at the prospect of the pink tissue robe. Ammi told him he could take it off once he reached the venue—but it must be worn in order to appease Dadi.

The pink tissue robe was a Bhakurajian traditional robe worn by all Bandian grooms in memory of our ancestor Achan Mian. The son of an extremely rich businessman, Achan Mian was a constant source of embarrassment for his father because he liked to play with his sister's plastic dolls. He also had an affinity with bright pink. Many advised Achan Mian's parents to marry him off as soon as possible so that other undesirable affinities may remain hidden. On his wedding day, however, Achan Mian refused to marry his bride—a woman who was twelve years older than him and who sported a moustache while he had none. He locked himself in his bedroom and refused to come out. His sister persuaded him by promising that he could wear his favourite pink robe, the one in which he felt he looked especially handsome. The sight of Achan in pink caused quite a stir among the Bhakurajians—though he looked like a pansy he was, nevertheless, man enough to marry the most shrewish and difficult woman in Bhakuraj. Therefore, Dadi insisted that Haroon Bhai wear the pink robe which had inadvertently become the traditional Bhakurajian symbol of machismo.

Things were rolling fast. Orders were delivered for Saima Apa's dresses. Cloth was bought and wrapped with matching bangles for her family. Dadi warned that she would not let Zeba Baji wear light pastels during any of the functions. 'You are so fair! Bright colours will bring out your complexion superbly.' They would also attract suitors like peacock feathers attract mates, which was the real reason behind Dadi's insistence on bright yellows, reds, greens and deep purples for the various functions. Zeba Baji resisted at first but conceded when Dadi attempted one of her faints and Abbu ordered her not to upset her about petty issues.

Haroon Bhai and Zeba Baji tackled the issue of the valima invitations. Haroon Bhai had turned into a lovesick moron by this time and tried to transfuse into the cards all his sentimentality towards Saima Apa. He wanted the invitations to be made of red velvet. The writing on them was to be in gold and was to mention something about marriages being made in heaven, and that by the grace of God the Bandians wanted to celebrate the arrival of a hoor to their family. Zeba Baji stared at him in horror when she realized he was not joking. She said that as far as celestial metaphors went, he should confine them to Saima's ears in the bedroom; the invitation would be a simple one stating that Mr and Mrs Bandian request the pleasure of everyone's company to the valima of Haroon with Saima. Bhai, though embarrassed, was too happy to take offence to Zeba Baji's comment that he was turning into a sap and agreed to her suggestion. The only amendment he insisted upon was that Saima Apa's name should come first. Zeba Baji rolled her eyes and complied.

Designing the cards, it turned out, was the easy part. Who to invite was significantly more complicated. We Bandians in one way or the other are related to almost everyone in the subcontinent. After immediate family and cousins and first cousins and second cousins, Abbu drew the line: he was *not* going to invite over a thousand people to their son's wedding because he simply could not afford the price of the Coca-Cola bottles. Dadi, content that Qurrat's family would enviously witness all the proceedings, did not put on too much of a fight. When the invitations were delivered, many indignant phone calls were made, primarily by my parents' second cousins who had only been invited to the valima instead of all the functions. Their premise was that if they were considered family, they should be treated like family and be invited to at least four of the six functions. Many refused to attend the valima and threatened to break their familial bonds. I wish temporarily invalid husband who had broken his ankle while jogging, while the last was too crotchety to survive a twelve-hour trip halfway across the world and feared the security situation in Karachi. Haseena Phuppo was convinced that she would get shot if she ventured anywhere near the Third World. But the excitement of those who *could* make it overshadowed the disappointment with the absentees.

The first to land in Karachi was Khala Ammi, Ammi's sister who lived in Doha. With her came my eldest and best-loved cousin, Naima, who was my age and a fellow comrade against Rania Phuppo's daughters who, to my dismay, were going to make a last-minute appearance at the wedding.

Rania Phuppo arrived with Robs (short for Robaba) and Maw (short for Mahwesh). They were a nauseating duo, two and three years older than me and believed themselves to be superior and more sophisticated because they knew more about boys and designers and because they received full-body waxes on a regular basis. When they arrived and hugged Dadi, she commented on how her babies had grown and looked straight at their large bosoms, well ensconced in tight kameezes. They of course took this as a compliment and strutted about more proudly than before.

One would think that I would have been delighted that my worldly-wise cousins had come to visit us after such a long time, but I was not. Robs and Maw looked down at us and constantly made fun of our cricket team and praised Tendulkar to the skies. They also suggested I get my curls bonded since they looked like a bird's nest on my head. And to add insult to injury, they told me that unless I did

It was lovely to have Hassan and Naima with us after such a long time, but it was miserable to share them with Robs and Maw who continued to be very patronizing at every turn, especially when they described my plaited hair as quaint and suggested that I get it straightened using this little thing called a flat iron, as if I didn't already know what *that* was. Worse, Rania Phuppo encouraged their belief in their own greatness by constantly telling Dadi and my mother how talented they were at school, debates, theatre and so on. Ammi never reciprocated in kind. I too was a good student and I had the singular ability to move my ears without touching them while simultaneously licking the tip of my nose with my tongue. But my problems were petty considering what my sister had to go through.

One would think that with all the wedding guests and planning, Dadi would put the issue of Zeba Baji's marriage aside for the time being. But no. Not Dadi. My sister's marital status was a burr in her cotton gharara that reminded her constantly that if something didn't happen soon, she would be bested by Qurrat and her insipid progeny.

My mother, who was up to her neck dealing with photographers, tailors and caterers, did not need to be badgered about finding Zeba a suitable match. How was she expected to search for a boy for Zeba? She couldn't go looking around in people's houses the way she had for Haroon.

But Haroon Bhai's wedding, it so happened, solved my grandmother's dilemma. Dadi realized with a jolt that while she had been agonizing over Zeba Baji's matrimonial prospects, she had not considered that she had perfectly eligible grandsons, two of them in the house at that very moment. Hassan Bhai was already engaged to a lovely girl in London. The match had been arranged, of course. Mansoor and Alam Bhai, on the other hand, were viable prospects. Dadi and Zainab Phuppo were seen whispering and scheming and looking speculatively at Zeba Baji. Zainab Phuppo was desperate to marry off at least one of her sons hoping that it would have a domino effect on her other offspring. Her older ones were far too independent and were too preoccupied in setting up their own business with their father to take seriously any talk of marriage. But Zainab Phuppo had reason to believe that as she had successfully dragged Mansoor and Alam Bhai to Pakistan, she would be able to go further and haul them into marriage.

Zainab Phuppo talked to my father about a match between Mansoor Bhai and Zeba Baji. Abbu threw the ball in Ammi's court and told her to do what she thought best. This was my father's standard response to any issue that he foresaw as becoming very tricky at a later stage. Ammi knew that my sister, tall, statuesque and quite stunningly beautiful when she was not scowling, would not be too pleased with the prospect of being wedded to Zainab Phuppo's short and rather rotund sons. It was a superficial reason, but it was the truth. She knew better than to say that to my Phuppo who was inordinately proud of being a mother of five boys, and Canadian citizens at that! Since they were equipped with a phallus and a blue passport, she considered them eligible catches and had often proclaimed that any girl would be lucky to receive a proposal from them. Therefore, Ammi decided to leave it up to Zeba Baji and Mansoor Bhai themselves. Matters sorted themselves out beautifully: Mansoor Bhai had lived in fear of Zeba Baji ever since she had beaten him to a pulp with the body of her Barbie doll whose head he'd taken off. So when Zainab Phuppo suggested that he marry Zeba Baji, he flatly refused and said that freedom from fear was a basic human right and one he intended to preserve.

However, the same suggestion was received with considerable alacrity by Alam Bhai. Alam Bhai, a full head shorter than Zeba Baji, was a highly self-conscious individual who thought the world of himself. He had come to Pakistan intending to live without the luxuries of air conditioning and high-speed internet in the faint hope that such extreme suffering would help him attain nirvana. He affected a philosophical disposition and when asked by my father what his plans for the future were, he replied that he was searching for the Truth. Abbu didn't know what to make of this so said, 'Good for you!' and went on to make golfing plans with Hassan and Mansoor Bhai.

All quests for enlightenment ended when Alam Bhai saw Zeba Baji at the airport. He embarrassed us all by proclaiming: 'Arey Zeba, you've blossomed since I last saw you!' and hugged her hard, in front of the entire scandalized Jinnah Airport public. Zainab Phuppo told him in the car that it was simply not done to hug or touch a woman in public here in Pakistan, even if she was one's wife. Alam Bhai laughed and commented alliteratively that these poor Pakistanis were provincial people and darted a quick glance at Zeba Baji to see if she had appreciated his wit. She was witnessed wincing.

Upon Zainab Phuppo's encouragement, Alam Bhai was persuaded to propose to my sister. There were several discussions as to how this should be done. Alam Bhai, like all good Eastern sons, never took a single step without first consulting mummy dearest. At first it was suggested that the parents should talk and gauge the response of both individuals. However, Ammi vetoed this plan because she knew she would be stuck having to say no to Zainab Phuppo who in turn would throw a fit, a talent she had inherited from my grandmother. So my mother suggested that the best approach would be if my cousin spoke directly to my sister and dealt with it as maturely as possible. Dadi was concerned that this direct approach would be a breach of the arranged way of things, but Alam Bhai was so dependent on his mother's approval for all actions that even the Direct Approach was pre-planned puppeteering and therefore perfectly permissible. So with a sadqa of a thousand rupees taken out for good luck and whirred around Alam's balding head, my cousin was dispatched to approach my sister with the intent of suggesting matrimony.

Zeba was reading *Pride and Prejudice* when he descended upon her. He plonked himself down uncomfortably close on the two-seater, put his ankle on his knee in an attempt to cross his legs—a Herculean feat considering how short they were. Slowly, he extended his arm along the sofa so that his hand rested just behind her neck. Zeba Baji tried to ignore his presence for as long as possible but since the muddy underside of his shoe was in grave danger of sullying her white shalwar, she looked up and asked, in her inimitably terse style, 'What?'

Momentarily unnerved, Alam Bhai opened his mouth to say something and then closed it to gulp. The roundness of his cheeks and bald head were emphasized by the downward movement of his head. He recovered quickly though, fuelled by the depth of his love for my sister. He sat up straight, cleared his throat and sallied forth with his very thought-out proposition:

'Mummy says we should get married. What do you think?'

'No.'

Before he knew it, Alam Bhai was staring at the drawing of Elizabeth Bennet refusing Mr Collins's proposal on the book's cover as Zeba Baji shielded her face from his to indicate that the conversation was over.

'Just stop reading the book for a minute, Janoo,' coaxed Alam Bhai. 'This is important. I know you must be feeling awkward about talking to me like this. You Eastern girls are like shy little flowers, wilting at the prospect of marriage. But in the West they are much more direct about these things than Pakistanis are.'

Zeba Baji gasped as her mind reeled with revulsion at Alam Bhai's endearment. 'Janoo' was one of those ambiguous epithets that can simultaneously be applied to infants and lovers alike. Used by Alam Bhai, almost eleven years Zeba Baji's senior, made it seem disgustingly oedipal.

'And so when Mummy asked me if she should ask Hussain Mamu for your hand in marriage, I said, let me talk to her.

I'm a modern man and I think intelligent, beautiful girls such as yourself should have the opportunity to make their own decision,' lied my suave cousin.

'You want my decision?' Zeba Baji interjected.

'Of course!'

'I think it is very civilized of you indeed to ask your first cousin who is young enough to be your daughter to marry you. But I think you need someone who is a little more Eastern: I think of you as a brother and I'm afraid my feelings for you are entirely platonic. Sorry.'

But Alam Bhai was unfazed. Mummy had told him to marry Zeba and marry Zeba he would. He laughed with all the energy his tiny frame could muster: squeezing his eyes shut, shaking his shoulders and the sofa along with them. He looked like a hideous, giggling hobbit.

'Now Zeba, I don't know if you've studied biology but I have, and it's extremely unnatural for eleven-year-old boys to be able to reproduce. So I am not old enough to be your father. Now listen, I know this must be sudden for you. I think the last time we met, you were five and so I don't blame you for saying no. Why, you hardly know me! But think about it, we share the same bloodline and in our culture, it's quite permissible for cousins to marry. It's so much more convenient. You'll be married, and you won't even have left the family. Now that I think about it, it doesn't make sense when people marry their daughters off into strange families. They have to enter a whole new world. With me, it will be like you never left home!'

'I can stay at home by not marrying anybody. Alam Bhai,

please don't make this more painful than it has to be . . .'

'Zeba, I'm your cousin and older than you, and I have seen a lot more of life than you have. And I know that girls need to marry; they aren't complete otherwise. My boss at the bank where I worked was a woman and I can tell you, I knew how frustrated she was without a man or children to satisfy her. She was a raving lunatic, I tell you. And you know what women like that do when they want a man but can't get him? They humiliate him by showing them that they have more power than them. If I had flirted with her, I would have received one promotion after the next. But I'm honourable and it was up to me to save her from herself. She might want to be compromised but I wouldn't be the one to help her. So I quit. I don't want that to happen to you. You're young and you still have time. You can have lots of babies, and I'll give you a house with a big lawn. And in Canada, it's fully air conditioned all the time! Not that you really need the air conditioning for most of the year, but there's heating, none of this load-shedding crap that's got us all melting like kulfis on a stove. And I'll make sure you have one of those high-tech kitchens where you can make meals for me and Mummy and Daddy. Sometimes for my brothers. Doesn't that sound wonderful?' His eyes shone with the picture of domestic bliss which his imagination had constructed before his eyes.

'That's right, Alam Bhai, I'm having an orgasm this very minute at the thought of cooking nihari for you.'

Alam Bhai blinked twice. I think one blink was surprise that shy, respectable Eastern girls knew what orgasms were.

This complicated his life considerably. The second blink was a manifestation of shock that they could say it aloud.

'Alam Bhai, I don't cook. I don't like children. I don't want to get married. So please, accept my apologies and since we have to coexist under the same roof for the next few days, we will pretend that we never had this conversation.'

But Zeba Baji underestimated the scope and depth of Alam Bhai's passion. He shared his mother's belief in his own eligibility and therefore did not take offence at my sister's refusal. He was a believer that, and I quote, 'the harder the climb, the more satisfying the journey!' And he fully planned to mount the summit that was my sister. He declared that he would make her see how wrong her decision was by being utterly charming to her until she was sobbing with desire and affection in his plump little arms. Therefore, he pursued her with the irritating resolve of a mosquito that goes after warm blood. He found frequent opportunities to converse with her and displayed a great deal of bullheadedness when rebuffed. When she made coffee, he offered to help. When told his help wasn't needed, he was the first to take the tray out of her hands because she was too delicate to hold such a heavy load. He was the first to drink it and the loudest to praise it. When Zeba Baji read a book, he peeked at the pages to read it with her. When Zeba Baji applied lipstick, he was in raptures but told her that her lips didn't need further enhancement, their scarlet splendour was enough. Zeba Baji, who was under strict instructions by my father not to be impertinent to his eldest sister's son, was slowly being driven to madness. She took to using the bathroom to read

was twirling Zeba Baji. Alam Bhai walked in and saw red at the sight of anyone touching the object of his affection. In a fit of rage he pushed Hassan Bhai, who fell on his buttocks with arms and legs still in the air and with his mouth open in shock and surprise. Dadi and Zainab Phuppo witnessed this in horror. A mortified silence ensued as it dawned on Alam Bhai what he had done. He blinked and looked at Hassan Bhai. The latter blinked and looked at him. A glance was shot at Zeba Baji. It was returned with a glare, which had all the devastating effect of a bazooka at close range.

I looked at Naima and I could see her trembling. And I couldn't control myself. It was as if a volcano was erupting inside me. I bit my lips to prevent the escape of the convulsions bubbling within. I shuddered and gasped. Similar sounds escaped Naima. We snorted and clamped our hands on our lips. But it couldn't be contained. Alam Bhai looked like a shamefaced rhinoceros and Hassan Bhai resembled a collapsed Humpty Dumpty. Zeba Baji was as rigid and white as the wall from which he had tumbled. I sat down and started laughing. Naima soon joined me, laughing so hard that barely a sound escaped her gaping mouth. My stomach hurt so much that I doubled over and yet, to my mortification, I couldn't stop.

Laughter, they say, is contagious. They also say that it's the best medicine.

They are wrong on both counts.

No one saw any humour in the situation. Dadi ordered Naima and me to get out of the room, shameless as we were. This gave rise to more hysterical laughter. Fati Phupps, who had arrived from Lahore on the morning flight, entered the room and immediately realized that something terrible had happened. Hassan Bhai's sprawled figure on the floor was also a good indication of the nature of the disaster. She immediately galvanized herself into action, and Naima and I were unceremoniously hauled up from the floor by our ears and marched out of the room.

She later told us that we had succeeded in escalating extant tensions and that Alam Bhai was furious. He had initially tried to cover his tracks by proclaiming it as an accident, and he was merely trying to participate in the dance since he thought there weren't enough men in it. Zeba Baji called his bluff and said that pushing didn't qualify as a dance step. This prompted an instruction from Dadi to respect her older cousin, which merited another nasty retort from my fed-up sibling, who expressed something to the effect of the difficulty in respecting people with very little self-respect to begin with. Upon which a furious Zainab Phuppo led Alam Bhai out of the room, saying that he was too good to waste his attentions on dancing girls. Apparently Zainab Phuppo shared Dadi's disapproval of respectable Shia, Syed girls dancing in public. The idea of her future daughter-in-law doing it made her especially uncomfortable—to her this was a Hindu tradition that respectable Muslims should avoid. Zeba Baji, on the other hand, was determined to party to the fullest at her brother's wedding. She calmly said that dancing and music was a special tradition of the courtesans of Lucknow, who happened to be both Shia and Syed, so she was following the example of posterity. Zainab

Phuppo then expressed surprise and stated that respectable girls never followed in the footsteps of courtesans. Zeba Baji wondered why they did not, considering that they were refined and more cultured than respectable Muslim women who considered it frivolity to apply perfume and whose sense of hygiene left a lot to be desired.

It took Dadi five minutes to calm down, but in those five minutes, she managed to say some nasty things. A bitter tirade was launched against stubborn, arrogant girls who would one day be too old to receive a decent proposal. She then said something about Zeba Baji becoming an out-of-season grape. She would lose her sweetness and shape and be too wrinkled and bitter to be plucked by any self-respecting man. Zeba Baji merely looked haughty and asked Dadi if she was quite finished. Dadi was extremely frustrated that Zeba Baji had managed to rebuff two perfectly respectable proposals and, by riling Zainab Phuppo, had eliminated the chances of receiving an offer from her other three sons as well. But she also realized that antagonizing her granddaughter would be counterproductive to arranging her marriage. In a huff she stuffed some paan in her mouth and watched as Zeba Baji helped Hassan Bhai to his feet.

In the midst of this drama, the time of the wedding approached. It is known to all but acknowledged by few that of all the wedding functions, it is the mehndi which offers the greatest opportunities for ambitious mothers to show off their daughters. This is because it has nothing whatsoever to do with Islam and everything to do with henna, dancing, singing and other revelry.

Haroon Bhai's mayun, as predicted, began with Dadi telling him that he was not allowed to see or talk to Saima Apa until the wedding. Since the nikkah and mehndi were two days away, Haroon Bhai was not devastated, and he circumvented Dadi's dictum by surreptitiously calling his beloved from his bathroom, which was becoming a valuable retreat from irritating relatives.

The milad was as painful as we expected. I wish Dadi had not insisted on inviting the sour-faced Shabnam Bibi who droned on and on in her sonorously nasal tones. Dadi was in raptures at the paeans paid to the Panjatan and kept putting forward one request after the other until three hours had passed and half of the crowd was consumed with boredom, the other with a migraine. Dadi insisted that Zeba Baji should join Shabnam Bibi as a choric back-up figure so that she would be in the spotlight, which was the only entertaining part of the evening since Zeba Baji did not have a lyrical bone in her body and lip-synced the whole way. An embarrassing moment occurred when Shabnam Bibi saw Naima and me whispering in the corner. She interrupted her naat and declared: 'The Prophet's family is here in this room and are observing your inattention. Do you want to go to hell? Now everyone in the room, say a resounding SALAWAT!' So we both shrivelled up into mortified silence while Robs and Maw snickered in a corner.

The nikkah was a solemn function, where only the immediate family was present. Saima Apa looked lovely in a plain red suit with silver circular designs printed on it—Bhakurajian style. Zeba Baji said to Fati Phupps that though traditional, Saima Apa's outfit was a pain to wear because it was so full of starch that it felt like one was wearing glitter paper. But Saima Apa withstood the ordeal with great fortitude, looking demure with the dupatta arched up over her head like a red triangle. Dadi was in her element, telling Robs and Maw to cover their heads at least on this occasion when the maulana was about to come. She also declared that the nikkah should be segregated and insisted that the men repair to another room, which was rather inconvenient for Auntie Shehla who had arranged for the whole affair to take place in her large living room so that everyone could witness the event. Too well bred to argue with Dadi, the men were shooed off into the drawing room. The maulana, a short, stocky individual with a jovial expression and ridiculously large glasses, arrived and read the nikkah in Arabic and asked Saima Apa whether he had her permission to make him her proxy so that he could say 'yes' on her behalf. She nodded in the affirmative, and the maulana went away, leaving us all to wonder whether the girl's part of the nikkah was over. We later discovered that it was. Naima and I felt cheated. Saima Apa had been exempted from The Test. This was the crucial part of the nikkah where a girl gave her consent. The emphasis is on *how* the consent is offered. It is the ultimate test of respectability. A truly modest young woman should be appropriately overwhelmed and be rendered completely unable to utter her assent in a steady voice. The tone must be tremulous, the pitch not above a whisper. The response, moreover, must only come upon the third question; only shamelessly forward wantons are bold enough to say 'yes'

when the maulana asks them whether they accept so and
so for their husbands. Dadi told us that at her nikkah, she
waited for the maulana to ask her three times and then
her aunt said 'yes' for her, while Dadi collapsed into her
mother's bosom who promptly started crying that her
daughter was now no longer hers. It was the sound of wailing
that usually signalled to the men that the girl had at last
agreed. In Saima Apa's case, there was no lamentation, it
was disappointingly clean, uncomplicated and legal and
we were most disconcerted at having been deprived of the
melodrama.

We recovered soon enough when we found a way for us
to sneak through to the men's section. We managed to sidle
along and peek through the door of the attached dining
room to observe the proceedings. Haroon Bhai was seated
between the black-robed maulana and Saima Apa's father.
The maulana recited more Arabic. He tapped Haroon Bhai
on the knee and my flustered brother said, 'I do!' in a loud
voice, whereupon the maulana stopped and told him that
he hadn't reached that part yet and recommended patience.
He continued and tapped Haroon Bhai again, and Haroon
Bhai opened his mouth again but shut it when the maulana
shook his head and continued the recitation. This occurred
a third time. Then the maulana suddenly declared that the
couple was married and that the girl's and boy's fathers
should accept his congratulations. Everyone got up at once
and started hugging each other, but Naima pointed out that
Haroon Bhai remained sitting where he was in the hope of
still being asked if he would have Saima for his wife. He

blinked a couple of times and then grinned broadly when my father scooped him up in a huge hug.

Once the maulana left, the ceremonies took place. Haroon Bhai was brought in and seated next to a smiling Saima Apa and we sang some songs as Dadi, followed by my parents and Saima Apa's parents and then the respective elders on both sides, fed sweets to the couple. Another red dupatta was placed on both my brother and his wife and a mirror was placed on their laps for the Ar-see-masaf. We all hooted when this happened, partly to embarrass Haroon Bhai and partly because no Bhakurajian function is rendered complete until the female relatives have hooted. Fati Phupps asked Saima Apa if she wasn't too disappointed in what she saw, at which Saima Apa shook her head and Haroon Bhai grinned broadly.

The mehndi took place that evening and it was this function on which Dadi pinned most of her hopes for my sister. Zeba Baji was set ablaze in a brilliantly orange and yellow gharara, courtesy Designer Dadi. We had decorated henna in various coloured earthenware pots and Zeba Baji was designated chief carrier, given the load of the largest and the grandest. The rest of us carried candles as we made our entrance into Saima Apa's huge lawn, where the ceremonies were to be held. Robs and Maw insisted that they wanted to lead the procession, which irritated me since I was the sister and I should have been in front. But Ammi said that we must be polite to our guests and told me to get in line behind them. Following them were Naima and I, then Zeba Baji with some of her friends. Haroon Bhai, wearing a dark blue shalwar-kameez, entered under the canopy of a bright

red dupatta, held above his head by his friends. Mansoor and
Hassan Bhai preceded them with a dhol player, doing the
bhangra. Alam Bhai sulked along behind them.

The henna was placed on the ground and all us cousins
danced around it, Naima and I looking like awkward
hooligans next to my sister, who was indeed, the tallest and
the most graceful. Robs and Maw swished and sashayed
most outrageously and batted their eyelashes at the hooting
boys who turned out to be Saima Apa's cousins. We then
settled down to sing songs and soon a small war was waged
between us and Saima Apa's cousins who tried to outsing us
through sheer volume and enthusiasm. Again, Dadi made
sure that it was Zeba Baji who played the dhol, because the
video camera shines brightest and most frequently on the
dhol player. She even made Zeba Baji initiate the ceremonies
with Haroon and Saima, both of whom were seated on a
wooden swing decorated with yellow-and-white dupattas.
This was a ceremony normally reserved for married women,
as they represented good luck. Widows and divorcées, having
bad kismets which were as contagious as the bubonic plague,
were persona non grata here. Zeba Baji's initiation of the
festivities was therefore an anomaly. But not even ancient
Bhakurajian traditions could stand in the way of Dadi's
ambitions. She sat on a sofa with Qurrat Dadi, constantly
commenting on how lovely her granddaughter looked, while
the latter nodded, feigning a look of boredom.

Robs and Maw were the first to dance. Dadi had wanted
Zeba Baji to start as this would be one more opportunity to
put her on display, but Rania Phuppo was adamant that her

daughters were anxious to show the world their brilliant choreography. The number was quite erotic. They jerked their hips from left to right with the sensuality of seasoned belly dancers. Their faces danced too: their eyes shone and their mouths smiled and pouted according to the lyrics of the song. They moved their sinuous bodies in perfect unison and when the dance ended it was the young (and old) men who cheered the loudest. Dadi looked faintly disapproving but Rania Phuppo expressed her pride by waving hundred-rupee notes above their heads to ward off any evil from her darlings. Zeba Baji, Naima and I followed with our dance, which was meant to be funny rather than seductive. In the middle, Abbu surprised us by jumping in with the bhangra. This launched a free-for-all where all of Saima Apa's and our cousins joined in, followed by Saima Apa and Haroon Bhai themselves. A protesting Dadi was dragged in by my mother and she hid her face in my father's chest as he tried to get her to dance by grabbing her hands and swinging them from side to side.

It was when dinner was served that all of Dadi's efforts bore fruit. Several women approached her about my sister, questions were asked concerning Zeba Baji's age, profession and culinary skills. Dadi glowed with all the pride of a goatseller on Baqra Eid who had managed to sell off all his animals, and lied brazenly about my sister's domestic achievements.

'Zeba? Arey, she cooks so well that I'm just left licking my fingers!'

'Sew? Arey, do you see she stitched that gharara herself!'

which was only technically true, since Zeba Baji had had to hem her shirt.

Zeba Baji was repeatedly summoned to say salaam to women who gave her intense once-, twice- and thrice-overs. Zeba Baji cooperated in the beginning but then retreated behind the stage on which Saima Apa and Haroon Bhai were seated so that she could be out of Dadi's sight.

The night before the rukhsati, Robs and Maw were more nauseating than ever. They kept looking at Haroon Bhai and snickering. I got tired when they burst into a new bout of giggles as we lay down to go to sleep.

'What's the matter with you?' I asked, in a manner that was not very gracious.

Robs rolled over onto her stomach and looked down at us as we lay on the mattress.

'Your brother seemed jittery at the mehndi. But then, tomorrow is a big day for him!' she said suggestively.

'Yes it is. So?'

'Well, I think,' Maw chimed in, 'that it's the *night* that he's looking forward to.'

And they fell into a new fit of giggling.

I remained quiet and looked at Naima, who also seemed perplexed.

'Uff, you both are so naive! You *do* know what happens on the wedding night, don't you?' Maw asked us.

'Of course we do!' said Naima indignantly. 'The groom gives his bride a new piece of jewellery. I know Haroon Bhai is going to give Saima Baji the most *gorgeous* diamond bracelet . . .'

'Uff ho! Silly!' interrupted Rob as she and Maw looked at each other. They reminded me of the evil Siamese cats in *The Lady and the Tramp*. 'They're going to have . . . sex.'

'No they are NOT!' I said indignantly, sitting up.

'Yes! They are! They are! What do you think the valima is celebrating? Why do we have a function after the rukhsati, huh? It's to celebrate the consummation of the marriage.'

This new piece of information was quite a lot to digest. I did have a somewhat nebulous idea about the facts of life, since no one talks about sex openly. What I didn't know was that there was such a time and restriction to the event itself. That we all knew exactly when and where my brother and his wife would be doing 'it' seemed quite scandalous.

'Well . . . what's it to you? Let them have sex. I'm not interested in things that don't concern unmarried women!' I proclaimed.

Oh, but I *was*. After Robs and Maw made some more fun of my 'Dadi-ness', they fell asleep. I however, kicked Naima to see if she was awake. An annoyed grunt indicated that she was.

'Naima, do you think that they have to do it *tomorrow* night?'

'I don't know. Probably.'

'Do you think they'll use their tongues?'

'I don't know. Probably.'

'What if they don't? Can we still have a valima?'

'I have no idea, to be honest. But I'm sure they've all thought of this before fixing the wedding date.'

I thought about Dadi sitting with my parents and

decreeing: 'Good boys and girls have sex on the birth of such and such Imam.' But I don't think it would have been discussed so explicitly. I once read in an encyclopedia that it was a Sumatran custom to air the wedding sheets of the newly married couple to confirm consumation. Would Dadi parade my brother's sheets around the house? I fervently hoped that she didn't. I fell asleep dreaming of Alam Bhai wearing a bed sheet like a Roman toga and sticking his tongue out at Zeba Baji.

The day of the rukhsati dawned and there was chaos all around. Too many women needed to use the bathroom all at once. Last-minute orders and confirmations crept up. Robs and Maw went to the parlour to get a blow-dry. But Dadi was serene. After all, she knew that this evening would provide her with another event to show off her granddaughter. This time, Zeba Baji had donned a bright red shalwar-kameez and was steered around speculative mothers of eligible sons by Dadi who held her firmly by the elbow. I accompanied her, partly out of sympathy and partly because I knew that it would be a highly enjoyable experience. I was not disappointed. My usually confident sister was quite disconcerted when one rather rotund auntie reached out and held Zeba Baji's chin, tilting her face and commenting to my Dadi: 'Mashallah! She's very fair!'

As Zeba Baji tried to disengage her jaw from the plump but firm grip that belonged to a blonde-haired, sharp-looking woman with cardamom-green eyes framed with kohl, a rapid round of questions was fired at her with the sweetest of expressions.

'How old are you, Beta?'

'Thirty-seven.'

'Arey toba, Zeba this is not the time to joke! My granddaughter has a great sense of humour. She's twenty-five.'

'Mashallah! And what have you studied, Beta?'

'English literature.' This honest answer was a result of Dadi sharply pinching Zeba Baji.

'From where have you studied?'

'St Joseph's Convent.'

'Ah, a girls' school. That's good. You know Gulbahar Auntie, I don't know what the world is coming to! Yesterday I met this girl who's studied in a co-educational institution all her life. Did you know what she told me? She said she had had three boyfriends already? Toba toba! And what are you doing currently, Zeba Beti?'

'Talking to you. Ouch! Teaching.'

'Very good, very good. I always say that teaching is such a noble profession and so convenient for marriage! I tell you, Gulbahar Auntie, this modern obsession that girls have developed for careers is just ridiculous. A smallish job-shob or charity work is acceptable. But girls nowadays neglect their husbands and children for their own selves. I tell you, the Day of Judgement is near!'

Dadi nodded vigorously in the affirmative and deftly disengaged herself and my sister from the conversation so that she could move on to the mother of yet another eligible candidate.

The candidate himself was present. A similar round of questions ensued. The mother had painted her face white but forgotten to extend the corrective cosmetics to her neck, which betrayed her by being distinctly brown. Her hair, like dry straw, had been wrested into a chignon as high as the Habib Bank building on I.I. Chundrigar Road. She raised one plucked eyebrow at my sister who reciprocated in kind. She then introduced her son, a handsome individual, smartly attired in black. Coal-black eyes were narrowed and the aquiline nose was turned up to look down at Zeba Baji. He curtly acknowledged my sister's presence with a nod and glanced at his mother with the arched eyebrow that was clearly ancestral.

Both Zeba Baji and I instantly disliked this arrogant individual, but Dadi was determined that some conversation was due so she sweetly suggested that Zeba Baji should say something nice to 'Bhai'.

Embarrassed, my sister glared at Dadi and then ventured forth with the safest topic that came into her mind.

'I hope you're enjoying the wedding?'

'It's tolerable.'

'Ah. Well, I'd try the Bihari kababs if I were you. They're quite delicious.'

'Oh, I've given up on the idea of actually enjoying eating at weddings. One is assailed by ambitious mothers and their eligible daughters with such nauseating frequency that it quite ruins the appetite.'

Zeba Baji clenched her fist. She made an attempt to leave but Dadi unwisely continued the conversation by interjecting that the eligible bachelor, named Noman, was a banker.

'My Zeba is a teacher, Nomi Beta.'

Noman looked bored and with a sigh asked the question expected of him.

'So where do you teach?'

'Karachi Grammar School,' said my sister, knowing how Noman would react.

The three words had a remarkable effect on the attitude of the eligible bachelor. His nose came down several altitudes, and he finally looked directly at my sister. His eyes widened in admiration and glistened with the joy of a starved man who stumbles upon a plump and juicy laddoo.

'Ah! And are you an old Grammarian?'

'I consider myself particularly young, actually!'

'Ha ha! I mean, what grade did you join in?'

'First,' lied my sister, who had actually only done her A Levels from there, but confessing this didn't suit her current purpose.

'Ah! I'm an OG myself. Which year did you graduate in?'

'1990.'

'I graduated in 1988! What a small world!'

'A little congested, I agree. When did you join KGS?' my sister asked.

'Grade five,' he said apologetically. 'I was at a school in Sharjah before that.'

'I see. So you're a mongrel.'

'Excuse me?'

'Well, you aren't a thoroughbred Grammarian. Mixed bloodlines. You know, because of the Middle Eastern educational experience.'

'Zeba,' interjected a frantic Dadi, 'I think Bano is looking for you.'

'I think, Madam Zeba,' Noman proclaimed, 'that you are a snob of the highest order.'

'I applaud your judgement and think you are an excellent judge of character. But snobs stick to their own kind. Can't risk sullying the bloodlines, you see. I'm a horrible Grammar-Nazi when it comes to such matters. But it was delightful chatting with you. As you heard my grandmother say, my mother looks for me and I must oblige. Do remember the Bihari kababs! Tata!'

My sister swivelled on one heel and marched off, leaving Dadi and me looking horrified and shocked. I ran after her—I could tell that she was livid by the stiffness of her posture. Dadi would also be quite angry with this unforgivable behaviour, but there was nothing she could do about it as all the cousins were gathering for the shoe hiding, a popular custom which had the potential to turn ugly. Our unfortunate ancestor, Lallan Mian found this out the hard way when his wife's sisters asked him for money and he refused to give any. Upon which his wife grabbed the leather shoe and threatened to beat him with it until he complied. When he refused once again, she came good on her threat. It was the first time that Lallan Bhai realized that his wife's bite was as bad as her bark.

A small group formed around the couple. Fauzia had already gotten a good hold of both of Haroon Bhai's saleem shahees and was pulling with all her might, encouraged by her cousins, while Naima was clutching my harassed brother's ankles to prevent him from slipping off the sofa. The negotiations started, Haroon Bhai pretending that he'd forgotten his wallet at home, though I knew that he had given about Rs 10, 000 to Hassan Bhai in anticipation of the event. Five minutes passed, five minutes of loud cheering and hooting and even taunting as one of Saima Apa's cousins told her to give up the idea of marrying a penniless man. With a great deal of drama, Haroon Bhai told Hassan Bhai to give them *some* money. A thousand rupees came out. Then another. Each time a note was pulled out, there was much applause. After the fifth attempt, the cheering reached a crescendo and Saima Apa was asked to induce her husband to produce a respectable sum of money. Saima Apa shyly nodded and Haroon Bhai faked an arrow in his heart and gallantly declared: 'Give it all away!' At which Hassan Bhai flung ten notes in the air amid shrieks of delight. It was all quite amusing but I noticed that Zeba Baji kept her distance, her arms crossed and her expression blank and unreadable.

Time came for Saima Apa to leave her house for ours, forever. Saima Apa hugged her parents and cried while Dadi looked smug and smiled into the camera and comforted Auntie Shehla by saying, 'Don't worry, I'll take care of her, she's my granddaughter, too, now!' which made her cry even harder.

We brought Saima Apa and Haroon Bhai home, making sure we were paid some cash to 'allow' them to enter our house. After another mini-milad and showering blessings on the couple, Dadi declared that it was time to leave the newly-weds alone. Naima and I exchanged significant glances.

It was three o'clock in the morning by the time everyone

go to bed and don't get out of it until morning!'

We obliged by fleeing to our bedroom. The next day, before the valima, neither of us could look at either my brother or his wife in the face without blushing furiously. Zeba Baji asked us what on earth was wrong, but there was no way we were confessing our attempts at voyeurism. She shrugged and walked off, getting ready for the final function of the wedding.

If my sister thought that the valima would be more enjoyable than the rukhsati, she was mistaken. The valima approached and she donned a sleeveless blouse with a cream-coloured sari, which Fati Phupps had brought for her in order to give her some relief from Dadi's selected clothes. Since Dadi knew it was better to relent than to argue with my aunt, she merely showed her disapproval with pursed lips, but later she had to admit that Zeba looked quite lovely with white motia flowers in her hair. Even Alam Bhai, who had not spoken a word to her since the undignified shove, went so far as to tell her she looked 'quite nice'. She steered clear of Dadi who knew better than to push her by subjecting her to more introductions. So my grandmother prudently remained on the sidelines and pointed my sister out to whoever accosted her.

She endured the public attention in silence, sticking close to Fati Phupps who was flirting outrageously with a man half her age, a man clearly besotted with this voluptuous, sophisticated woman wearing an off-shoulder blouse, which revealed a plump cleavage. Dinner was served and all the ammas who had until now been concentrating on eligible bachelorettes directed their attention to the food, upon which they descended with great determination. Things were particularly frantic in the prawn section where the freshly fried pieces were consumed at a much faster rate than they were being prepared. Kishwar Begum, a cousin of my mother's and newly arrived from London, stood aside contemptuously and let everyone else serve themselves, while commenting loudly on how Pakistanis could never learn the art of getting into line.

Into the fray lumbered a hefty figure, a middle-aged woman who looked like she could jump up and down a hundred times with a grown man perched on each shoulder. She shimmered in her shiny blue shalwar-kameez as she shoved dainty aunties left, right and centre. After heaping her plate high with biryani, kababs, prawns and nan bread, she waddled to the table where Zeba, Fati Phupps, Naima, Hassan Bhai and I were seated. She heaved herself down and commenced eating. Her four chins multiplied into six every time she looked down at her plate. Slowly looking up, she scanned our faces with her beady eyes, which focused on my sister and remained solidly on her. The crudeness of her eating habits, however, diverted one from the frankness of her gaze. She chomped on the chicken breast, holding it firmly with both hands, her fingers coated with dirt-brown gravy that oozed down to her elbows and smeared the thick, black hair on her arms. As she masticated the meat with open mouth, the separate grains of rice and chicken were visible as they turned into gooey mush. After the bone had been de-meated and gnawed so that it was a shrivelled remnant of its past glory, it was chucked down under the table with an expert flick of the wrist. Naima gasped and Fati Phupps pinched her on the knee, telling her to contain her reactions to the events around her. One more piece of meat was devoured, the bone flicked under, this time making contact with Hassan Bhai's ankle who jumped and enclaimed: 'Oh, for heaven's sake!'

Madam Adiposity slowly moved her thick neck, her gaze shifting from Zeba to Hassan, who was instantly intimidated by the size of her substantial hands, which came down on the white tablecloth with a resounding thud.

'Did you say something, boy?'

'No!' lied Hassan Bhai, slumping in his seat to avoid her gaze.

Her relentless stare resumed its focus on Zeba Baji, having the same effect on her as the Eye of Sauron on Frodo Baggins. My sister was paralysed like a fly watching the approach of a spider whose web it is enmeshed in. Fati Phupps took pity on her and suggested to her that they should find another table. The corpulent one finally spoke.

'Are you this girl's mother?'

'Yes.'

'How old is she?'

'Why do you want to know?'

'Because I have a son who's thirty-three years old. Is she spoken for?'

'Um, look Bibi, it's horribly embarrassing for my daughter to be sitting here. Zeba Beta, why don't you get up and get me some prawns while I talk to Auntie?'

Zeba Baji got up with great gusto and made to leave

from the scene when the fat woman interrupted with an instruction.

'Haan, larki, get me some prawns as well. As well as some extra biryani. In a separate plate. And some Sprite. Diet.'

Zeba Baji, thoroughly bemused, nodded and escaped with no intention of ever returning.

Fatima Phuppo said, 'Look, my daughter is not interested in getting married right now, she's too young . . .'

'She looks old enough to me. Old enough to bear children. What else does she need to do?'

My aunt, a self-proclaimed feminist who took every opportunity to oppose such chauvinism, was aghast. Her eyes nearly exited their sockets. Her mouth remained open as she turned as red as a tomato. She inhaled loudly and was about to splutter out a response when the mammoth matron continued:

'Besides, my son is present here. I want him to see her. If he likes her, then we can talk further.'

'My daughter might not like your son.'

'She will.'

Naima and Hassan Bhai watched in horror as this woman, clearly accustomed to getting her own way, took out a cell phone from her purse and dialled a number. She let out a robust burp and was gearing up for a second one when she barked: 'Usman? Come here.'

I often wonder how Usman knew where to find his mother, 'here' being slightly vague. But then, such an immense target can hardly be difficult to sight. After a few minutes he arrived, a wraithlike individual wearing a starched shalwar-kameez with pink and gold embroidery on his collar and sleeves. He was only a few inches taller than his seated mother and looked at us all with a morose expression. He was as thin as she was fat and when he stood next to her the contrast seemed especially ridiculous. They looked like the number 10. Or the number 18, since, to be fair, the mother did have some semblance of a waist.

'This is my son,' proclaimed the woman as she rested her hand on her knee, sitting with all the pride of a landlord showing off his lands. 'Where did your daughter go?'

Fati Phupps suddenly had an epiphany.

'Acha, acha, this is your son? Mashallah. Very good. What did you say his name was?'

'Sardar Usman Butt.'

'I see. I hope you don't mind, but are you Sunni?'

'By the grace of God, yes, we are.'

'Oh dear, well, we are Shia. Descendents of the sixth Imam. You understand that we don't marry into Sunnis. Unless you have a Shia husband? That would change things considerably.'

The woman scowled, the sides of her mouth turning downward in utter contempt. Her son revealed similar revulsion, which was exhibited by his spitting on the ground.

'We most certainly do not!'

'Not even a distant relative? But you simply must produce one Shia relative so that I can convince Zeba's father to approve the match!'

'Arey Bibi, you must be mad to think that we would marry into Shias! Even if you converted, you could not have my

Usman! May Allah forgive you for your sins. Chalo Usman, take me home.'

She surged forth with indignant effort, almost overturning the table on all of us in her attempt to get up. Usman helped her by ineffectually grasping her elbows. We watched them plodding away and breathed a sigh of relief. Fati Phupps exploded.

'What was that? Can you believe that woman? Of all the nerve! I'm going to write an article on Ms Kalashnikov right there. Who says it's the men who oppress the women of this country? We ourselves are our biggest enemies! Did you see her son? He looked like she sits on him every day! I just can't believe that people like that still exist! Women like that should be put in prison I tell you!'

Zeba Baji, seeing it was safe, plopped down next to Fati Phuppo and cooled her down by making her take a few sips of water. Hassan Bhai winked at her.

'Mubarak ho! Fati Phupps warded them off. Waisay I must say that our Usman was indeed a prize catch, wasn't he? Excellent sense of style.'

Zeba Baji hugged Fati Phupps tightly and proclaimed her a gem. Fati Phupps declared that she was starving and suggested that we, too, partake of the prawns before they finished.

Thus ended the final function of Haroon Bhai's wedding. We were all relieved at the prospect of some rest, but Zeba Baji's misery was not about to end. Because, as everyone knows, the mothers who are *really* interested in getting their sons married wait till *after* the wedding to arrange marriages.

her, breakfasting with her, going to the office with her and returning home with her. They dined together and they, of course, slept together. This is not to say that they didn't spend any time with us. All meals were a family affair, but it was fairly safe to say that the days when Haroon Bhai belonged to us were gone. A new woman occupied most of his time and attention. It didn't bother me as much in the beginning because I was shamelessly obtuse and didn't allow myself to miss their company since I was in it all the time. I routinely plonked myself down between them on the sofa to watch television. I monopolized Saima Apa when she joined us for tea or food. She was a fascinating new acquisition who knew plenty about make-up and weight loss, the two subjects a pimply, overweight teenager like me could not stop discussing. I didn't give them any time to relax privately. I asked Saima Apa whether I was invading her space and naively expected her to tell me the truth. My poor sister-in-law, forced to be diplomatic, told me 'not at all'. I told her to tell me to buzz off whenever she wanted to and congratulated myself for having dealt with the situation quite cleverly, not knowing that it was probably impossible for any girl to tell any in-law, no matter how young they may be, to buzz off.

Ultimately, my own stupidity settled the situation when I barged into their room unannounced to find them locked in a passionate embrace. I screamed and Saima Apa dived under the covers and buried her head and Haroon Bhai told me to please get the hell out and respect their bloody privacy. I ran out in tears and tore out his picture from the frame in my room and burnt it. I felt betrayed because the physical intimacy that I had so briefly witnessed seemed to set the seal on the fact that Haroon was my brother second and somebody else's husband first. The fact that my brother had scolded me, *me*, his favourite sibling, in front of Saima Apa was a further source of mortification. I am ashamed to admit that no matter how much I admired my sister-in-law, I never actually considered her 'real' family; she was an appendage to us 'original' Bandians. Witnessing this intimacy forced me to reanalyse the situation with realistic eyes, and I didn't like the conclusion that stared me in the face.

Saima Apa tried to coax me out of my embarrassment but I treated her with significant animosity and looked at her as if she were a loose woman. Zeba Baji ultimately sat me down and we spoke woman to woman. Would I like it if Haroon ignored his wife and paid all his attention to me? I replied that I should like it very much. That received a sharp admonition not to be silly. I sulked for a while and then said that I wished I could handle change as well as she did. That evoked an uncharacteristically open response.

'Oh, Saleha. I wish that were true. But I hate change too. One day I'm going about my own business and the next I'm dragged around by Dadi for a grand display and auction. One minute I'm single and proud of it and all of a sudden I'm considered incomplete because I don't have a man to take care of me. Did you not see how rude I was to that idiotic Noman? I mean, just because he was an arrogant prick didn't mean I had to act catty. But it hurts, being carted out in front of men and their nauseatingly smug mothers.'

I wanted to continue with this conversation but it was

clear that my sister did not want to reveal any more feelings. She shrugged and returned to her usual curtness by informing me to buck up and stop being a prude around my brother and his wife. Eventually, I cultivated a healthy respect for their privacy, which I took care never to invade.

The dynamic that evolved between the three generations of women in the house was too subtle to analyse and, therefore, difficult to resolve. The mother and daughter-in-law relationship is a very strange and complex one. The mother takes an active part in searching for her son's wife. Without her approval, nothing can take place. If it does, then it enters the shady and scandalous realm of The Love Marriage—and hence all resentment against the newcomer is deemed justified. But even with arranged marriages, a shift of attitude takes place after the wedding. The ugly green monster rears its head and the son who was once so willingly shared becomes an unwilling rope pulled in all directions in a nasty tug of war.

Dadi was more transparent about her dislike of having to share her darling grandson with another woman and made it a point to say to Haroon Bhai whenever she saw him that he had changed and that she felt alone and that she missed her Fareed Beta. When that didn't have the desired effect of separating her grandson from his wife's side, she added Abbas Phuppa to the list of the regular people that she proclaimed to mourn on an hourly basis. That got her a hug and a kiss from Haroon Bhai, but not much else. She soon changed tactics. She took to waiting for the couple at the door as they arrived from the office every evening, holding a small bottle of mustard hair oil in her hand. When they arrived, she bid Haroon Bhai to come and have his champi done. While this happened, she complained to him how she hardly saw him any more, that a man should have some more control over his impulses and should not be like a rotund aubergine on a tray, swaying wherever it was tilted. All this occurred in front of Saima Apa, who smiled politely and went to shower and change while Dadi monopolized her grandson and jealously guarded him from any company but her own.

I never expected my mother to act possessively. For the most part she didn't, but it was clear that she was having a tough time accepting Saima Apa as part of the family because the latter had supplanted my mother in Haroon Bhai's eyes as his favourite woman in the world. She stayed quiet, but shot hostile looks at her daughter-in-law when she thought no one was looking. One day, however, she turned pale and pursed her lips in anger when Haroon Bhai proclaimed that Saima Apa made the best biryani in the world. That honour had belonged to Ammi alone. She took to watching the saas–bahu serials on television and loudly reviled the daughter-in-law for her injustice to the mother-in-law. Dadi and Ammi drew closer together and found a new kinship against a common threat. Zeba Baji, unruffled by these goings-on, kept herself busy with her books and her friends and was least perturbed by the new addition to the family.

Had Saima Apa left things up to Haroon Bhai, she would have alienated three-fourths of her female in-laws because he really did show absolutely no balance when it came to wife and family. But my sister-in-law made it a point to spend more time with all of us individually. When she had time, she helped my mother with the cooking. She asked Dadi to show her photographs of her childhood days in Bhakuraj, a request fulfilled with great alacrity. Slowly but surely, the antagonism we had begun to feel abated. It would be tempting to say that we accepted her as one of our own, but that would be untrue. We settled into a delicate truce, which was seriously jeopardized when Saima Apa and Ammi had an argument about Haroon Bhai's favourite colour. Ammi said it was lavender. Saima Apa said it was black. Both stood their ground and my mother was incensed that her daughter-in-law, who had known her son for only a year, pretended to know more about Haroon Bhai than the woman who had given birth to him. Dadi plunged into the argument by insisting that she had raised Haroon Bhai and that his favourite colour was mauve. The three argued vociferously until they summoned my harassed brother and demanded to know which one was his favourite. He said purple and fled. Saima Apa, embarrassed, followed him. Zeba Baji had been witnessing this with an amused expression and said to Dadi and Ammi, 'If you two don't loosen your grip you're going to lose not just your daughter-in-law but your son as well.'

'Look at this chit of a girl telling her elders how to act! I'll have you know I know exactly how to handle myself as a mother-in-law!' announced Dadi.

'That's exactly my point. Stop being her mother-in-law. Stop trying to be her mother. Treat her lovingly or don't treat her at all. And the same goes to you Ammi. She's not your daughter; she will never be. But she obviously loves Haroon and for his sake wants to get along with you. But if you continue to flare up the minute she acts like Haroon's wife, she's going to stop caring about you. Be her friend, stop arguing with her and give her space. Else she'll get some on her own by moving out. You know I'm right. Didn't you say something of the sort to Dadi before Haroon and Saima were married?'

She left both mothers-in-law feeling uneasy. Logically, my sister's words made sense. But the irrationality of heaving emotions did not always bow to logic.

Saima Apa soon got a reprieve from their attentions when proposals poured in for Zeba. Having married one offspring off, they channelled their energies towards making the same arrangements for the other.

Dadi's round of introductions initiated a series of inquiries about Zeba Baji. This was the first phase of the process when a number of personal questions were asked concerning Zeba Baji's age, profession, future plans, citizenship status and extracurricular activities. When satisfactory answers were given to all the questions, things went on to the second phase in the drawing room.

The first phone call came from the daughter of Dadi's friend, with whom Dadi sat at the Imam Bargah during Moharram. When the phone rang, Ammi picked it up, accidentally pressing the speaker button so that I overheard the conversation.

'Hello? Am I speaking to Mrs Bandian?'

'Yes, you are.'

Awkward silence followed by uncomfortable clearing of the throat.

'Jee, hello, Mrs Bandian. My name is Sanober Haq; we met at your son's wedding. Your mother-in-law introduced us to you and your husband, I hope you remember?'

My mother had absolutely no idea who she was talking to. But of course, one mustn't be rude and acknowledge the lack of recognition.

'Of course Mrs Haq! How are you?'

'I'm fine! How are your son and daughter-in-law?'

'They're fine! Very happy. And your husband? Is he fine?'

'Oh yes, he's fine. And your mother-in-law? How is she?'

'She's fine.'

Painful Pause. Both ladies knew where this was going but did not know quite how to get there. It wasn't that Ammi was trying to be difficult, she was simply unaware of how much information she should offer since the role of the daughter's mother was a novel one.

The girl's mother, as a species, is very different from the boy's mother. The former is as passive as the latter is active. She is bound by many rules. If broken, they would be detrimental to her daughter's marital future. She must not volunteer information about her daughter unless asked by the boy's mother; to do so would make her seem eager and pathetic. She must on no account withhold information if sought by the boy's mother because this puts her daughter in a suspicious light. She must walk a precarious tightrope when it comes to tone and attitude. While she may want to attract proposals for her daughter, she must act with haughty reserve. She must be receptive to inquiries but never seek them out. She must always listen and nod but never initiate.

She must convey that her daughter is a prize to win, but must never seem to outwardly anticipate the distribution ceremony. Thus my mother was decorously taciturn as she waited for Mrs Haq to broach the topic of introductions.

'Yes, well, your mother-in-law introduced us to your daughter Zeba. How is she doing? Very pretty girl, mashallah.'

'Zeba is fine.'

'Oh good. That's fine.'

Once it was established that everyone and everything was quite fine, Mrs Haq proceeded to ask Ammi about Zeba Baji. After the answers were deemed satisfactory, she proceeded to tell Ammi about her son, a thirty-year-old industrial engineer in Dallas named Furqan. He had done his master's from the University of Indiana and was making about $80,000 a year. My mother blushed with embarrassment at the mention of the salary but did not say anything. I soon found out that it was considered quite acceptable to reveal the financial status of a suitor as the financial capability of the boy is deemed very important and is the basis of making a good match. They hailed from Ajmer Shareef and had been based in Karachi for the past thirty-five years. Furqan had two sisters, the older one married and the mother of two boys. The younger was studying home economics. Everything sounded quite good and Ammi looked very pleased until Mrs Haq put her foot in her mouth. In fact she swallowed it whole.

'You see, Furqan is coming down this summer to Karachi for two weeks and I would really like him to meet Zeba. We've also looked at about four other girls to show him. He's not too picky and should like at least one of them!'

Ammi responded with silence and Mrs Haq seemed to realize she had made a fatal gaffe.

'Oh, I mean, there are such few good girls around! You know how it is with boys these days—they have such high standards! But mashallah your Zeba is on top of the list. I am sure that once Furqan sees her, he won't want to take a look at anyone else!'

It was a poor save, but at least she was trying. Ammi curtly informed her that she would let her know when they could come over. She was highly offended that her daughter was on any list at all.

'After all,' she said to Dadi, 'I also went around and looked at girls but I never categorized them on any basis. I don't care that her son is highly qualified—she's a very ill-mannered woman!'

'But the boy seems like quite a catch!' said Dadi whose eyes gleamed at the prospect of getting Zeba Baji engaged before her arch-rival's granddaughter got married. 'Bahu, you are too naive—the world does not operate by your rules! Why, people get their sons engaged and then break their word when they see a better girl come along! It happened in Bhakuraj all the time. My own sister was betrothed to our first cousin, but then along came Rajo Bibi, who paraded her daughters in front of him. Now what was my sister to do if her breasts were not as big as watermelons? Bas, Bhai Naseeruddin broke off the rishta with my sister and married Rajo Bibi's youngest. Never had any sons. Serves him right. And Mrs Haq was just being honest! What are mothers supposed to do if their sons live in Amreeka and only come for two weeks? Even when you go shopping, you see at least five or six samples of clothes before selecting one, don't you? Getting a good proposal is very difficult these days, Bahu; you must not get angry at little things like this. After all, Mrs Haq was just being honest. I think you should call her and let her come as soon as possible.'

Ammi was still not completely convinced, but Abbu said it might not be a bad idea to let the family come over. 'The mother might be tactless but the boy might be decent enough. No one is asking you to make a decision anyway. Just let them come, no harm in it.'

Thus, it was decided that Mrs Haq and her daughters would come and visit us the next week. They would be seated, as all subsequent families who came, in the drawing room.

Dadi set about choreographing the drawing room meeting with all the fastidiousness her frail form could muster. In her excitement she remembered how she had been presented to suitors who came to see her in the village of Bhakuraj.

'I came from a respectable Shia, Syed family and our family practised the veil. No man was allowed to look at me directly. So my mother, your Par Dadi, seated me inside my room at an angle so that my reflection was caught by a mirror which was placed inside the courtyard. That way, suitors and family saw my reflection, but never my actual person. There I sat, with a dupatta on my head, looking at my hands and toes. Gone are the days when girls used to have a sense of modesty about marriage. Now they want to go out to restaurants and talk and date! Arey wah! If you've done that much, why don't you go and sleep around with whoever comes to you with a proposal!'

'Yes, but if we slept with them, we wouldn't want to marry them,' replied Zeba Baji with a naughty wink at me.

'Why is that so?'

'Because most men are terrible in bed. They pay no attention to a woman's needs.'

'Are you listening to your daughter, Bahu? She's speaking like she has a lot of experience! Wah wah! And let me tell you something, these new ideas about women's needs are just mordren nonsense. The only need a woman feels is the need to hold her child in her arms and to keep her husband well fed and contented!'

'But Dadi, don't you think a woman should get some pleasure now and then?'

'What is this pleasure-shleazure business? Women are supposed to fulfil their duty to their husbands silently and patiently. And let me tell you, this pleasure-shleazure nonsense is just something they put in those novels that you bury your head in. Respectable women don't think about pleasure. Toba toba. Why, on my wedding night with your Dada, I . . .'

But we all ran out before we had to hear any more. Dadi's Bhakurajian stories were very entertaining, but details about my grandparents' wedding night were not something we wanted to hear.

Dadi tried to convince Zeba Baji to sit demurely in front of a mirror. My sister said absolutely not. My Dadi said that she had become disobedient. My sister said that she would agree to a mirror but Dadi should not blame her if, at the time of the grand viewing, she saw a poster of G.I. Jane instead of her granddaughter's reflection. Dadi, knowing my sister was capable of pulling off a stunt like that, decided to concede to the mordren zamana. Zeba would meet her perhaps-future-in-laws normally, face-to-face. But, there were a few rules on how she should conduct herself:

1. Like a Good Eastern Girl, she would be brought in with a dupatta on her head, accompanied by both Saima Apa and me who would support my sister's overwhelmed person by the elbows.

2. She must not wear red, which would make her look too eager to be wed. Neither must she wear black, which would indicate reluctance. A light-pink-coloured shalwar-kameez, with full sleeves, would do just fine. After all, one must look pretty while pretending to be demure. Under no circumstances must her lipstick be red. Dadi hated red lipstick with a passion and said that it was the colour prostitutes used to lure men into their beds. This abhorrence arose from the fact that long ago, Fareed Chaccha had brought home a female friend with scarlet lips to meet Dadi. After Fareed Chaccha went missing, the colour became associated with the Sunni son-stealer who had appropriated her son and was not willing to let him go.

3. Zeba Baji would say a shy 'salaam' to Mrs Haq and sit quietly next to her daughters, never initiating

conversation but always answering all their questions in a quiet whisper. She would serve tea and refreshments personally. After making sure all had eaten, she would excuse herself and exit the drawing room.

4. She would not discuss politics or literature under any circumstances because this would reveal her in all her opinionated glory. Good Eastern Girls should never have strong opinions of their own, only those of their husbands or in-laws.

Zeba Baji listened to Dadi's dictums in silence and then locked herself in her room with the phone, where she presumably called a friend and complained bitterly about life. The day arrived for Mrs Haq to come and Dadi was in her element, instructing me to dust the drawing room and telling Zeba Baji to make the samosas and to start taking a greater interest in household affairs.

'Naureen makes the most delectable gajar ka halwa! And she can cook a meal for fifty people in an hour! And look at you, you can't tell turmeric from mustard powder! How do you expect to get married and please your in-laws if you can't cook! There's a good girl now, slice those potatoes. Arey Bhai, don't put that much salt—do you want Mrs Haq to choke?'

Zeba Baji was about to say that that was precisely the plan, but a sharp look from Ammi quieted her. She had received a lot of flak from Abbu and Ammi for being so rude to Alam Bhai and upsetting Zainab Phuppo with whom relations remained strained. She didn't want to upset my father and mother by further rudeness and, therefore, prudently kept her mouth shut. That is not to say she submitted to any of Dadi's instructions.

The day of the drawing room arrived glorious and sunny. Dadi was full of energy as she prayed and blew and bossed all of us around. She said that she had a good feeling about what was to happen.

The entire second phase was a disaster. Mrs Haq and her daughters arrived forty-five minutes late and unapologetically ensconced themselves on the sofas. The older daughter, Amina, was statuesquely emaciated as she fussed over her seven-year-old son, Momin, who wore a permanent frown because he had been pulled away from *Ninja Robots* under duress and was not ready to be a sport about it. The younger daughter, Zehra, looked permanently stricken and sat in one corner with her arms and legs crossed to ward off all evil.

Conversation was stunted as the boy occupied most of our attention. He decided that he would entertain himself by examining any trinket catching his fancy. Ammi clenched her fists and pursed her lips as her favourite porcelain ballerina was picked up and dropped to see if it would survive the fall. Amina casually asked him not to be naughty and continued telling a nervous Saima Apa how difficult it was to get decent maids for one's offspring, because they all insisted on getting married just when you needed them the most.

Despite all instructions to wait demurely for someone to fetch her and bring her in, like a shy feather on a gentle breeze, Zeba Baji marched in wearing a black sleeveless shalwar-kameez. She was unaccompanied. Her blood-red lipstick stood out against her pale skin. Dadi gasped and crossed and uncrossed her legs, but could do no more in front of the guests.

Introductions were made and we all shifted uncomfortably in our seats as Zeba Baji took to heart Dadi's advice to be reticent and only answered any questions put her way with a nod or a shake of the head, with an occasional shrug of the shoulder thrown in. When asked about a hobby, she succinctly replied, 'Sleeping.' When asked if she liked children, my sister glanced at Momin and said, 'Hate them.'

Ammi coughed and asked Zeba Baji to get some refreshments. A trolley was wheeled in and parked in front of Mrs Haq. Then my sister returned to her seat, leaving my mother and Mrs Haq to wonder what the hell she was doing. Dadi was livid, but kept quiet while I distributed the plates and the pakoras. Zeba Baji, oblivious to all the animosity aimed in her direction, stared with a dreamy look in her eyes at the chandelier.

Momin went slightly mad at the sight of the tea trolley. He waddled to the chutney dish and plonked his entire hand into it, proceeding to rub it all over his clothes and on Ammi's carpet. Amina decided that she had had enough and marched over and knelt down, holding her son firmly by his shoulders.

'Momin, Beta, look at me.'

Momin obliged.

Amina brought her face very close to her son's, tilted her head and scowled at him. Her eyelids shrank to make way for distended eyeballs and dilated pupils.

Momin returned this frown with a pout and a jerk of his head, while he tried to shrug away his shoulders from her grasp.

Amina got up, satisfied that she had put the fear of God in her son and calmly returned to her plate. Her ineptitude as a disciplinarian was a thing to marvel at. The incorrigible brat returned his attentions to the trolley and decided he wanted to pour some tea for himself. He touched the scalding kettle and let out a loud wail. Amina returned to his side and coaxed him to go with her to wash his handsy-wandsies with nice cold water.

She received a violent kick in the shins.

Mrs Haq laughed and said something about today's children. But my sister, a teacher with a no-nonsense attitude, had had enough. She surged up from the sofa and knelt down in front of Momin.

'Momin sweetheart, look at me. I suggest you shut up right now, before I set my doggy on you to eat you.'

All in the room let out a collective gasp.

'That's right! I have a big dog outside and he's twice your size and he's got big, ugly teeth like Donatello's knives and he drips poison. All I have to do is call him here and he'll eat you up! So, are you going to be quiet while I wash your hands? You know, my dog really likes to eat fat little boys with chutney on their hands.'

Momin threw his head back and wailed in violent terror as my sister gently led him to the bathroom, washed his hand and covered it with toothpaste. A much more subdued child was returned to his mother. Amina clasped her child to her chest and glared at Zeba Baji as if she had just molested her firstborn. Mrs. Haq looked at my Dadi and my mother, the latter sitting with her forehead resting against the palm of her hand in a posture of despair and embarrassment.

Zehra, silent thus far, surprised everyone by speaking and suggesting that they take her nephew to the hospital to make sure there weren't any serious burns. They hustled off into the night, Momin's wails of wanting to play with the doggy fading away into the dark night.

It was hardly surprising that the Haqs did not want to proceed to the third phase. We never heard from them again. We sometimes bumped into them during Moharram at the Imam Bargah, where Amina would tuck her darling behind her and hold the alam of Hazrat Abbas high up to ward off Zeba.

Zeba Baji did not get into serious trouble for disobeying Dadi because everyone had expected her to act up in some small way or the other. I overheard Ammi tell my father that it was quite a miracle that she had consented to meeting a family at all. In spite of her surliness, she received a whole flood of proposals, so no permanent damage was done.

I wondered why people were so attracted to Zeba. Naima said it was because she was fair. Her skin was so white that many suspected Irani blood somewhere in the mix. The other factor, my cousin declared knowledgeably, was that Zeba had long hair. 'People can't resist a girl who is as attractive and beautiful as your sister. She's the poster child of the perfect bahu until she opens her mouth.'

Even Dadi was proud of the number of proposals Zeba earned and was positive that it far exceeded the amount Naureen had received. She tried to pry out of Qurrat how many people came to see her granddaughter, but Qurrat said she couldn't remember. Dadi was incensed at the answer. 'As if her granddaughter got countless proposals! She probably just got five or six. That's why Qurrat refuses to tell me.'

If I were Zeba Baji, I would have thought Naureen lucky to receive calls from just four or five suitors. It certainly wasn't pleasant going through the drawing room phase week after week. It would have been nice if Dadi and Ammi had some kind of screening process to weed out undesirable inquirers, and Ammi, for her part, did try. When a woman told her that her son was as handsome as Amitabh Bachchan and was looking for an Aishwarya Rai, she told them that their stars would not meet. Dadi called the woman behind Ammi's back and told her to bring Amitabh on over. That was an interesting get-together, especially when the woman went on and on about the amazing attributes of her attractive son and, as his crowning glory, declared to Zeba Baji that he even owned a BlackBerry. Zeba Baji merely looked at my mother with a 'Why?' in her eyes.

Zeba Baji bore being put on display with apparent stoicism. But I noticed that her eyes flashed with anger each time a new family came. She continued her minor rebellions, refusing to serve any refreshments, wearing what Dadi deemed were shameless clothes. My sister's wardrobe played a great role in fending off proposals. Some thought she was too fast and said so to her face. Other families took her reticence as addlepatedness and declared she was too slow mentally. This they were tactful enough to say softly to my mother, who reacted with great indignation and suggested that they leave as soon as possible. It was amazing how unrestrained people were in passing negative and positive comments about my sister to my sister's face. Some women went so far as to lecture her about the benefits of marriage and bid her to not display her reluctance in such an obvious fashion. 'After all,' uttered one irate auntie who was miffed because Zeba refused to look at her son, 'it's not as if you are the cream of the crop.' Zeba Baji laughed about it later, saying that she was probably more curdled milk rather than anything else.

A few months passed and people came and went. Dadi despaired, taking the lack of progress in the third phase as a direct insult to the family image.

'What's wrong with us?' she asked my mother. 'My Hussain is a doctor and we live quite well, we have an impeccable bloodline and she's beautiful. I'm telling you, if you could tell her to talk a little more and wear something more substantial than that scrap she puts on in front of people, someone would want to deliver a formal proposal. That Qurrat looked at my Zeba with her evil eye. I don't blame her completely. Naureen looks so plain in front of my beautiful granddaughter. I think it's time to burn some spices.'

Zeba Baji's matrimonial affairs had me preoccupied with the whole business of marriage. I was more certain than ever that arranged marriages were the only route available to decent, respectable girls. Still, it seemed quite upsetting that a drawing room was the only court of romance available.

Being surveyed by boys and their mothers and their fathers and their sisters didn't seem an ideal route to matrimony.

But what did I know? All I was supposed to do was go to school and study hard and not fail at math tests. I was to avoid all distractions, including male company. I was expected to sit at length with Dadi and listen to her stories about Bhakuraj. This in itself wasn't such a pain, but I was about to turn sixteen and had other minor rebellions on my mind.

The injustice of life hit me full force when I was told that I could not go to my friend's sixteenth birthday party. He was a boy and we were teenagers and that was the age, apparently, where all sorts of hanky-pankiness commenced. So I was forbidden to attend the party being thrown at his house. I cried myself hoarse and sulked and went on a hunger strike for five whole hours, but to no avail. Dadi suggested that I should give him toffees at school and wish him in class. I replied that we were no longer five years old. She told me that was precisely the problem.

So I snuck into my mother's cupboard and read all the Harlequin Romances that she pretended she didn't read. Every time a man and woman met and had passionate sex, my heart soared with excitement and anxiety. The heaving bosoms and pulsating veins had me in a frenzy. So what if these forbidden pleasures were not allowed for respectable girls from respectable families? This was as close to breaking the boundaries of tradition as I could have gotten and it was all sinfully delicious. And I found out that, in fact, tongues were an integral part of the process.

Ammi discovered my latest preoccupation and forbade me from entering her room. I moped around the house, watching all my friends go to mixed parties while I, respectable, conservative-and-proud-of-it Saleha Bandian was not allowed to have normal teenage fun. It wasn't fair. After a while, I began to get on everyone's nerves so Ammi decided to enroll me in French classes at the Alliance Française. My idle mind was indeed playing host to devilish notions of romance which she wanted to quell immediately. Dadi was most concerned about my mother's choice of language. After all, was not French the language of love? But Ammi was not quite as paranoid, and she was happy to have me out of her hair for a while.

Dadi, meanwhile, burned red chillies around Zeba Baji's head and declared enigmatically that there had been no odour so Zeba was, indeed, suffering under the yoke of some evil influence. She said several prayers on her prayer beads and blew on Zeba Baji every five minutes until she was dizzy and had to lie down. But it seemed that her blowing was fortuitous, for it brought forth a proposal from none other than a fellow Bhakurajian!

Syed Gulzar Rizvi belonged to parents who had been born and reared in Bhakuraj before shifting to Lahore, Pakistan. Dadi was in raptures when she heard that the thirty-eight-year-old was still single and eligible. Her ecstasy increased manifold when she heard that he was a successful banker and soon to be promoted to vice-president.

'What's to wonder about it? Just say yes! A Bhakurajian Banker! Shia! Syed! What more could you want?' she said to my mother. So enthusiastic was she at the prospect of this particular proposal that Abbu had to be recruited to calm her down.

'Amma Jan, I know you are excited, so are all of us. But we can't possibly say yes to this Gulzar chap without seeing him and his family first! And you seem to be forgetting that they haven't sent a proposal. They've just expressed an interest. We can only say yes once they've asked. You see that, don't you?'

It was a foregone conclusion for Dadi that Gulzar Rizvi, nicknamed Gullan, would fall head over heels in love with Zeba.

Gullan Jee made quite an impact upon Zeba Baji when she first saw him from behind the kitchen door as he entered the drawing room. His step was rather dainty, like a ballerina trying to twirl on an egg shell. The Bhakurajian influence was apparent. He wore a white shalwar-kameez, full of starch, with pink embroidery reminiscent of Achan Mian. His full head of hair was well slicked and reeked of sesame oil. He placed a red handkerchief over his face when Zeba Baji came in. She took one look at her suitor and turned red with repressed laughter. Saima Apa hurriedly encouraged her to sit down and drink some water so that there would be no further embarrassing outbursts. Gullan Jee pretended a dainty cough and in doing so, brought his head forward in an affirmative nod. Thus did he indicate to his mother, whom he called Amma Jee, that the girl had met with his approval. Amma Jee looked at Dadi and smiled. Dadi beamed. And it was considered done and sealed. A few more looks would have set the time and date, as these Bhakurajian kindred spirits needed no words to express what was in their hearts and minds. But Zeba Baji wore an amused expression, correctly indicating to my mother that Gullan Jee was being regarded as nothing but a joke.

Gullan Jee had an annoying habit of never saying anything directly. When I had served refreshments and he had partaken of the tea with his little finger pointing firmly northwards while he held the teacup, he attempted to make conversation with me, his future sister-in-law. He asked, 'So, Saleha Bibi, have you seen that Indian movie *Kal Ho Naa Ho*?'

It was a perfectly innocent question but the manner in which it was asked, with a tilt of the head and a knowing look, made me think he was asking me whether I thought if there was going to be a 'tomorrow' for him with Zeba Baji. I wanted to say, 'Not a chance!' but desisted out of the fear of Dadi.

Dadi was in raptures after Gullan Jee and his family left.

'Such a good boy he is! Why, he reminds me of your grandfather when he came to ask for my hand in marriage—after he had swept me off my feet, that is! Arey Hussain, his mother knows how to make tikias and bachkas, puris and khurmis, Bhakurajian style. Imagine my Zeba going to a Bhakurajian family! She will learn all our ways and traditions! I used to be afraid that our way of life would be dead and buried with me but now I know that it will live on through my granddaughter.'

My grandmother wiped a tear from her eye and glared at

Saima Apa, who was calmly helping my mother and sister put away the leftover food in the refrigerator. Saima Apa had offended Dadi's sensibilities once by saying that she didn't care too much for Bhakurajian cuisine because the spices used were too pungent for her taste. Her palate was made for milder stuff. Moreover, she hated that most of the chutneys and pastes were doused liberally with dill and mustard oil. It soon became clear that the Bhakurajian ways were not going to be continued through the offspring of Haroon. The possibility that they could survive through Zeba filled Dadi with gratitude towards God and resentment towards her granddaughter-in-law.

Abbu listened warily to Dadi's song of praise for the Rizvi family. He glanced at my mother, who gave him a can-you-please-reason-with-her look. Gullan Jee, despite his Bhakurajian heritage, had failed to make a serious impression on us. He reminded me of an ancient relic thawed from deep freeze for Dadi by her prayers. He was what I imagined my Dada to be like. The idea of Zeba Baji marrying him was simply ridiculous.

We all let the matter slide and hoped that Amma Rizvi, Gullan Jee's mother, would not call, deterred by Zeba Baji's untraditional get-up of yet another sleeveless kurti with jeans. But alas, the phone rang; Dadi picked it up and beamed when hearing the official proposal of marriage from Amma Rizvi. Luckily, she remembered that a girl's grandmother, bound by the same rules as the girl's mother, could not appear too eager. She thanked Amma Rizvi for her compliment to her granddaughter and told her that we would get back to her after consulting with Zeba. She put the receiver down, clasped my sister to her chest and said, 'Mubarak ho, my lal, you're betrothed!'

Zeba Baji jumped out of her embrace and demanded to know what she was talking about. Betrothed to whom?

'Why, to Gullan, who else? I haven't said "yes" yet but I will in a week. Hussain will make the necessary inquiries about the family and the boy's work in Lahore. But I don't think there will be any obstacles to the two of you marrying.'

'Except that I wouldn't marry him even if he were the last man on earth!'

'Arey? What do you mean? Bahu, what is your daughter telling me? She's letting go of a good Bhakurajian boy for no reason at all! Give me one good reason why?'

'For starters, he's old. Secondly, did you see how he covered his face with that preposterous handkerchief? Who does that any more?'

'Good modest boys who are honourable and don't ruin girls' reputations by sleeping with them and getting them with child, that's who!' shouted Dadi, her voice quivering with fury.

'Dadi, are you seriously telling me that you expect me to marry that memento from the past? I can't even look at him without laughing!'

'Acha? Well, laugh at the fact that he's a successful banker in Lahore. Laugh that he's widely respected. At the fact that he respects his roots—unlike you who scoff at them! And why shouldn't you? You've made it clear that all your Bhakurajian ancestors and I are clearly beneath you. Nitwits we are, isn't that what you think? And have the fear of God in your breast, my daughter, for you are arrogant beyond words! Do you think you are above every man that steps into this house? Remember what I told you about Chandni Bano! There's a lesson to be learnt from her life!'

Chandni Bano was the Shrew of Bhakuraj. Her father was in despair at her refusal to marry. She hailed from one of the village's richest families, who owned a full fleet of cows and goats and many acres of farming land. She was famous for her fair complexion. It was said she bathed in aloe vera and cream which her servants whipped up for her every day. She was intelligent as well, a voracious reader well versed in the politics and issues of her times. Many a suitor was flayed alive by her scornful looks and vicious words. But her pride was her downfall as she said no to one proposal after another. Soon she grew old and her father died and left all his possessions to his brother's son. Chandni Bano, in order to retain her way of life, was forced to marry her snorting, decrepit first cousin who was often seen expectorating phlegm and scratching his groin in public.

'Dadi, I don't want to marry Gullan Mian. I would never fit into his family! And he parts his hair down the middle!'

'Zeba, no one wants to live alone. We women are built to have children, to create families. How are you going to have a family of your own if you insist on saying "no" to every good proposal that comes along?'

'Dadi, I can't stand the idea of marrying this man. I wouldn't know what to say to him. He's very different. We'd have nothing in common.'

'You will once you get married. And who says you need
to say anything to him? Why, my sister married a man who
refused to talk to her. They had ten children and were hailed
as the ideal couple. This mordren nonsense about soulmates
doesn't exist! If a woman was her husband's soulmate, why
would Allah promise him a different hoor in heaven? Why
not his wife all over again? It's a social and religious obligation
that you must fulfil, to have children and to raise them as
Muslims. This love-shove business that you and Saleha are
going on about is just impractical, I tell you!'

'I need time to think about it,' stalled my sister.

'You have a whole week!'

'I'm going to a teacher's workshop in Islamabad at the end
of the week. I'll let you know what I think after I come back.'

'But he's leaving for Lahore after that! How will we get
you engaged?'

'I don't know. That's not my problem. Dadi, I've said I'll
think about it. Please don't rush me. If you want an answer
soon, it's a definite "no". I think it would be in everyone's
interest if you let me think it out. You might get the answer
you want.'

Thus the matter was dropped for the time being. Amma
Rizvi called, and Dadi was apologetic when she said that
her granddaughter needed time to think about the matter.

'After all, today's girls do make their own decisions! And
my Zeba gets very overwhelmed at the notion of marriage;
I've raised her with the highest ideals of modesty. Why, the
thought of even talking to a man makes her blush so prettily.
But it was so nice to meet your family! Give my love to Gullan

and tell him to call me to say salaam from Lahore!'

Dadi knew better than to tie Zeba Baji to any knot, but before she left for Islamabad, Dadi did urge her to come back with 'good news' for her frail, old, dying, loving and eternally well-meaning grandmother. The next seven days were passed consulting numerologists on the mathematical aptness of the match. More prayers were said, more spices were burnt. And on the seventh day, she awaited the return of her wilful granddaughter with unbridled excitement.

Zeba Baji had yet to step into the house when Dadi came out on the porch, her arms akimbo, and demanded: 'Well, what's your decision?'

Zeba Baji was visibly irritated. She had hoped that Dadi would have forgotten about the whole affair.

'Dadi! Can I at least step inside?'

'After you tell me that you are going to say yes to Gullan!'

'I've decided I can't make a decision without speaking to this chap personally, one-on-one, no chaperones present.'

Dadi hyperventilated and would have successfully managed the Third Faint of her life had she not realized that there was no Haroon Bhai or Abbu to catch her on her way down. So she settled for raising her hands above her head, calling for my mother to come listen to her wayward daughter, and then beating her chest as if she were doing maatham at a majalis.

'Arey Bahu! Arey wah! Look at what Zeba is saying? It has come to this! My granddaughter, a girl from the Bandian family whose women were known for their purdah and modesty, my own flesh and blood, wants to go and *talk alone*

to a prospective suitor? The End of Days is coming! Imam
Mehdi! Come down and save us from these immoral times!
Bahu, this is your fault! You and your mordren ways have
corrupted your daughters! Look at this one. Shameless!'

It took us fifteen minutes to calm Dadi down. I massaged
her shoulders only to have my hands slapped away multiple
times while Ammi made her drink cold water. After the
choking and spluttering abated and her breathing returned
to normal, my grandmother refocused her attention on my
sister, who was watching her impatiently.

'So this was your plan all along? Wait for Gullan to leave
and then spring this on me! O Allah! What will I say to
Mrs Rizvi? I told her my granddaughter was too shy to talk
to boys. Now what do you want me to do? Call her and say
my granddaughter has had a brain transplant and wants
to talk to your son on the phone?! What will she think of
our family?'

'I don't just want to talk to Gullan on the phone. I want
to meet him again. Not in the drawing room. In a restaurant
for coffee or something like that. I want to see how he
conducts himself under normal circumstances.'

This announcement generated yet another bout of hysteria
from my grandmother.

'Normal circumstances? Do you think that he is retarded
that you want to take another look at him? What do you
want me to say to him, pray tell? Shall I tell him that my
granddaughter is summoning him for inspection?'

'Why not? After all, if he had said he wanted to see me
again, you'd have flown me all the way to Lahore to walk and

talk and sit in front of him. Why don't I have the same right?'

'Because you are a girl and should be thankful that he wants to marry you at all!'

'Dadi, I've kept my promise. I thought about the proposal and I've decided I can't come to a decision unless I have met him again. I want to see if I can talk to him. My worst fear is that he just sits around with that handkerchief on his mouth while his mother does the talking for him.'

'What's to be afraid of? That's how boys from respectable families behave!'

'In your time, maybe. I, on the other hand, want an intelligent conversationalist, and I may be putting too much value on his ridiculous appearance. So I want to meet him. If not, then I don't have any problems with calling the whole thing off. Now, I'm famished. I'm going to take a bath and then fix myself a cup of tea.'

With this announcement, my sister picked up her suitcase and marched upstairs to take a shower. Dadi was not going to let the matter go quite so easily. She demanded to know why my mother was not forcing her daughter to say 'yes' to quite possibly the best proposal she would ever receive. Ammi said that she didn't know if Gullan was the best to come along because there might be better ones in store yet. Dadi demanded to know what would be better than a Bhakurajian boy. My mother replied that someone who wasn't quite as attached to his roots as Gullan would probably be better.

'What is that supposed to mean? You think he's odd because he respects the traditions of our ancestors?'

'Amma, Hussain appreciates and follows the traditions of

his ancestors. But he does not go around in a shalwar-kurta with a handkerchief over his nose and mouth. That did seem a little odd to me as well. Plus I didn't like Amma Rizvi. She seemed sharp.'

'I don't know what you mean. She reminded me of myself!' Ammi kept quiet.

'Amma, I don't think Zeba's demand to meet Gullan again is unreasonable. Okay fine, we won't let her meet him alone; we'll send Haroon and Saleha along with her so that it's not so scandalous. But think of this, she hasn't said "no" yet. And maybe after meeting Gullan, she'll like him! You of all people know that forcing Zeba to do something is the best way to ensure that she will *not* do it.'

Dadi thought about it for a second. Actually, she thought about it for more than a second—she spent a whole hour on this line of reasoning. Her paan-dan was summoned and her eyes once again took on that faraway look as she masticated the tobacco-lathered betel leaves. Later, I found out that she had called Amma Rizvi and told her that she felt it was unfair to let Gullan say yes to marrying Zeba unless he met her once again.

'After all, he should get to know the woman he is going to marry before anything formal is declared. We don't break engagements in our family. Ask him if he would like to meet my Zeba once more?'

Of course, Gullan did and said that he would be flying to Karachi for a meeting in about three weeks. The twain would meet then.

Chapter Eleven

How Everything Went Wrong

As we waited for the anticipated meeting between Zeba Baji and Gullan, things fell into a lull of routine. Dadi bided her time, praying fervently to God and asking the Prophet and his family to put in a good word for her. Ammi puttered about in the kitchen and Saima Apa and Haroon Bhai spent a lot of time on their own or with Saima Apa's family. Dadi was annoyed because she believed that Saima Apa should spend more time adjusting to her new home, rather than wasting it visiting her parents. Of course, if Zeba Baji were to get married, Dadi would expect her to visit every day of every week for at least two hours, not including weekend visits which should last the whole day.

I continued my French classes, which plodded along slowly. I tried to pronounce my r's as gh's without bringing up phlegm in my throat. It would have been hopeless had it not been for my new teacher, Mr Anwar Butt, who took me aside and helped me with my pronunciation.

Mr Butt was five years older than me. Tall and lean, with a thick mane of dark hair that reached his shoulders, he looked like the forbidden rebel that I had read about in Ammi's romance novels. His teeth were tobacco stained from all the cigarettes he smoked and my heart skipped a beat when I saw him smiling at me amidst curls of smoke, which his thin, almost cruel lips conjured. He told me to pucker my lips and roll my tongue to say '*caotchouc*' and I almost fainted with excitement.

Later, when I came home, I felt wretched, as if someone had reached inside my stomach and squeezed my intestines so hard that I felt like doubling over. I couldn't wait to go to class again, to see him again.

Was I in love? No, this couldn't be love, could it? To fall in love was immoral. It led to love marriages. Good, sensible girls didn't fall in love, I told myself. I repeated: respectable girls only fell in love with fiancés picked by their parents. I was violating a very firm family rule.

My imagination went into overdrive with all kinds of hypothetical scenarios. I felt all my Bhakurajian ancestors shaking their heads at me for soiling the family name. I saw Dadi having a heart attack and dying when I told her that I had selected Anwar to be my husband. I imagined accidentally bumping into Anwar and feeling his firm body next to mine. I would say something charming that would endear my personality to him forever. He would then show up at my house with roses and ask me out. What would happen then, I couldn't really see in my daydreams. Sometimes I would picture Dadi thwacking him on the head with a saucepan. Sometimes I would picture her welcoming him inside and interviewing him, finding out he was Shia and Syed and approving the match. Other times I would imagine us running away to Bengaluru.

I tried to find out if he was Shia. If he was, then I would have a sanction to flirt with him, but I found out from another student that he was a Sunni. And that he had a girlfriend who was three years older than him with whom he had been going steady for the past two years.

All my fantasies fizzled into thin vapour. I was left with a steady, throbbing ache in my heart and misery and guilt for allowing myself to fall in love like a fool. I felt as if I were a snag in the evolutionary Bandian process, that I was defective somehow. No wonder they didn't allow us to fall in love. It was a ludicrous emotion. It made us act idiotically. It made our brains stop functioning and allowed the inner retard to take over. Of course! What wisdom there was in the arranged way of life! That way one only fell in love with someone who was committed, someone who dedicated his life to you. Not someone who cavorted with cougars and smoked Benson & Hedges all day!

While I was feeling miserably sorry for myself, my sister seemed ecstatically happy. She hummed while working. This was very unusual, even if the song was the highly unsentimental *Shut Up and Drive*. She was extremely pleasant to everyone at home, including Dadi, towards whom her attitude softened considerably. She took over my role as chief masseuse and since her hands were softer and more delicate than mine, Dadi was in heaven and solicited her

services many times a day, surprised like the rest of us when
Zeba complied with a smile each time. Dadi thought it was
because Zeba was having a change of heart.

'Press my shoulder, right there, aaaahhh yes! Good girl!
I always knew that you would come to your senses! A boy
like Gullan is like one in a million! Only a fool would let
him slip. See, now that you've had so many days to think
about it, the idea seems to appeal to you, doesn't it? I knew
it would. You must listen to your elders, Zeba, they have the
benefit of experience on their side . . . Arey, don't press so
hard, you want to break my spine? Hai, I'm just waiting for
the day you get married. Then I can die in peace.'

On and on Dadi went, talking about Gullan and Zeba and
how many children she should have and how she must give
up the idea of working after marriage because she needed to
stay at home to help in the kitchen and have babies. To
all this, Zeba Baji listened quietly with a far-off look in her
eyes, as if she were really imagining what it was like to be a
wife and mother.

As I was wandering around one day, wondering what it
would be like to run my fingers through Anwar Butt's hair, I
heard Zeba Baji talking to someone in the bathroom. Since
she was whispering and clearly didn't want to be heard, I
plastered my ear against the door and heard her ask her
friend at the other end of the line how it was going to work
out at all since she was Shia.

I could not believe what I was hearing. I positioned my
ear next to the keyhole for better reception.

'Saba, he's not Shia! You know what my family is like!

They'll flay me alive! And I don't feel very comfortable taking this relationship too far. This guy is coming to see me in a month or so. I'd feel like a hypocrite dating someone else when I've given my grandmother my word to give this guy a fair chance. Who? You know that guy I told you about, the one who kept on snivelling into a handkerchief? I know, I know, but I promised Dadi! Yes, I know I'm lying to myself but I have to at least try and give Gullan a fair chance. What? No, no, Gullan is not his real name; it's Gulzar, I think! Oh God, why couldn't I have met Omer earlier!'

My mind reeled at the import of what I'd just heard. Zeba Baji was besotted with a Sunni, and not just *any* Sunni, a man named none other than Omer! This was devastating. This was not happening! I had to stop this! But stop what? It seemed pretty obvious that Zeba Baji was trying to put the brakes on herself. But how far had the relationship progressed? Who was Omer? Where had Zeba met him? What did he do? It would be disastrous if he were a fellow teacher. The only thing worse than a Sunni was a penniless Sunni teacher.

My eavesdropping put my mind in further turmoil. At first I nursed hopes that perhaps Zeba Baji and I could join forces and marry the Sunni men of our dreams together. It was always better to rebel in company than alone. But Anwar's girlfriend made my dream impossible to realize. Did this Omer fellow return Zeba's feelings? If he did, then God knows what my sister would do. Had they dated? If so, how many times? And behind Dadi's back! How had she managed it! I veered from admiration to jealousy to fear for my sister's future. A billion questions revolved around in my head, but I couldn't give voice to any of them because my sister was a very private person and would skin me alive if she found out that not only had I sneakily overheard her conversation but was being bold enough to question her about her private matters.

I decided to enroll in a bit of amateur espionage. I noted the time Zeba Baji left for work and when she returned, when and how frequently she went out with 'friends' and how many times she disappeared into the bathroom with the cordless phone. It became routine for her to go out in the evenings with the same Saba and return just before dinner. Saba had long been a good friend, but she had never provoked this elation, and I guessed that someone else was responsible for my sister's cheerful disposition. At night, when she thought everyone had gone to bed, usually after eleven, she would take the cordless and slip into her bathroom and whisper and talk, a perpetual laugh in her voice. I didn't need to listen to the conversations. It was clear that Zeba Baji was fast becoming more and more attached to this Omer fellow, and that was all I needed to know. What she expected to happen was beyond me; each day I marvelled at how my extremely sensible sister was investing in a relationship that would bring nothing but heartache.

The months passed and the time for Gullan to arrive came nearer. I noticed that my sister's demeanour changed. Her bouts of cheerfulness became interspersed with silent moroseness. She became cranky and snapped at me when I accidentally spilt orange juice over the newspaper before she had read it. She treated Dadi with a greater degree of patience but the measure of affection she displayed decreased considerably. I decided that I would swallow my fear of her wrath and try and talk to her.

So one fine Sunday morning when Dadi was snoozing and Ammi and Abbu had gone to Sunday Bazaar and Haroon and Saima Apa were at her mother's house, I went to my sister's room. She was surrounded by test papers. She checked them with massive impatience, grumbling under her breath that children were becoming more linguistically challenged every day. I offered to help her tabulate the marks and she gladly dumped a stack of test papers on my lap. We sat in amicable silence until Zeba Baji rapped her pen against her forehead and proclaimed: 'I'm absolutely sick of my job and my life! Saleha, don't ever make the mistake of becoming a teacher. It's thankless, it doesn't pay and it stunts your mental growth! Not to mention that you eventually go blind trying to focus on these ridiculous phosphorent inks students use these days.'

I expressed an appropriate amount of outrage. Temporarily appeased, she went back to work. But eventually her mind wandered, and I caught her looking at the ceiling, observing the travail of a gecko which was trying to slither behind a frame on the wall. It froze into stillness each time one of us moved or shifted in our seats. I decided that the time was right to tactfully and subtly coax my sister into a confession.

'What are you thinking about?'

'Nothing in particular.'

'Are you thinking about Gullan?'

'No.'

'Are you thinking about Omer?'

My sister shot a sharp glance at me and pinned me to my seat with her glare.

'What the hell did you just say?'

'I know you are dating someone named Omer. I heard you talking to Saba about it on the phone. In the bathroom.'

'And what were you doing lurking behind the door?' asked my sister in a tone dripping with scathing sarcasm.

'I . . . had to use the bathroom too. So I stood outside and was waiting for you to come out and I heard you talking to her.'

'Why you interfering little wretch! You were spying on me! That's why you've been acting like my shadow for the past few weeks! Who gave you the right to meddle in my private life?'

'Zeba Baji, I wasn't spying—I overheard your conversation, honest. And I haven't told anyone. But I just wanted you to know that I understand what you're going through and that your secret is safe with me.'

My attempt to placate her worked partially. Zeba Baji blinked, looked down at her paper and absently corrected a spelling and added a comma here and an apostrophe there. She looked at me again.

'What do you mean you understand what I'm going through?'

'Oh, because . . . because I think I'm in love with someone as well and he's just a bit older than me and I'm hopelessly, devastatingly enraptured with him but I can't express it to him because he's Sunni, too, and he has a girlfriend and he doesn't know I exist, partly because I don't talk to him that much because what will happen if I talk to him, nothing will come of it will it now? So all I do is sit and stare at him and feel stupid because what kind of an idiot falls in love with someone Sunni who doesn't give her the time of day. It's a horrible feeling and I feel like I'm one of those desperate girls who scale the walls of the school to go on a date with sleazy men who wait for them in their cars with tinted glasses. And I'm not desperate or frustrated but then why am I acting like it? You must know the feeling and I just want to jump off the terrace and break my leg so that someone can feel as sorry for me as I do for myself.'

I started crying and launched myself into my sister's arms. I had gone with the noblest of intentions of patting her back in comfort while she expressed her woes to me, but talking about Anwar let loose all the emotions I had cooped up inside. Zeba Baji held my heaving self in her arms and stroked my hair. I looked up, thinking that my outburst had moved her to sympathy. Instead, she was valiantly trying to suppress a laugh. I exploded with rage.

'You think I'm dumb, don't you? I hate you! I came here to let you know that you and I are in the same boat and you're laughing at me! I hope that you are forced to marry Gullan and smell like sesame oil for the rest of your life!'

I would have flown off the bed and out of the room had not my sister grabbed my shoulders, pulled me into a bear hug and continued to laugh until tears had come into her eyes.

'Uff, Saleha, you're retarded! Adorable but retarded!

Now listen to me, I don't think you're in love—you have a crush. And it's not immoral to have those feelings towards someone. It's the most natural thing in the world. It's going to last for a while, and it'll be wonderful and terrible all at once and then one day you'll wake up to find that you're over it. I've experienced it many times. Enjoy it! This is the fun of being young!'

'I don't think you should underestimate the extent of my devotion for him. I can't stop thinking about him. I've even lost my appetite.'

'Really? Is that why you've been finishing off that box of Ferrero Rochers as quickly as you can? Saleha, liking someone or even loving someone isn't immoral. Nothing to be ashamed of. And I'm not laughing at you. I'm laughing at how earnest you are and how seriously you're taking all this, as if you were going to go to hell just because you fancied yourself in love.'

'But you know how Dadi goes on and on about good girls guarding their honour and their eyes? I can't take my eyes off Anwar.'

'Oh ho, Anwar is it?'

'Yes. And he has the most beautiful hair! And he doesn't even know I exist! I . . . I even dreamed of kissing him you know! I'm totally going to go to hell!' I started crying all over again.

'Look, Saleha, Dadi has a point to the extent that girls should not throw themselves at the first boy they see and act in a way that they lose their dignity and self-respect. But if this Anwar gentleman is good-looking and smart and

articulate, then I'd be worried if you weren't interested!
And you're acting maturely, you know that you like him but
because nothing can come of it, you're keeping silent about
it. Though God knows why you haven't discussed him with
me or any of your friends. Let me say it again: it's the most
natural thing in the world! Liking someone is nothing to be
ashamed of. You haven't committed a crime!'

'Then what about you? Why haven't you said anything?
And what were you thinking? You're going to be killed! Do
you have any idea what this will do to Dadi? And Ammi and
Abbu will be livid as well! You know that Omer is a Sunni
yet you're talking to him? Isn't that wrong?'

Zeba Baji was silent for a while.

'I've met him a few times. But I haven't been in touch with
him lately. Gulzar Rizvi will be in town in a week or two and
I've given my word to Dadi to give him a fair chance. I can't
do that when I've got someone else on my mind.'

'So you do like this Omer?'

'Yes.'

'Are you upset because you've not been meeting him for
a while?'

'Hmm . . .'

'Do you love him? Do you think you can ever love Gullan?
Will you say yes to Gullan if he acts normally? What will
you tell Omer?'

'I have no idea. I'm not thinking about it. What'll happen
will happen. I've decided to wait and see. And I want you
to drop the subject now. Don't talk about it with me or with
anyone else.'

I wanted her to continue but Zeba Baji made it obvious that she was more interested in discursive essays than this conversation. I was about to go when a thought popped into my mind.

'Zeba Baji, Omer isn't a teacher, is he?'

'Why do you ask?'

'Because it's bad enough that he's Sunni. He must have *some* redeeming quality?'

'You are outrageous, you know that? He's a doctor. Now scoot!'

I hopped off and skipped away to write an ode to Anwar's cigarette. But my preoccupation lessened when Gullan Jee called Dadi to say his weekly 'salaam' that evening and informed her that he would be arriving in six days' time. This threw my grandmother into a vortex of excited activity that sucked in whomever passed by her room. I was the first to walk in after the phone call and was cheerfully told that my future brother-in-law was to arrive, and I should select an outfit for the meeting because I was to be the official chaperone. Then my mother was told to decide which place the meeting would be held and to start preparing for the ensuing engagement because Dadi considered the meeting to be a mere formality before she could call Amma Rizvi and say 'yes' on Zeba's behalf and then call Qurrat Dadi and gloat. Haroon Bhai and Saima Apa were informed that they were to accompany me in my role as the protectoress of Zeba's virtue because my person was deemed insufficient for the mammoth task of preserving respectability.

The next day, doubts crept in.

and Zeba trying to talk to each other with Dadi sitting in the middle, her snowy white hair glowing in the candlelight, chewing paan enthusiastically as she interrupted time and time again to tell Zeba Baji to draw her dupatta properly over her bosom, or ask Gullan what Bhakurajian dishes he liked so that she could teach my sister how to make them.

But it came to pass that the excitement of Gullan's arrival proved a little too much for my grandmother who went into a dead faint three days before he was due to arrive. I was organizing her week's medicines for her when I saw Dadi get up from her bed where she had been frantically reciting on her prayer beads for Zeba's marital future. She collapsed in front of the bathroom door. I screamed and called for Ammi, putting Dadi's head in my lap, trying to revive her by slapping her hard on her cheeks. Ammi ran in and took charge, first by ordering me to stop assaulting my grandmother on medical pretexts. Then she slapped me because I had declined into a state of hysterical hyperventilation. Dadi was in a daze, her eyes rolling over so I could only see the whites through the semi-open lids. Eventually, some water on her face made her wake up, and we lifted her frail form on to the bed. Ammi rushed to call Abbu at the hospital while I sat by Dadi, holding her hand. It was strange to see her lie absolutely still in her crisp white sari on the equally white sheets of her bed. Stillness was not something I associated with my grandmother. Her wrinkled face looked tiny and frail, as if she were wrapped in a cocoon, which was threatening to enfold her entire person. It struck me how fragile my indomitable Dadi was, even with her fierce spirit and forceful opinions pervading all that we did.

Because she was unwell, Dadi let Ammi take the reins and organize the meeting between Gullan and Zeba. My sister was clearly stricken and apprehensive, especially because she did not want to do anything to antagonize my grandmother in her frail state. Saying 'no' to Gullan was definitely one of those things. It was decided that we would meet Gullan Jee at a nearby coffee shop in the evening. All us siblings were to accompany Zeba, but Haroon Bhai slyly concocted clever plots to provide privacy for the would-be couple.

'Okay, it's going to be like this: when he comes, we will all get up to say hello. Let me direct the seating arrangements. I want Zeba to sit directly opposite Gullan at the table, it will make conversation easier. Then I'm going to make an excuse and go to the bathroom. Saima and Saleha, five minutes later I want you to find some reason to leave them alone for ten minutes. Saima, why don't you ask a friend to come and drop by at the coffee shop at the same time? That way you'll be able to say hello and Zeba and Gullan can talk. Saleha, you tag along with Saima. In exactly fifteen minutes, I'll come back and stand in such a way that only you can see me. If you want more time, touch your eyebrow. If you want to be rescued, scratch your nose. If you can't decide and want me to do some interviewing of my own in front of you, pull on your ear. If you want me to scoot but Saima and Saleha to intervene, touch your lips. If you want Saleha and not Saima, pinch your cheeks. If you want Saima and not Saleha . . .'

'Haroon, will you please relax? Just give me half an hour alone with him. Then come and rescue me.'

When we left for the coffee shop two days later, we

received our blessings from a beaming Dadi who lay on her bed with her prayer beads. She clasped Zeba Baji to her chest and said, weeping, 'I'm so proud of my guriya! Make me happy! Try not to speak too intelligently. Let him ask all the questions and just provide the answers as briefly as possible. Don't let your brothers and sisters leave your side. Give my love to your future husband!'

If my sister felt trapped, she didn't show it. She exuded confidence, but I knew that the higher her head and the more confident her stance, the greater the turmoil within her. She was not one to show her emotions but rather dealt with whatever came her way with an almost blasé indifference. She sat rigidly in the car and stared out the window while Haroon Bhai rattled one instruction after another on how we needed to be disciplined and follow his orchestrations to the letter. After all, he had been put in charge of the entire affair and didn't want to botch it up.

He baulked when he found out that Gullan had arrived before us, had already booked a table and that he was accompanied by Amma Rizvi and his sister, Shabban.

A clever wife lets her husband make all the plans and then takes over when he encounters reality. While Haroon Bhai let out a frustrated 'Oh, for heaven's sake!' under his breath and looked defeated even before going to battle, Saima Apa rallied forth. She exclaimed that it was delightful to meet Amma Rizvi again as she introduced Zeba Baji to Shabban, who had not been present at the drawing room stage. She sat with Amma Rizvi and made me sit next to Shabban, and it was my duty to keep her occupied with conversation. Haroon

Bhai looked helpless and frantic and sat next to Gullan and talked his head off while Zeba Baji sat right opposite them, glaring at him because he was not making any effort to include her in the conversation.

Shabban was conservative, unmarried and thirty-five years old, a combination that made her a singularly unpleasant conversationalist. Clearly she detested sitting next to me, an inconsequential teenager, when she was determined to sit next to and grill Zeba. I asked her all sorts of questions about Lahore and the cultural activities that took place there and did she attend them frequently? To which she coldly replied that she didn't drive and did not have time for such frivolous pastimes. But then how did she spend her time, I asked. Did she work? Bhakurajian girls in her family did not work. They either got married or spent their lives taking care of their fathers and brothers. I asked her how she felt about my sister working. She told me not to bother her with cheeky and precocious questions. I spluttered out an insincere apology and focused on making a butterfly pattern on my plate with the salt and pepper shakers.

So far, Gullan and Zeba had not exchanged even one word. Saima Apa saw how Haroon Bhai's garrulous presence was becoming a significant impediment to any communication whatsoever. She suddenly declared to Amma Rizvi that Dadi was extremely unwell. Amma Rizvi, who had been scanning my sister with razor-sharp eyes, expressed genuine concern. Saima Apa told her that her grandmother-in-law would feel so happy if she met Amma Rizvi. Would Haroon do Amma Rizvi a favour and drive her down to meet Dadi? Dadi was too weak to get up and had been so lonely; seeing Amma Rizvi would revive her spirits. Haroon Bhai looked confused but got up anyway, inducing Amma Rizvi to do the same. Shabban looked mutinously at my sister-in-law.

'But how will Amma come back? We can visit Dadi Jan after we've finished our coffee.'

'Goodness, no, Haroon would be delighted to drive Auntie Rizvi to Dadi. We can all meet up at our house later. I'm sure she would love to meet you, Shabban, and I know she would be thrilled to see Gullan. Haroon, we'll meet up at home—Gulzar Bhai will take us there, will he not?'

Gullan frowned but nodded in the affirmative. Haroon and Amma Rizvi left and Saima Apa focused her attention on Shabban, who had taken Haroon's seat next to Gulzar. She sat stiffly, her lips pursed with disapproval, especially when she got a closer look at my jeans-clad sister and saw a very untraditional female specimen of the Bhakurajian kind. Saima Apa tried to stimulate the conversation between Gullan and Zeba.

'So Gullan, do tell us what you do in your spare time?'

Gullan looked down at his hands and then straightened the collar of his white shalwar-kameez as he replied: 'I actually don't get that much spare time. Banking hours, you know.'

Zeba Baji tried to tiptoe into the conversation.

'I have a friend who is a banker. He works all kinds of odd hours when it's time for auditing, but other than that, he's home by six or seven at the latest.'

Shabban leapt in aggressively.

'My brother is a very hard worker. He's not like other lazy bankers who saunter in at ten and leave at six. Gullan has breakfast right after Fajr and then he goes for a walk and then he's at the bank by eight. He comes back at ten. My late father used to say that success only accompanies the hard worker. Not upstarts who use connections and external influences to procure the job. I say that people like that may be able to get a job but are they able to keep it? No they aren't! Because they are lazy and they deserve to be fired.'

This lecture had a very depressing effect on all of us. Gullan kept looking at his hands and then took out a handkerchief from his pocket and wiped his forehead with it. Zeba Baji crossed her arms and looked at Saima Apa. I couldn't handle the awkwardness of the situation any longer. I decided that it was time to get rid of Shabban. So I accidentally spilt my lukewarm coffee on her clothes.

Everyone surged to their feet, including an outraged Shabban. I acted appropriately apologetic and guilty. I must say that I gave an Oscar-winning performance of mortification because Gullan sprang to my defence, saying he had seen the cup slip and that it was an accident. Shabban clearly wanted to give me a tongue-lashing but enough of a scene had already been created, and everyone was looking at us. So Saima Apa suggested that Shabban accompany her to the bathroom where she would help wash off the stains. A frowning Shabban was led away by my extremely sympathetic sister-in-law, holding her kameez in the air to avoid the stain from seeping into her shalwar as well.

Gullan underwent a metamorphosis in his attitude as

soon as his female relatives left the scene. He sat up straight, crossed his hands behind his head and looked directly at my sister for the first time. Zeba Baji asked him with a smile, 'So when you get some free time, what do you do in it?'

'I read the newspaper. I sleep. Not much. Spend time with my mother and sister.'

'Oh. Do you watch any television?'

'No. It sends me to sleep.'

'I see. Any books you like to read?'

'I said that I read the newspaper. Sometimes I read the *Times*. When I have the time.'

He smirked at his own wit.

'Hmm . . . ha ha! Is there anything you want to ask me?'

'Not particularly. I know you are a teacher.'

'Yes, I teach English.'

'I hated that subject. I burned my copy of *Macbeth* after my O Levels.'

'Ah.'

Silence.

Gullan put both his hands behind his head again and stretched his legs under the table and stared at my sister. Zeba Baji grew distinctly uncomfortable under his frank gaze. She crossed her arms and legs and leaned back in her chair.

'What about eating? Do you like dining out?'

'I eat whatever my mother and sister make for me. I don't like restaurants. Too expensive. And there's nothing as glorious as a home-cooked meal.'

'Well, all of them aren't expensive, are they? I don't really know that much about Lahore but I know there are great roadside dhabas where you get delicious Pakistani food!'

'It's very unhygienic. I don't like sitting out on the road. Gives me a wheezing cough. And all that smoke activates my sinus.'

Zeba Baji stopped trying. She and Gullan stared at each other until Shabban and Saima Apa arrived. The former sported a wet kameez front, which she fanned in the air. Zeba Baji suggested that we all head home before Shabban contracted a cold. Gullan Jee called for the waiter and paid the bill.

He didn't leave a tip.

Gullan and family sat with Dadi for two hours. Amma Rizvi was extremely solicitous and went so far as to say that she hoped Zeba Baji was taking excellent care of her elderly relative. Dadi was quick and effusive in her praise and declared my sister a veritable Florence Nightingale as she looked at my sister knowingly. Amma Rizvi declared that Bhakurajian girls were famous for the way they took care of their husbands and their mothers-in-law. She also asked for a glass of water and when Zeba Baji brought her one, she told her that Gullan had lots of female cousins who thought the world of him and who showed exaggerated care and attention to her, naturally, because she was his mother.

My Dadi tilted her head, held her chin with her forefinger and thumb and asked, 'And why shouldn't they show consideration? You being the mother of such an eligible bachelor!'

Amma Rizvi smiled complacently and sipped.

When they left, Dadi was over the moon. She asked Zeba what she thought of Gullan. I was afraid that my sister would flat-out refuse, and Dadi would have a stroke, but Zeba just shrugged her shoulders and said, 'Whatever you decide Dadi. I'm beyond caring.'

Dadi mistook Zeba's indifference for modesty and held her hands up for prayer.

'Hai Allah! My granddaughter is going to marry a Bhakurajian! You've answered my prayers! I'm going to make a journey to Imam Raza's Tomb after they get married! Then I'll go to Karbala! Then I'll do Umrah! All this in thanks to your munificence to a sinner like myself!'

But Haroon Bhai was soon to interrupt my elated grandparent.

'Dadi, Zeba might not have any objections but I do. I don't think she should marry Gullan.'

Dadi stopped short in her prayers and looked at Haroon Bhai as if he'd just declared the arrival of the Apocalypse. So shocked was she that she forgot to palpitate, hyperventilate, throw a tantrum or fake a faint. She just looked at my brother—who sat on her bed, put his hand on her knee and spoke gently but firmly. 'I know that you like Gullan. I think he's decent enough. He might make someone a good husband, but not Zeba. I talked to him quite a lot today and he doesn't have much of a personality. Besides, the only subject he can talk about is himself. Never once did he ask me a question about what I did or anything. Zeba's into literature and movies and God knows what kind of artsy-fartsy nonsense. She would be very frustrated as his wife.

Not to mention that I think his mother and sister would make Zeba's life miserable and he would let them because he's fundamentally spineless.'

Dadi didn't know how to react. She looked at my parents who looked back blankly at her. I decided to throw my own two cents in.

'I agree with Haroon Bhai, Dadi. When Shabban was present, she wouldn't let Zeba Baji talk to Gullan, she was so possessive. And she told me that women in her family didn't drive or work. I mean, who are they? The Royal Family of Saudi Arabia? And I didn't like the way Gullan stared at Zeba Baji when his relatives were not there. It was slightly lecherous. So I don't think he'll make a good husband or brother-in-law or son-in-law.'

Dadi looked at Saima Apa and said that at least Saima should have the good sense to realize that Gullan was a matrimonial prize of the first order. Saima Apa looked at Haroon Bhai, bowed her head and said, 'I have no opinion, only that of my husband.'

Dadi flew into a rage.

'Don't try that with me, you insolent twit! What do you think, I'm dumb? You have plenty of an opinion in other matters, but when it suits you, you echo my idiotic grandson who's lost his mind completely!'

We all stared at Dadi in horror. She was quite capable of being nasty, but always indirectly, insinuatingly. Never had we encountered this unadulterated, confrontational rage. That she called her darling grandson idiotic was an indication that something was not right. She was not well.

Abbu immediately brought Dadi a glass of water to drink. She flung it away.

'Haan, haan, try and calm me down by drowning me. You all want me to die! That would be convenient for you, wouldn't it? Then you'd go and date-shate all you want and then marry non-Muslims and get married in sleeveless ghararas without chaapa on them! You scoff at all the traditions of Bhakuraj because you think they are foolish. Well let me tell you, it is these same traditions that have made each one of you who you are. I'm going to call Rizvi Begum and say "yes" and you are going to listen to what I say, because I'm your elder and I know what's best. That is that!'

Because she was working herself into a fine fury, we decided to let the matter drop. Abbu tucked Dadi in bed, as it was late at night. She was reminded to wait for Amma Rizvi to call. After all, it was the boy's prerogative, not the girl's, to take the first step even in the fourth phase. The next day, as we were all having lunch, the phone rang. Ammi picked up the cordless on the table and handed it to Dadi, who turned on the speakerphone. It was Amma Rizvi, who inquired after Dadi's health and the discussion remained on that subject for the next fifteen minutes and concluded with an exchange of compliments for each other's families. Then Amma Rizvi broached the subject of Zeba.

'Your granddaughter is really pretty. Gullan liked her well enough. But I can't say the same for Shabban and me. After all, we're from a conservative set-up and if Zeba were to come into our family, she would have to give up wearing jeans and Western clothes because they are a sign of the devil. And there would be no need for her to work; Gullan earns enough to support all of us. The problem is that she is advanced in years and might not be ready to make that adjustment.'

We glanced at my tight-lipped twenty-five-year-old sister.

'Both Shabban and I think that the other one, Saleha, would be young enough to mould and she would fit into our set-up with great ease. As for the age difference, well so many of our ancestors in Bhakuraj fared so well in spite of it. In fact, I say many a marriage fared well because of it.'

I choked on my chicken and Saima Apa had to thwack me on the back to induce my respiratory system to resume normal functioning. My future flashed before my eyes, a lifetime cooking Bhakurajian cuisine with Amma Rizvi glaring at me and Shabban sitting on Gullan's lap to prevent any new woman from taking her place in her brother's life. I threw a frantic look at my mother who also was visibly appalled. Dadi turned pale and spoke with silent fury.

'Rizvi Saheba, you are my sister and therefore I do not want to be rude. But it's extremely uncultured of you to come for one daughter and give a proposal for the other. It simply isn't the Bhakurajian way. I hope you have a safe trip to Lahore. Goodbye.'

She clicked the power button and looked at a dazed Zeba.

'Well, that is that. Pass me the bhurta.'

Chapter Twelve

How Zeba Was Discovered

After the Gullan episode a lull descended on the entire marriage process. Dadi was seriously disillusioned by the ill-mannered actions of her fellow Bhakurajians. Also, she was not well. Spells of dizziness were accompanied by bouts of rage. Though still a force to be reckoned with, she was just not as active as before, needing more time to lie down and rest. I was extremely worried about her.

She still told me her favourite stories from Bhakuraj as she oiled my hair so that it would grow nice and long. When my time came she thought I also would attract many a suitor. Dadi firmly believed that long hair was important. She told me that sometimes, prospective in-laws would go so far as to measure the span of the girl's braid with their hands. Dadi proudly boasted that her braid had been as long as seven handspans, and her mother-in-law had had large hands. After that, she was made to stand on a weighing machine because no one wants a fat daughter-in-law. The size of Dadi's

I once had objected too vociferously for not being allowed to wear orange to my friend's birthday party. Dadi sat me down and told me that in her time, Moharram meant no television and no music for a month, so I had better be thankful that she was only putting limitations on my wardrobe and not other aspects of my life. When I asked her how she had watched television when her father couldn't afford one in those days, since it was still a novelty, I was again told to hush up and not ask inconsequential questions.

Moharram was a busy month for my grandmother, whose religious fervour rejuvenated itself with the force like that of the Indus river during the monsoon. There were additional prayers to be said, the Quran to be read and clerics to be heard on television. There were three majalis to attend at the Imam Bargah: two for the women in the morning and evening and the other for the men at night. Sundays were especially hectic as there was a majalis in Nishtar Park right after dawn. There were processions to be viewed and food to be cooked on which Abbu said a fateha so that it could be fed to the poor. We asked Dadi to slow down and cut down on a majalis or two because she still seemed frail and irritable, but she told us that not even we could keep her from grieving for her beloved Imam and his family.

It is no coincidence that Shia girls receive the majority of their proposals as soon as Moharram and Safar end and the happier month of Rabi-ul-Awwal approaches. Hawk-eyed mothers routinely zero in on five or six prospects who attend the Imam Bargah during the first twelve days. There is plenty of opportunity to take a good look at girls. After careful viewings and several inquiries, mental lists are made of families to be visited.

Zeba Baji often managed to escape such inquiries. Since I was with her, I, too, could detect the attention she attracted and we both usually swerved away from Ammi and Dadi and walked in the opposite direction to confuse the approaching girl-hunters. It was a diversionary tactic we learnt from the gazelles on National Geographic. The herd had to be broken up to save them from the hungry leopards. Some of the more determined mothers were not fazed and decided to approach my sister directly.

One example of such a woman was Mrs Amir, who clamped her hand down on Zeba Baji's shoulder as we sat, moved to tears by the story of Karbala, in a majalis on the ninth of Moharram. My sister jerked her head up and exchanged a wary look with a hook-nosed, bright-eyed woman who curled her lips down to ask, 'Excuse me, is your name Sadia?'

Zeba Baji gave her a bemused expression, which did not dishearten the spirited Mrs Amir who just had to have the information she required.

'I asked you if your name was Sadia, Beta!' she persisted gently, as her hand tried to squeeze the information out of Zeba Baji's shoulder.

'Jee, there is a majalis going on!' my exasperated sister reminded her.

Mrs Amir withdrew her arm, not because my sister had revealed something unknown to her but because she was shushed by the women around us who were irritated at having the talk disturbed.

'Acha acha! I will talk to you later,' she relented and leant back against the wall with a sense of expectation.

As the end of the majalis approached, my sister's shoulder became, yet again, the target for another heavy thump by the same hand.

'What is your husband's name?'

'I don't have a husband and this is not the time . . .'

'Acha so you are unmarried? Where is your mother?'

'I don't know!' Zeba Baji nearly yelled.

'Well, I have a son who is working in London . . .' Mrs Amir began, only to be admonished by other women who insisted that all conversation should take place after the maatham was over. They were clearly as annoyed as my sister at this inopportune interrogation.

As soon as the maatham ended, Zeba Baji ran outside to avoid being accosted again. She had underestimated the resolve of Mrs Amir who followed her outside and who again asked, 'Oh ho! Where are you off to? Acha beta, tell me, where is your mother?'

'She's somewhere inside.'

'Haan, haan! She's an old friend of mine. Tell her that Mrs Amir sends her salaam. In fact, why don't you give me your number, and I shall say hello to her myself!'

'I don't remember it.' Zeba Baji had run out of patience and creativity when it came to lying.

'Don't be coy; give me your phone number! Besides, I have something very important to talk to your mother about!' exclaimed Mrs Amir with a lilt in her voice, much in the same manner Abbu used to have when he used to come home and tell us he had a treat for us in the form of a new toy or a car ride.

'583 . . .'

'Not your landline. Your cell number.'

'0333 . . .'

'And make sure you give me the right number! In fact, let me give you a missed call so that I can make sure it is the correct number. Is that your cell ringing? Good!'

My sister looked at me frantically. She resembled a meerkat trapped into a corner by a salivating hyena.

We eventually received a phone call from Mrs Amir. Zeba Baji handed the phone to Ammi and Mrs Amir abandoned all pretence of prior friendship and mentioned that she had taken a liking to my sister and was very interested in her for her son who was in London. Ammi was a little taken aback by her proactive methods but after finding out that the boy was three years younger than my sister, simply said 'no' and hung up.

Things remained uneventful and appropriately morose until Zeba began to act suspiciously—she smiled to herself and hummed. This was most uncharacteristic of my usually surly sister. And then, one night I noticed that the bathroom light was switched on. It was 2 a.m. Omer the Doctor had returned.

While I was very happy for my sister, a conflict of tsunamic intensity wracked me from within. I felt I owed it to Dadi to be scandalized by my sister's behaviour, but I couldn't manage to feign the outrage expected of me. According to conservative Bandian standards, Zeba was obviously acting immorally, or as Dadi would term it, like a prostitute. Dating a Sunni man was an act that threatened to sully the pure arranged-marriage history of the Bandians. I didn't want Zeba Baji to become another Iraj, whom Dadi still condemned. Just the other day Dadi had said about our wayward ancestor, 'How selfish she was! Only thought about her happiness. I ask you, did she have any regard for her parents' sensibilities? Did she feel any regret that due to her, they could never look anyone in the eye again? Uff, the shame that she brought upon that family! Three younger sisters she had, and all remained unmarried. Who would give a proposal to a family that had been smeared with such dishonour? Independent thinking women with minds of their own! Toba toba, may Allah forgive us all!'

However much I reminded myself of the immoral Iraj and tried to convince myself that under no circumstances was a love match to be tolerated, my mind kept wandering to those five horrible seconds when my future had flashed before my eyes. A future when I thought that Dadi might say yes to Amma Rizvi's proposition and betroth me to a snivelling, oily-haired suitor. It had felt like I was about to be delivered a death sentence. I thought it remarkable that Zeba Baji had held out for as long as she had. Had I been in her shoes, I would have thrown up repeatedly all over the place and descended into a state of permanent anxiety and depression. But she had endured his noxious presence and the acidic company of his sister and mother and had left it up to Dadi. How could she have known that Haroon Bhai would unwittingly come to her rescue? If Gullan was the best offer to come along, then could she really be blamed for wanting to choose someone for herself?

But she couldn't be stupid enough to start a relationship that she had no intention of pursuing because that would bring certain heartache. There was only one conclusion—she intended to pursue it. But how in heaven's name would she hide it from my parents and grandmother? Did she intend to hide it forever? It would be a convoluted universe in which she could expect to introduce a self-chosen Sunni man to my parents and live to tell about it. The idea was simply absurd. It was suicidal: like Evil Knieval trying to jump off the Empire State Building without a parachute and hoping to land on his motorcycle and drive through a hundred hoops of fire.

If my sister had agonized about how to introduce the topic of Omer the Doctor to my parents and Dadi, she needn't have. Matters were taken out of her hands when Dadi, on her way back from a majalis at Qurrat's house, felt nauseous and asked Abbu to buy an anti-emetic for her at the chemist's. As she waited in the car, her eyes wandered to the window of a restaurant where she saw my sister sitting with another man, feeding him ice cream with her spoon and accepting a taste from his.

I had been unaware of the target of Dadi's furious glare as I was engrossed in a game of Space Impact on my cell phone. I looked up in surprise as Dadi let out a loud gasp and got out of the car. I saw the direction in which she was going and froze in terror as the unsuspecting objects of her wrath came into my line of vision. I clambered after Dadi, who was marching towards the restaurant, a tiny, frail soldier wearing a black gharara, en route to fight a valiant jihad to protect the virtue of her wayward granddaughter. I caught up with her and suggested that she calm down and rationally consider that maybe Zeba Baji was having a meeting with a colleague? Dadi gave me look that silenced me; a look telling me not to think of her as a senile old fool just yet.

She climbed up the makeshift box-stairs and shoved the glass door open. A pleasant-faced waiter with a Charlie Chaplin moustache and a liberal paunch welcomed her and asked her if she wanted a table for two. She withered him with a look, and he stared after us, clearly unnerved at the sight of an enraged eighty-year-old and her frantically gesticulating granddaughter who was indicating that he get out of the way and retreat into safety. Dadi asked him how he slept at night, running an establishment providing errant young couples with ice cream as they went down the path of the damned.

She then swerved on her feet and marched toward my sister's table. Zeba Baji had her back to us and did not see us approach. The person sitting opposite her had a clear view of my approaching grandmother's imposing presence but didn't seem too perturbed, as he probably thought she was coming after someone else. She stopped at their table, her arms akimbo and asked, 'What is going on here?' in a menacing tone similar to the one adopted by the ferocious officers during a change of guard at the Wagah border. He jumped up and stood straight, like an errant cadet found out by a superior.

He was certainly nice looking. Tall, extremely thin and clean-shaven, he had a receding hairline which made him look serious and mature. In normal circumstances, one would have described his expression as one of thoughtful confidence. At the moment he was sporting a look of abject terror inspired by my grandmother's wrath. I noticed, even in these dire circumstances, that he had an impeccable sense of dress and was wearing the smartest brown shoes I had ever seen.

If Omer was terrified, my sister was furious at this interruption. She, too, got up and looked at Dadi, then me, and then at Dadi again, trying to figure out how on earth we had found her out. Dadi repeated her question. 'What antics are these? *Is this what I think this is?* Is my granddaughter, the little girl I changed and fed and raised with good Muslim values ACTUALLY OUT ON A DATE? During MOHARRAM?!'

Each question was delivered in a pitch louder than the last and the final word came out in a loud shriek. I nervously looked around and saw that we were making a spectacle of ourselves. Several teenagers looked frightened, others sympathetic. At a corner table, two women in their mid-fifties or so were shaking their head and letting out a 'tsk'ing sound to show that they sympathized with my grandmother.

Zeba Baji put her hand on Dadi's shoulder and hissed: 'Dadi, we're in a public place, and I don't want a scene.'

'Arey wah! Will you listen to her? I'm making a scene? *I'm making a scene?* I'm bringing order to my house, that is what I am doing! The scene was created when you and this boy here were sitting together, alone and unchaperoned and *feeding each other ice cream!!! IN MOHARRAM!!* What about that scene? That is okay? But if your grandmother comes and asks you what you are up to, she is creating a scene?' Each question dripped with sarcasm as corrosive as toxic waste. I could see the green vein in Dadi's temple throbbing like a sparking KESC wire, about to detach itself from her head. I didn't know what upset her more—that Zeba Baji was on a date, or that she was doing it in Moharram. She was working herself into quite a pitch while all who observed her stared in fascinated horror. Dadi decided to make her indignation public. Looking around, she saw a number of teenage couples sitting together, most attired in Western clothing.

'What country do you think you belong to? Dating-shating openly like shameless creatures! You should be ashamed! Bursting out of your blouses, piercing your foreheads and lips and speaking English like it's your mother tongue? These are not Pakistani values! If you stopped watching Amreekan movies and started reading the Quran, you would realize what a sin you are committing!'

Her audience shifted uncomfortably. The boys began to peruse their menu cards with a newfound enthusiasm while the girls crossed their arms over their chests and stared away in the opposite direction. The pot-bellied waiter signalled the manager so that he could do something to deflate the situation. Zeba Baji gave Omer an apologetic look and picked up her handbag and said, 'Dadi, I think it's time to leave.'

'Time to leave? *Time to leave*? TIME TO LEAVE? You shouldn't have COME here in the first place!'

Zeba Baji didn't say anything but led Dadi out of the cafe, as she ranted and raved, declaring that the End of Days was

'I said to myself, no, no, that cannot be my Zeba. My Zeba would never deceive me by acting so indecently! Here I am, praying night and day to Allah to arrange a good match for her and there she is, going against all our ways and meeting strange men in strange places! And look at her clothes! Pink! Not even light pink! Almost maroon! What are we Syeds coming to if our own daughters wear maroon in Moharram! All she can think about is ice cream and ice cream parlours! Telling us she's going out with that Saba! I never liked Saba. Typical Sunni thing to do, to help your friend to indulge in indecency during Moharram. I tell you Hussain, these Sunnis want to sabotage our ways! And Saba managed to do it very well! Did I think my Zeba was gullible enough to be tempted to sin in Moharram, the most sacred of all months? No, I did not. But I was wrong, wasn't I? My Zeba was dating, wearing maroon in Moharram and then telling me not to make a scene! She should be thankful she has a grandmother who's looking out for her well-being! Who will save her from herself? Hussain, this is your fault! Did I not tell you to put her in a convent school for college? But NO, you wanted her in a co-educational school! What had you told me? She should be used to boys! Well, look how used to them she is now! Comfortable enough to go ahead and date them! No one listens to me. Now look, your disobedience to my wishes is bearing such bitter fruit! Eating ice cream! From A MAN'S SPOON! When? In MOHARRAM!!'

This was the general rant as we drove home. Zeba Baji remained expressionless and rigid, staring outside the window while Abbu also listened silently. I could sense that my father was furious at my sister because his grip on the steering wheel was so tight that his knuckles had turned pale. My sister was in deep trouble, and I wanted to offer whatever comfort I could. But what could I do? Dadi's taunting, questioning, demanding and accusing voice filled the car. It took a lot of strength to keep silent and listen, even though her fury was contagious and by the time we reached home, all of us were shaking with rage and shock.

Abbu installed Dadi in her room, telling her not to worry, he would take care of the matter and that she should rest because she was looking pale. She said that she doubted my father's ability to take care of any matter. If he had taken care when Zeba was young such a day as this would never have come. Ammi, who had heard the commotion from upstairs, ran down and asked Zeba Baji what was going on. Was everything all right? My sister remained silent. Dadi's voice could still be heard, scolding Abbu and then finally breaking into tears, the abject despair in her voice revealing just how deeply betrayed she felt.

When her voice faded away and we presumed that she had drifted into a fitful sleep, Abbu emerged from her room, closing the door behind him and telling Zeba Baji to come to the living room. Ammi could bear it no more.

'Hussain, what has happened? Will someone please tell me what's going on? Why is your mother so upset? And Zeba, where did you come from? You were going window shopping with Saba. What has happened?'

Abbu looked at Zeba and snapped out terse instructions through clenched teeth.

'Start explaining.'

Zeba Baji looked up from her lap and in a clear, steady voice said, 'Ammi, Dadi was upset because she caught me dating.'

My mother let out a loud gasp and put her hand on her chest.

'Dating? You? But surely you weren't? She must be mistaken!'

'She wasn't mistaken,' replied Zeba. 'I *was* out on a date. I've been meeting him for a few months. I met him in Islamabad, when we were at our teachers' conference. He was staying at the same hotel and visiting a friend.'

'What is his name?' asked my father.

My sister remained quiet. She was trying to muster up the courage to deliver the final blow.

'I asked you what his name is!' said my father in a near-shout. Ammi tried to calm him down by telling him that screaming wasn't going to help anyone. Abbu told her not to interfere and directed his glare at my sister.

'His name is Omer Khan.'

A shocked silence descended upon my parents as the significance of what had been revealed became clear to them.

'I don't think I heard you right,' my father said in a soft, menacing whisper. 'Could you repeat his name?'

'Omer Khan. And yes, before you ask me, he is a Sunni.'

A loud wail came from Dadi's room where she had evidently been listening to our conversation. Abbu put his head into his hands and my mother asked my sister what on earth she was thinking. Zeba Baji remained silent.

Ten minutes of tense silence ensued as Abbu rubbed his temples with his fingers, trying to calm himself down. When he finally looked up at Zeba Baji, his face was red and his eyes flashed with fury. He ordered my sister to her room and told her to stay there until he had figured out what to do with her. Zeba Baji got up slowly, squared her shoulders and walked out, her eyes shimmering with unshed tears. Abbu seldom showed his displeasure and his fury traumatized all of us.

That was a silent day, with Zeba Baji in her room, not daring to come out to face my father's wrath. Abbu brooded in front of the television and my mother hovered around him, trying to soothe him, to placate him while she told me to keep checking on my sister and making sure that she was not hungry. When Haroon Bhai and Saima Apa returned, I told them what had happened. Dadi also heard their arrival and called my brother into her room, where she clasped his shoulders and wept and said that chaos had come to their household and someone had cast the evil eye upon our family.

'First my Fareed taken away by that red-lipped Sunni! Now Zeba as well! What have I done to deserve this fate?' she kept asking while Haroon Bhai awkwardly patted her back and looked at Saima Apa.

My sister-in-law silently went to Zeba's room, outside which I had been tiptoeing all day long. She saw my sister's tear-stained face and gave her a huge hug, offering silent support. I too went in and sat on the bed, telling no one in particular that if they were hungry then I could make them french fries.

Saima Apa smiled at me but said she didn't think anyone was in the mood for a meal. She and my sister talked softly for a long while.

My sister revealed, through sobs and tears, that although she'd cut off all communication with Omer when the time to meet Gullan had arrived, knowing that Omer existed and was interested in her didn't help Gullan's cause much. She'd known Omer for three months and wanted desperately to marry him. He returned the sentiment. They shared a deep connection. Her being a Shia wasn't an issue for him, partially because he wasn't too religiously inclined. She hadn't dared talk about the future because she was afraid of how all of us would react.

I left Zeba Baji and returned to Dadi's room where she was still sobbing into Haroon Bhai's shirt. I gave her a reassuring smile and asked her if she had had her medication.

'Arey I don't want any medicine! Is that all you can ask me about? Plying me with God knows what kinds of pills to finish me off. Be patient! My heart cannot withstand the blow that Zeba has delivered to it. Just wait. I will die soon. Then this family will go to the Sunnis. That's what you all want, isn't it? To be rid of my conservative ways so you can marry whoever you please and dress however you like and skip majalis in Moharram! Don't worry, it will happen soon.'

Haroon Bhai temporarily lost his patience.

'Dadi, we are all trying to be supportive. Now, you are a brave girl, aren't you? We need you to be strong about this. I'm sure Zeba is as unhappy as you are and we need to discuss this as a family. But we can't do that if you keep weeping like this! Look how red your face is! We need you to be our leader, to help us through this! You have to be our rock at a time like this. You see that, don't you?'

Dadi brushed away her tears and wiped her face with Haroon Bhai's tie.

'I'm trying to be strong but I'm so tired! You all make fun of everything I say! We do things in a certain manner so that our values are retained! And when you don't, you see what happens? And then when everything collapses around me, you tell me to be strong!'

'Dadi Jan, this isn't about you right now. Let's all go to the living room and discuss this calmly and rationally. We will get through this. We just need you to calm down.'

Dadi muttered that she would like to know how she was supposed to calm down when the sky was falling all around her. But she decided to dry her tears and proceeded to the living room. I was sent to summon Zeba Baji so that we could all talk about what had happened and arrive at some sort of resolution.

Chapter Thirteen

How Everyone Fought

With heavy hearts we all sat down together at the family meeting. I felt torn inside as I trudged upstairs to call Zeba Baji to the lounge.

On the one hand, I understood why Dadi was outraged. Hadn't she made her position absolutely clear? Was not Zeba Baji threatening to overturn the well-established order that my grandmother fervently believed in? There was a way things were done and that was that. The traditions particular to our family had evolved through generations and for Dadi, the ways of her ancestors were sacred. Zeba Baji was breaking two inviolable rules by finding her own mate and not selecting him from the Shia clan. In the village of Bhakuraj, she would have been ostracized.

On the other hand, it seemed unfair to judge her actions by pre-Partition Bhakurajian standards. It was true that in our very traditional and conservative set-up many of our relatives broadly stuck to the old ways, believing that they were far superior to the nonsensical values that prevailed in the modern age. We Bandians from Bhakuraj were proud of our collective identity, but maintaining this identity could sometimes become a struggle, especially for someone like my sister who had a mind of her own. While she, too, loved to hear the stories of Bhakuraj, she treated them as obsolete anecdotes merely meant to amuse, but for Dadi they were a code of life. Zeba had formulated her own codes from the very beginning and this was her first break from the ancestral umbilical cord.

Was she wrong to do this? In uncertain times when everything was unknown, our values were all we had had, but for someone like my sister, this cord must have felt like a noose.

Zeba Baji descended the staircase slowly, her face expressionless. All eyes were upon her as she took her place on the single seater in the corner, the hot seat where the criminal was to be interrogated.

But it was Ammi who first spoke, her voice soft and almost sympathetic.

'Okay, Zeba, start from the beginning. Who is this Omer and when did you meet him?'

Zeba took a deep breath and said, 'We met in Islamabad. It was a week-long conference for teacher training, as you know, and I was staying at a hotel. The first day was quite hectic so I went down to have some coffee to unwind. Omer and I met there at the coffee shop the first evening and started talking. It was perfectly innocent; I didn't think anything of it. But then the next day when I went down he was there, too; we talked again and I found that we had a lot in common.'

'You mean other than shameful behaviour?' Dadi interjected.

'Amma Jan!' protested my mother.

'Ek toh he's stalking her and then she's finding it romantic! I tell you this girl's completely lost her senses!' exclaimed my indignant grandmother, who was hushed by all of us. Haroon Bhai asked her to give Zeba Baji a chance to finish what she was saying.

'Well, yes, I think he wanted to meet me and after the second meeting I also wanted to keep talking to him. So we did. When I returned to Karachi, I told you to let Gullan come and I didn't intend to see Omer again. But Saba and I ran into him at a CD shop and we exchanged email addresses. Then we exchanged phone numbers and got talking. I did meet him without telling you but when Gullan called and said he was coming in three weeks, I told Omer I wouldn't be able to meet him or talk to him.'

'Wah wah! What a favour you did us! Calling Gullan and leading us all to believe that you were serious about the match when you had someone else on your mind!'

'Dadi, what do you want me to do?' exploded my sister. 'Was it my fault I met Omer in Islamabad? No. Was it my fault I liked him? No!'

'Look at how innocent she is acting? It wasn't as if someone was forcing you to meet him and talk to him! Exchanging emails and phone numbers! Meeting him behind our back . . . was that respectable behaviour?'

'All I did was share a cup of coffee with him! Communicate with him! We've only shared meals together.'

'Respectable girls don't go on dates with men their families disapprove of!'

'And do respectable grandmothers flaunt their granddaughters to be examined and inspected by men and their mothers like cattle? If they do then I want none of this respectability, it's highly overrated!'

Dadi gasped and put her hand on her heart. Tears of anger crept down my sister's cheeks as she glared accusingly at Dadi.

'Hussain, look at what she is saying! Hai hai! As if I was cheapening my own granddaughter! You ungrateful girl, I have prayed and worked hard to arrange a good match for you and you accuse me of being a . . . a . . . PIMP! Who told Gullan's mother "no thank you" when she suggested he marry Saleha instead? Who has safeguarded your virtue by making sure you met men with your entire family as chaperone? Never in my wildest dreams did I think that I would receive such accusations in return!'

'Did you have to be so goddamn ingratiating to everyone? Do you know how demeaning it is to be put on display in front of insufferable women while you praise their idiot sons? You were practically ready to beg if it meant getting someone to marry me so that you could settle some ridiculous score with Qurrat Dadi!'

Abbu got up and pointed a finger at my sister. 'Zeba, you are talking to your grandmother and my mother. She is the elder of our family and I suggest you mind your manners.'

'You want me to be polite to her when she practically made a spectacle of me every single week? Fine. But what about you and Ammi? Why did you remain quiet when I was put on display in front of men with whom you knew I would never be happy? Why did you let Dadi continue with Gullan for as long as she did? I'm your daughter and you *never* for one minute considered my feelings in the matter. Why did you never once take my side?'

'Zeba, that is simply enough! Other girls marry men chosen by their parents!' barked my father, his face turning a deep red.

'What can I do if you can't see that I'm not like other girls?' asked my sister brokenly, her eyes filling with tears. 'I feel like a freak because I don't fit into your notion of what it means to be a Bandian! I don't want to get married for the sake of producing children. I want a companion. I want love.'

'LOVE!' gasped Dadi. 'No one in our family has married for love for generations!'

'Dadi, Omer and I love each other. I know he wants to marry me. If you could just for one moment step out of what was done in the past and pay a little consideration to my happiness . . .'

'Absolutely out of the question! You want us to reward you for behaving like a wanton!'

'You think I like doing this? What a legacy you've given us, to suppress all natural emotions and think that loving someone is impure. How can you expect me to be quiet and let you decide my future when you show absolutely no regard for what I want? If this family had been slightly more willing to talk to me about love I wouldn't have lied to you all. I wanted to tell you so badly! I'm in love for the first time, and I couldn't even tell my own mother about it for fear that she would look at me in horror. Saleha just had her first crush and she could only cry about it because she felt like she was betraying you. Look how respectable we are! You've forced one daughter to agonize silently about something that should be exciting and wonderful, and the other to go behind your back because that was the only shot at happiness she would ever have!'

With this impassioned declaration Zeba Baji stormed up the stairs and locked herself into her room. I blinked after her, furious that her exit had left me exposed and in the same depth of trouble as her.

'Oh ho! Not one tamasha but *two* under my very nose. Who is your boyfriend, Madam Saleha? And when are you going to sneak off to meet him? Tonight? Make sure you let us know so that we don't walk in on YOUR hanky-pankiness.'

'Dadi . . . I . . . Zeba Baji shouldn't have . . . it's not . . .' I spluttered frantically as I saw three pairs of glaring eyes aim their ire at me. 'I don't sneak out with him. I don't do anything with him, really.'

'Who was Zeba talking about, Saleha?' asked Abbu through gnashed teeth.

'J-just my French teacher.'

Dadi let out a long moan. 'HAI! My youngest molested by a teacher! French! That's all they are good for—love and romance-shomance and defiling innocents! Wait till I file a case against him.'

'Dadi Jan! He didn't do anything! I just . . . it's just that I told Zeba Baji that I thought he was cute, that's all.'

'Cute. Cute. CUTE! He's a TEACHER! You are supposed to respect your teachers, not have dirty thoughts about him. This is what love does—it blinds us to inappropriate behaviour! What goat-like behaviour—lusting after your teacher. What does it say in the Quran? Your teacher is like your parent. YOU'RE LUSTING AFTER A PARENT! Do you hear? Bas. From today no more French! You stay at home and learn how to sew a kameez!'

'Dadi! You . . . you're being ridiculous!' I screamed. Abbu got up and dragged me by the elbow and told me to get out of his mother's presence if I could not observe the rules of decorum and decency. I fled the battleground, leaving Abbu baffled, Dadi furious, Ammi confused and Saima Baji looking extremely uncomfortable and not knowing how to respond to her first in-law family feud.

I spent the next few days feeling angry at Zeba Baji for blurting my secret out. I also felt sorry for her. Love was horrible. Well, it was probably horrible for her to love someone and to be told she couldn't marry him. As for me, I wasn't *in* love with Mr Butt any more. The crush had gone away after two weeks, just as Zeba Baji had predicted it would. He was a brilliant teacher but he tended to giggle by turning his face upwards, giving his front-row students, i.e., me, a generous glimpse of his nose hair, yellow teeth and purple tongue. If love cannot survive nose hair and an unattractive mouth, then it isn't love at all. My infatuation dissolved as steadily as the curls of his cigarette smoke.

We settled into an uncomfortable cold war after that initial disastrous attempt at communication. Abbu curtailed Zeba

Baji's driving privileges, because he wanted to discourage her from meeting Omer. So she went to work and came home and locked herself in her room every day, refusing to talk to anyone. Abbu worked overtime and Ammi tried to console Dadi who had assumed, with great gusto, the identity of a misunderstood martyr.

'Who am I to say anything any more?' she proclaimed as Ammi fed her her daily medicines. 'My granddaughter thinks I am villain number one! She should have shot me in the head when I was, what did she say . . . *throwing* her on people, if she thought I was so evil! The other one calls me ridiculous. This is the thanks this generation gives to its elders! Did you hear the way she talked to me? I've never been spoken to like that ever before! Hai, I will pray for my death so that I cause no more misery! How did I know that securing a future for my granddaughter was to cause suffering to this family? If I'm such a criminal, why didn't you send me to jail? Or better than that, you can send me to one of those old-age homes that are coming up here! That is the fate of us old people, to be flicked away like an unwanted fly from a bowl of milk!'

And on and on it went. When I came into her room for her daily massage, she routinely turned her scathing sarcasm on me, too.

'Come come, another forlorn lover! Should we wash your feet and drink the water now that you've attained the purity of love? Now you will be coming to me five years from now and declaring you want to marry a Hindu! What kind of an example is your sister setting for you? She will be the destruction of this family! Your mother should have controlled her when she had the chance, but no! Cultivating independent thinking skills! Look where all this independence has got her! Fancying herself in love with a Sunni! Too many American movies, that's what I think!'

Zeba Baji's impulsive declaration concerning my feelings carried some consequences for me as well. I had to undergo a thorough investigation every time I asked to go to a friend's house. Abbu tried to make me drop out of French class but I went on a hunger strike and threatened to shave my head after he said that he questioned the wisdom of sending me to a place where I was clearly distracted by less intellectual pursuits. Ammi intervened and told Abbu that he was being needlessly harsh. He replied that if he had been harsh when we were young we wouldn't have come to this day. Ammi replied that for once he should think for himself and stop quoting his mother like an African parrot. And so my parents had a fight. Dadi egged Abbu on, insisting that he should not listen to my mother's absurd and ill-placed 'liberal' notions. So Abbu slept for a week on the living-room couch, though Dadi did say he could share her bed. Ammi put her foot down. Abbu could sleep wherever he wanted, but I was not to stop learning an important language just because I had a schoolgirl crush on my teacher. Hence, I was allowed to continue with my classes.

Resentment can be contagious and all of us caught the disease. I resented Abbu and Ammi for fighting with each other instead of working towards a solution for Zeba Baji— one cannot be scolded out of love. I resented my sister for bringing me in the line of my Dadi's ire. I resented Haroon Bhai for being such an escapist ostrich, hiding away from our problems instead of being a supportive son. I resented Saima Apa for being happy while I was sad; it didn't seem fair. Haroon Bhai avoided us and resented Zeba for causing such a stir, thereby making his first year of married life less about him and more about her. Ammi resented Abbu. Abbu bristled at Ammi's accusations of his being a mama's boy, mostly because they rang true.

Things were not helped by Naureen's upcoming wedding. Dadi went through another rant for my benefit when she got off the phone with Qurrat Dadi, who had invited our family to the dholki. There were songs to be learnt and dances to be practised, and considering the overall mood we were in, it came at a most inconvenient time.

Dadi bemoaned the fact that Naureen, who was plainer and came from a less reputable family than Zeba, had the good fortune to get married first. How hard Dadi had worked to prevent such a time from coming! Now Zeba Baji would be the joke of the family—twenty-five and a spinster!

'And everyone will come and ask me why she's not getting married, and I'm supposed to keep quiet and say it's her own kismet! Her own kismet be hanged! She is the luckiest girl in the world, to be born Muslim, Shia and Syed and a Bandian to boot! What is the point in telling people how many proposals she got? Is there any use of receiving eligible bachelors in your house when your granddaughter is actively damning her own soul to hell and her life to spinsterhood?'

When the subject about who was to attend was broached

during dinner, Zeba Baji declared that she didn't want to go. Dadi said there was no question about it, she had to go.

'What will people think? That you're jealous because you're not getting married and Naureen is! You have to go to save face! Say whatever you want to me, I'm evil, I'm a villain, but I will still fight to protect you from shame in the family!'

Zeba Baji glared at Dadi and said she was busy that day. Dadi asked busy doing what, she'd like to know! Zeba Baji said she wasn't meeting Omer, if that was what Dadi was insinuating. Dadi said that was because Abbu had taken away her car keys. Zeba Baji remained quiet. Dadi, not one to back down, asked her if she was talking to Omer on her cell phone. Zeba Baji remained quiet. Dadi told Abbu to ask his daughter what she was up to on the phone with her room locked. Abbu looked at my mother and remained quiet. Dadi didn't let it go.

'What's the point of talking to him? You're not going to marry him, not with this family's approval!'

Zeba Baji got up abruptly, her chair making a sickening screech as it was dragged back along the marble floor, and left the room, her food unfinished. I felt my anger flare up yet again.

'Why must you goad her Dadi?' I demanded to know before I knew what I was doing.

'Oh ho, look who's finding a tongue like her sister! Be quiet and finish your saalan! It's not your business!'

Although pursuing the path of non-confrontation would have been wise, I nevertheless persevered.

'Why isn't it my business? She is my sister. And by the way, all of you are acting really immature!'

Ammi told me to be quiet or leave. I complied with a huff and followed my sister out of the room. Eating amidst such hostility was giving me cramps in my stomach anyway. I went to the TV room and started watching an old tape of *Perfect Strangers*. Saima Apa joined me twenty minutes later and asked me how I was doing.

'How do you think I'm doing? We used to be such a happy family and now we're biting each other's heads off! Why did Zeba Baji have to date Omer? Why does Dadi have to be so rigid? I wish both of them would just go away and leave us in peace!'

'I know what you mean, Jan,' sympathized my sister-in-law. But I was not in the mood to be polite.

'How could you know what I mean? You and Haroon Bhai are never around! You just come here to eat and sleep. The rest of the time you spend at your mum's house or with your friends! You don't know what it's like to be a part of this family!'

Saima Apa turned red, then made an excuse about needing to take a bath and disappeared into her room. I felt petty and miserable and couldn't do anything about it. I had needlessly hurt her feelings. Anger ate away inside me and my pride prevented me from going up and apologizing. But it didn't stop me from feeling guilty.

The strength of a family lies in how they ride out the hard times. By this standard we were proving to be selfishly weak. Someone had to do something. I took a deep breath and marched back into the dining room where Abbu and Ammi were still eating with Dadi.

'I have something to say and I think you should hear me out,' I declared.

'You will say nothing if it means disrespecting your grandmother or your parents,' replied my father, not even looking up from his plate as he swiftly scooped up aloo gosht gravy in a neat little ball and inserted it into his mouth in a matter-of-fact manner.

Momentarily nonplussed, I stood there, my hands crossed behind my back, rocking myself to and fro on my heels as I decided my next move.

'Okay, yes, I was rude to Dadi and I'm sorry. But I have something to say and I want you to talk to me like an adult and not as a child.'

Abbu looked up from his plate and gave me a cold stare. I held my ground, returning his look with an expression I hoped resembled some kind of courageous patience. Finally, he pointed to my chair.

'Fair enough. Be seated.'

I sat down and gathered my thoughts. Dadi gave me a look and then rested her cheek on her hand and said, 'I hope you're not going to tell us you're marrying a Parsi now, are you?'

'No Dadi! What I want to say is this—I know you are feeling disrespected by all of us. I know you've told us what is right from wrong and for the most part we've listened to you. Or we try to listen to you. But you must listen to us too. I know you think that what Zeba Baji did was wrong.

Maybe it was. Okay, it definitely was. The point is that it has happened, and she's found someone for herself that you don't approve of. Are you going to keep her locked in her room forever? You know as well as I do that she's never going to marry anyone. What's worse? Marry a Sunni or not marrying at all?'

'She will get over it once she stops talking to that boy.'

'But why should she stop? She loves him!'

'How many times do I tell you? There is no such thing as love!'

'Didn't you love Dada?'

'I was fond of him. That's all there is, fondness and companionship, none of that bookish nonsense about "soulmates" and whatnot; all that is just a product of hormonal imbalances!'

'But Zeba has spent some time with Omer and she knows him, and he seems to like her. She will be unhappy without him. I know that it has never been done in our family but that doesn't mean it can never be done.'

'It *will* never be done! I know more about these things than you young people and the strongest of attachments can dissolve once you put space between the people involved. Now leave it at that!'

I tried to change tactics.

'Dadi, he's a doctor. Imagine how rich she'll be!'

Dadi looked at me thoughtfully. 'So is that what you think I am looking for? Money? We have more than enough money here, thank you. We don't need to marry any Sunnis to get it!'

'Dadi, the only thing Omer doesn't have is a Shia label.

Abbu has that, so does Haroon Bhai and yet none of them pray. They don't even go to majalis if they can help it. What's the difference?'

Dadi shook her head once again and took another bite of roti. She asked Abbu how his day went at the hospital, signalling that she was not willing to pursue this discussion any further. I sat helplessly and listened to Abbu's story about a particularly difficult patient he had encountered who refused to be injected because she was scared of the needle, even though she badly needed the antibiotics. It was clear that the discussion was over.

Chapter Fourteen

How We Were Shaken Up by a Whirlwind Intervention

Days went by and it seemed like eons. No one talked to each other. Or when they did talk to each other, they feigned an exaggerated civility that seemed more offensive than a slap on the face.

It was worst between Dadi and Zeba Baji. At dinner time, Dadi would ask her to pass the salt. When Zeba Baji complied, Dadi would heave an exaggerated sigh and say, 'Haan Bhai! You have already rubbed salt on my wounds. At least let me use some of it for my food.'

Abbu and Ammi were also waging a cold war with each other. While they were back to sharing the bedroom, they barely spoke because Ammi felt that Abbu was taking an extreme stance by curtailing my sister's freedom of movement. To contradict him directly would only make him dig his heels in. She adopted a strategy to make his insides quiver with the ice of silent treatment. Abbu responded by communicating primarily with Dadi, who validated his reaction vociferously. Ammi got even angrier.

Zeba Baji retreated into her room and her books and refused to talk to anyone unless necessary. Saima Apa was distant with me. It wasn't unexpected after my angry accusation. I felt miserable at having alienated her but refused to apologize, considering it against my pride.

It was clear that we were stuck in a rut and we needed someone to pull us out of the morass of negativity into which we were gradually sinking.

I was brushing my teeth on Sunday morning when I heard the doorbell, followed by Ammi's shriek. I rushed downstairs to find her hugging Fati Phupps, who seemed to have been conjured out of thin air. I blinked thrice, not believing that she was really there, then ran to the foyer and gave her a tight hug.

Fati Phupps appeared the epitome of purpose, attired in a midnight blue sari, strings of jasmine flowers in her hair that swung against her face as she fished out a hundred-rupee tip from her purse for the taxi driver for lugging her three heavy suitcases from the car to the front door.

'Hello Saleha! Your skin has cleared, good! I've got some foundation for you, it's time you started using some make-up. Can someone pay the taxi-wallah please? I don't want to see his face; he's been looking down my blouse in the rear-view mirror all the way from the airport. There, thank you Saleha. Well! Here I am! Now why is everyone looking at me like that?'

'Fati, what are you *doing* here?' Ammi asked, giving her another hug.

'I'm here to talk some sense into my mother dearest, that's what! What? You honestly think that Zeba would meet someone wonderful and not be allowed to marry him and I wouldn't find out? She calls me while crying her eyes out and I ask myself what purpose have I in the world when my niece is upset? So I take a week's vacation and book the first flight available to Karachi! Don't you worry, dear sister-in-law, I shall save this household from the fatally narrow-minded! Now, where is my mother? I have quite a few bones to pick with her!'

Leaving her suitcases on the front step, Fati Phupps marched to my grandmother's room where Dadi was resting on the bed. Dadi sat up with the agility of a guilty teenager when Fati strode into her room, as if unhinged at the waist.

'What has happened? Why are you here? Has someone died? Has someone hurt you? I told you living alone is not a wise idea for women in this country, but will you listen to me? No you won't. You tell me what has happened, I will fix everything! Now tell me what's wrong before I die of a heart attack!'

Fati Phupps was quick to assure her mother that everything was fine and that she was not in any mortal danger, nor was her person under threat of rape or any other method of bodily violation due to the manner of her dress and the nature of her work, a constant apprehension harboured by my grandmother.

'Amma, I am fine, relax! Now what about over here? Are things fine here? I've heard some disturbing news!'

Dadi glanced sideways at her spirited daughter.

'What do you mean? What have you heard?' she asked, reaching for her paan-dan.

'I've heard from your granddaughter that you and my brother are making her life exceedingly difficult. Is that true?'

My grandmother directed her furious gaze at me. On seeing the accusation in Dadi's eyes, I hunched my shoulders and held up my hands and backed away. 'I didn't call her, Dadi! I swear! I didn't think of it!'

'Acha! So now the whole world is involved in this disgraceful fiasco! The more I'm trying to protect Zeba's reputation by keeping the entire affair private, she's making calls to the whole world saying God-knows-what about her own grandmother!'

'Oh, I see, Amma! I don't qualify as family? I'm the "whole world"? Is that how you would refer to your own flesh and blood?'

If there was anyone in the entire world that Dadi was scared of, it was Fati Phupps, because her temper was legendary. My aunt's fury reportedly rivalled that of my Par Dada Jee—Bakhtiar Bandian—who we were told had been torn from his mother's bleeding uterus under the influence of Jupiter. He had been the most successful darogha that Bhakuraj had ever seen simply because criminals were too afraid of him to commit crime. Dadi often commented that if there was such a thing as reincarnation, which of course there was not, then Bakhtiar's soul must have entered Fati Phupps's body. She, too, had been a rebel from the start. Her temper was quick to ignite and hot as coals in a Quetta stove.

Dadi no doubt remembered all this when my aunt confronted her about Zeba Baji, and she knew that if she dismissed Fati Phupps as she was dismissing the rest of us, there would be hell to pay. Therefore, she was avoiding confronting my aunt in argument. But Fati Phupps, it seemed, was on autopilot and expressed her indignation in no uncertain terms.

'It's absolute nonsense I tell you! Marrying young girls to vile-smelling strangers merely because they have the right pedigree! Now, I am going to go upstairs and wipe the tears from Zeba's eyes. Then I'm going to call Omer and have a meeting with him. If I like him, and I think I will, I will ask him to bring his parents to this house. You will meet his parents, and we will decide as a family what is to be done!'

'Arey wah! Who are you to march in here and tell us all how to live our lives? And why should I not be proud of the examples *most* of my daughters have set? My Haseena had never even *seen* her husband before the Ar-see-masaf! She didn't even talk to him until the nikkah had been read!'

'She didn't talk to him afterwards either! If she's the model of matrimonial bliss then God help the rest of this family. For goodness's sake, Amma, she calls her husband Mian. Mister. *Mian*. Not once by his name or some endearment!'

'That is how women from respectable families address their husbands!'

'Really? I think it's because she never got around to asking his name because *he* won't talk to *her*! The only reason she's not gone batty is that she shares the same indifference towards him! What a successful marriage!'

'Just who are you to take me to task like this?' asked my grandmother, tears welling up in her enraged eyes.

'I'm your daughter, that's who! I'm the one who practically raised Hussain when your arthritis kicked in! I was present at Zeba's birth. She was born into my hands! She's like my own daughter!'

'Look at the way you're talking to me! I'm your mother, Fatima, show some respect! What does the Quran say about the rights of the parents? You're not allowed to even say "uff" to me!'

'Well, I don't say "uff" to you, do I?' asked Fati Phupps coyly.

'You say many other things! When I die you will regret all that you have said to me!' Dadi spluttered, shaking with fury.

But Fati Phups was immune to this emotional guilt trip. Their inflamed exchange was interrupted by my sister, who had heard Fati Phupps's resounding speech all the way from her bedroom. She ran into the room and hugged my aunt from behind, laughing and crying at the same time. Fati Phupps's demeanour softened immediately and she went from raging lioness to protective mother hen in a matter of seconds.

'My poor baby! Now don't you worry, I'm here. We'll sort this mess out. Don't you worry! This is what is going to happen. First we will get someone to go and take my suitcases to the guest room. Then I'm going to bathe. Then I'm going to get you to call Omer. I shall speak to him. And then . . . well, we'll take it from there!'

And off went my mother, sister and aunt, talking and making plans while Dadi, shocked and helpless, could only watch them. I offered her a massage and was told to leave her alone and shut the door behind me.

Fati Phupps did, in fact, speak to Omer two hours later. And she did it under Dadi's nose. She barged into her bedroom while Dadi counted her prayer beads with a martyred expression on her face. His number was dialled and he was put on speakerphone as usual.

Fati Phupps introduced herself to Omer and asked him what his intentions were towards Zeba Baji. The voice on the other end, soft but confident, replied that his intentions were honourable. Fati Phupps grew impatient and told him not to dither about the issue. Did he or did he not want to marry her niece? Yes, said the voice, he did want to marry Zeba very much. Fati Phupps declared that in that case, she wanted to meet him to judge whether he was a suitable choice for Zeba.

'We have many questions to ask you, as you may know. You might have several questions for us. If you wish, you can bring your parents along. But I think it's better if I meet you in person somewhere other than this house. What say you?'

'I think it is a good idea. I will come and answer all your questions. My father has already met Zeba and likes her, so there is no one to persuade on my front. If you want to reassure yourselves on account of my person, I am more than willing to meet you wherever you would like to meet.'

'Good boy! Sensible answer!' my aunt nodded, giving Zeba a nod of approval. 'What about your mother?'

'She passed away when I was twelve. It's just me and my father.'

'Terribly sorry to hear about that! Now Omer, Zeba will call you as soon as I've decided where and when I shall meet you. It was good talking to you. Goodbye!'

Fati Phupps hung up without waiting for Omer to say anything more, as it was her custom to summarily end a telephone conversation when she decided it was over, whether or not the person on the other end agreed with her. She looked at my sister with a wicked smile.

'No mother-in-law. Clever girl!'

Zeba Baji declared that that was *not* why she had chosen Omer. Fati Phupps declared that whether it was intentional or not, a woman who chose to marry a man without a mother showed excellent sense. Dadi shook her head and prayed to God for the souls of her headstrong offspring and grandoffspring.

While arrangements were made to meet Omer, Fati Phupps unpacked a month's worth of saris and silver jewellery, her regular mode of attire. Zeba Baji was visibly happier; I was glad that someone had finally broken the dread and gloom that had permeated our house. I was also anxious about Abbu's reaction to the proceedings that had taken place, but needn't have worried, for Fati Phupps had a knack for dealing with him. He was quite shocked when he arrived home that evening to get a quick hug from Fati Phupps.

'Fatima Baji! What are you doing here? Is everything all right?' he asked frantically, searching her face for any sign of sadness or injury.

'Hussain! There you are! You've lost weight! Good to see

you! Now that that's over with, I want to tell you that you are an imbecile!'

My father blinked and stared at his sister, who was now dressed in a lovely olive green sari.

'I beg your pardon?'

'You have it! Now, Zeba has told me all about Omer. I've talked to the boy and you and I are going to meet him tonight for dinner at that Thai restaurant I've been meaning to go to. Amma knows about this, and she will have to agree to whatever you and I decide, whether she likes it or not. Now, for your daughter's sake, develop a spine and talk to this boy and see whether he will make a good husband for her. That's that! You have about an hour to shower and get ready!'

'Now look here Fatima Baji, I know what I am doing. Zeba has gone behind our backs and broken several rules and embarrassed us all! We shall not encourage this ridiculous match at all. She's far too young and too headstrong to make a decision in this matter. That is that!'

'Yes, yes, very good. Your daughter is shameless and deserves to be stoned. Shall we entomb her in a stone wall and wait for her to starve to death? Be sensible, Hussain. She is your daughter. She is headstrong. She knows her own mind. She broke a few rules. Don't make me remind you of your antics when you were a boy! I can tell your wife quite a few college stories. Who pulled you out of your scrapes? Me! So remember what it is like to be young! These things happen! Get off of your high horse and go upstairs for heaven's sake and get dressed! You smell like a hospital!'

'That's because I've *come* from a bloody hospital!' protested my father as Ammi physically pulled him into the house and pushed him up the stairs to get ready. He descended in half an hour and spluttered out some objections at being woman-handled in this manner when he came down to meet a foot-tapping Fati Phupps impatient to get going.

'What's wrong with being handled by me when you've been letting Amma influence you to make the decisions all this time? I'm merely here to make sure you come to an independent decision about the future of your daughter! What about the wishes of your daughter? Or your wife? Act like a father who gives a hoot about his daughter's happiness. When you do that, I'll leave you alone to live your own life. Until then, I'm here to give you some sense of perspective! Now are you ready? Good. Let's go! I'm starving!'

My father was dragged out the door by my aunt, declaring that she should show him some respect and that there were ways things were done in this family and he was respecting tradition because it made us who we were. Fati Phupps retorted that it made us blundering morons, that's what!

That was the last I heard of their conversation as they got into the car and drove away.

How do I describe the state our family was in during those hours of the agonizing wait? Ammi and Dadi both fled to their respective prayer mats, the former praying for her daughter's happiness, the latter fervently imploring all Twelve Imams and the Panjatan to intercede on her behalf and prevent this most disastrous of matches. She sat in the middle of the living room with her prayer beads clicking away at furious speed as she rocked back and forth, taking God to task and asking Him what business He had in trying to sully the Bandian bloodline.

'What will it look like on our family tree? How will I be able to live down this disgrace?'

Haroon Bhai said that it was usually the male descendants whose marriages were recorded and therefore she would be saved that particular ignominy. Dadi gave an impatient snort and told him to go away because he didn't know what he was talking about. After that, he and Saima Apa lolled about until they could take no more and declared that they were leaving for ice cream and did anyone want to come with them? We all declined because we wanted to be home when Abbu and Fati Phupps came home.

I tried to distract myself by checking my email, disappointed that all I had in my inbox were a few spam messages, including an invitation to buy a penis enhancement cream, which I immediately deleted. I attempted to eat away my anxiety with ten Ferrero Rochers and a cheese sandwich. I then agonized about my weight and tried to undo the effect of the compulsive binge by jumping with a skipping rope, thereby promptly contracting an excruciating case of cramps and doubling over in pain and lying in misery for the next hour until it subsided.

While my digestive system gave me grief for abusing it, my sister took to the terrace on which she paced for two hours. She then came back inside, asking me what was wrong with me. I lay moaning on my bed, staring in horrid fascination at my bloated belly, which resembled that of a pregnant woman. I told her to leave me alone and she complied. When I recovered, I went to Ammi's room to find my sister lying down on the floor, with her head in my mother's lap. Ammi stroked her hair and told her that everything would be all right, just wait and see. Zeba Baji buried her head in Ammi's stomach, letting out a muffled apology for the way she had spoken to her and blamed her for being a bad mother. Ammi remained silent for a while and then said she hoped Zeba Baji understood that her mother had not talked to her about such matters, so she had no idea how to approach the subject of love and sex either.

'I just want you to know that I did the best I could. And I also want you to know that your father does care about you. He asked me yesterday whether he should meet Omer or not. So he was considering it. You mustn't blame him. He's done things in a certain way all his life. All of us have, and to change that doesn't come easily for us. And if it is so hard for us, imagine how difficult it must be for your grandmother, who is so old that she can't even imagine doing things differently. We're all trying to protect you, in whatever way we think is best. You must understand that.'

Zeba Baji nodded and said that she did. She hugged Ammi tightly and kissed her on the cheek. She thought for a while and suddenly cringed. 'Ammi, what if Abbu doesn't like Omer?'

Ammi told her not to borrow trouble.

We heard a car pulling in and rushed downstairs to the door, to discover it was only Haroon Bhai and Saima Apa who had returned with a pack of ice cream to cheer everyone up. I helped scoop out the mango ice cream, Zeba Baji worked on the chocolate. It was hard work as they were frozen solid. I hacked away at it with a spoon until yellow mini-icicles flew all over the kitchen floor. Ammi told me to stop helping, as I was creating a mess rather than being useful. Haroon Bhai microwaved the ice cream for a minute and Zeba Baji scolded him for doing so, telling him that microwaving plastic containers made them carcinogenic. Haroon Bhai merely rolled his eyes and told her to stop behaving like a doctor just because she wanted to marry one. Saima Apa arranged the bowls in a tray, and we all settled down to eat in the living room around a still-praying Dadi. When Haroon Bhai asked my grandmother what flavour she wanted, she declared she was diabetic and it was just like her family not to think of her disease and to eat sweets in front of her.

'But Dadi, you are not diabetic! You just had some gajar ka halwa a few days ago!'

'I am indeed diabetic! If you gave me even a fraction of the attention you gave your wife, you would know it!'

Haroon Bhai opened his mouth to argue that Dadi was mistaken, but kept quiet when Ammi signalled him to let it go. Dadi had been diagnosing herself with a new illness every day for some time now, placated only when Abbu gave her a placebo at the end of the day. Yesterday, it was herpes. The day before that, it was vertigo. Dadi had always been a bit of a hypochondriac, but of late, she seemed genuinely convinced that she had contracted a horrible ailment and was outraged when none of us believed her.

Soon, we heard another car pulling into the driveway

and hurried to the door once again. Abbu and Fati Phupps sombrely got out of the car. My heart plummeted to my stomach. They hadn't liked him. I looked at my sister who had turned pale. Ammi suggested that we all proceed to the living room to discuss what had taken place. I was told to get some ice cream for my aunt and father. When we had all settled down, Dadi demanded to know what had happened.

'Arey, have you no consideration for your old mother's nerves? What happened! Tell me at once!'

'The Thai food was terrible. There was this dish called cao phat gai. Really tasted like an exploding cow, I tell you. Quite nauseating.'

Silence followed Fati Phupp's review. Dadi asked her daughter if she had taken leave of her senses, telling her about blown-up bovines instead of telling us about the Sunni boy.

'First you chuck me out of my granddaughter's life, then you tell me about Thai food! What did I tell you about spinsterhood? It drives you mad eventually!'

Fati Phupps said that it was really up to my father to make the final decision, as Zeba was his daughter.

Abbu leaned forward, his elbows on his knees as he laced his fingers together.

'Amma,' he said to Dadi, 'I met Omer tonight, and I kept in mind that in all this time not one Sunni has married into the family, that not one girl has married of her own accord, and I still think that this is how things should remain.'

Dadi beamed, her expression victorious as Zeba Baji stiffened in her seat.

My father continued. 'That is how things should remain, but the fact is, life doesn't turn out as we expect it to. I went tonight expecting to meet a boy with no manners and culture, considering that he was threatening to steal my daughter from under my nose. However, I met a man who told me he cared very deeply for my daughter. He was confident, respectful and polite. I also think he will make Zeba very happy.'

Zeba Baji's eyes glistened with tears. Dadi's blazed with rage.

'Hussain, what are you saying! He's a Sunni! He has corrupted your daughter! And yet you are defending him?'

'Amma, he is far better than many of the proposals we received on her behalf during these past few months. Now I'm not saying that there aren't good Shia boys around. There are probably many of them, but somehow, we haven't come across anyone suitable. I have been asking around and doing some investigation of my own about him, and I've found out that Omer is a promising pathologist. His department head, Tariq Maqsood, says he has high hopes for him. He earns quite well.'

'A pathologist! Those are the doctors who perform post-mortems, aren't they? Toba toba, you're getting our daughter married to an undertaker with a medical degree! Well he can dissect my dead body because that is the only way he can get to my granddaughter!'

'Amma, let's not be melodramatic. Pathologists do far more than post-mortems. Besides, they don't cut up family members. There are usually hospital policies about such things,' interjected Fati Phupps.

'Who says he's a family member? Hussain, have you considered that Zeba's children will be Sunni? That they will know nothing of our ways?'

'That they will be Amma. That they will be. But I don't think it is correct to stop a good match because of what may be written on a piece of paper in the distant future.'

'A good match?! Have you all taken leave of your senses! What am I hearing? Have I taught you nothing Hussain? Is the word of your sister now more important than that of your mother?'

Abbu got up and hugged his mother, who tried to push him away but failed as she collapsed into angry tears.

'Centuries of tradition go down the drain because my granddaughter has no self-control? See my own son send her into a Sunni family! See the day when my family becomes a laughing stock because a girl from my own family is marrying for love! What will people say? That I couldn't control the girls of my house; that they are fast. God knows how many boys they've dated! How will we get a decent proposal for Saleha? Have you thought about her?'

Fati Phupps intervened.

'Amma, you've made your decision known—you won't support this match. We cannot force you to. We can only ask you to reconsider your opinion about this affair. But we are going to have dinner with Omer and his father tomorrow. If you wish to be there, we would be glad. If you don't, then we will have to get Zeba married without her grandmother's blessing because her grandmother cares more about what people will say than her own granddaughter's happiness. Now, let's go lie down. You can think about it as you go to sleep.'

Fati Phupps took a gentle hold of Dadi and led her to her room. Dadi looked frail and weak, a vanquished warrior grown weak with age and constant opposition. I felt uneasy. I looked at the ceiling, waiting for it to wrench open and let through the thunderbolt that God would strike us with for going against the dictates of Dadi.

Zeba Baji got up from her seat and went to my father who received a tight hug and an emotionally charged whisper: 'Thank you, Abbu.' Abbu's eyes became teary. He patted her awkwardly and suggested she better get some sleep. It was late and they had a long day ahead of them. Everyone retired to their respective bedrooms. Fati Phupps took my bed as I lay on the mattress on the floor.

But I couldn't sleep.

All this while, my loyalties concerning Zeba Baji's marital future had been squarely with my sister. But now I felt guilty for crossing Dadi, for making her cry. Ammi was right; Dadi was merely looking out for what she believed would make Zeba happy. What would she be feeling right now? For years what Dadi said went. She had made all the important decisions in the house. Abbu deferred to her not just because she was his mother, but because she was older and wiser than us. To be told by the very family she was watching out for that she was wrong and that they would not consider her feelings on a matter that was very important to her would have been like receiving a punch in the stomach.

I crawled out of my mattress and slipped downstairs into Dadi's room. She lay alone on her bed, a tiny little figure huddled in her sheets. I could hear the steady clicking of the prayer beads and knew that she was awake. I crawled in beside her, wrapped her in my arms and whispered, 'Dadi, I love you! Don't be angry. Don't hate us. Please come with us to meet Omer. It would mean a lot to Zeba Baji. It would mean a lot to all of us.'

Dadi shifted to make more room for me. I expected her to say something on the lines of what did it matter if she was present or not, her opinion no longer mattered. But she stayed quiet. A tear emerged from the corner of her eye and glistened on her cheekbone before it slid down her face. I hugged her tighter.

'Dadi, tell me about Achan Mian again.'

She merely rolled over to the other side. The ticking of her alarm clock was the only response I got.

Chapter Fifteen

How Things Began to Change

My legs felt as if someone had parked a lorry on them. I opened my eyes to find myself lying next to Dadi on her bed, my arms around her waist. I tried to move but was unable to do so. Putting aside the hysterical notion that God was punishing me through paralysis, I looked down to see Zeba Baji's head on my calves, her arms folded as she lay horizontally across the bed so that her torso was resting against Dadi's feet. Sharp little pricks tortured my legs and toes. My legs were asleep and needed to be awakened, like my sister. I whispered her name and got no response. I tried to move my legs but they were in a deeper slumber than her. I sat up sideways and nudged her. She responded by opening her mouth and drooling on my pyjamas.

I thwacked her on the head and wiped the saliva off with her braid. She responded by jerking awake, looking frantic and then asking me loudly if I had a death wish when she realized I was the source of her rude awakening and that her hair was still in my hands. I replied that I had the right to restore the circulation of blood to my legs and it was a wish for a healthy, mobile life that had motivated my actions and she had no business chiding me for my instinct of self-preservation.

Our little spat had the effect of awakening my grandmother, whose cotton shalwar-kameez rustled as she rolled over to see what the turmoil was all about. She squinted, puzzled to see her two granddaughters in her bed, one holding the other's braid.

'What is going on here? Why are the two of you in my bed?'

I let go of Zeba Baji's hair and thumped at my feet with my fists, letting out a moan of agony as a sensation like that of a ticklish fire assailed my leg.

'Dadi, my legs are asleeeeep!' I wailed.

'Then walk on them to wake them up! How many times have I told you not to create a commotion so early in the morning? That's right, take a few steps! Feeling better, aren't you? Silly baccha!'

I walked around the room, chided into silence. Dadi nodded her head in amused exasperation and declared that I was quite hopeless and that I would have amounted to no good if she had not been there to take care of me. She glanced at my sister and suddenly her smile faded away and her expression changed to one of hurt disapproval as she was reminded of the previous night's discussion.

'Well, what are you doing here?' she demanded.

'Dadi, I wanted to apologize to you.'

'Oh really? What are you apologizing for? For accusing me

of destroying your life? For going ahead and calling Fatima to help you destroy yours? For brushing me out of your life like unwanted dirt on the floor when you felt that I was getting in the way?'

'For hurting your feelings. We are meeting Omer today, and I know you disapprove. But I'm here to ask you to forgive me and to give him a chance. I can't imagine taking such a big step in my life without your being present. Please Dadi! Please be there for me, even if you think I'm making a mistake.'

Dadi shrugged and said she would come if she felt like it. Besides, what was the point of being there when her opinion was not counted in the first place? Zeba Baji let out a sigh and walked out of the room, leaving me to pace to and fro to induce my feet to carry my weight without wobbling at the ankles.

Dadi displayed her displeasure at our impending meeting with Omer and his father, Mr Shahid Khan, by choosing to remain in bed all day. Ammi asked her if she wanted breakfast in bed and was told that a woman in mourning did not partake of such frivolous luxuries. Abbu insisted that Dadi needed to eat something because she couldn't take her blood pressure medicine on an empty stomach. Dadi said women with broken hearts didn't give a thought to blood pressure medicines. Fati Phupps asked her when she would stop being melodramatic. To which the curt response was: 'When you start wearing sleeves.'

Haroon Bhai too failed in coaxing my grandmother out of bed. He entered with a bottle of oil and asked for a champi, only to be told that he was beginning to go bald and no amount of hair oil could help his cause. My brother, who was inordinately vain about his good looks, accused Dadi of imagining things. But Dadi said that that's what happened when a man married and became a slave to his wife. His hair fell off as a manifestation of the loss of his masculinity and virility. Haroon Bhai emerged from the room with one hand on his head and the other clutching the bottle of coconut oil and looked at Saima Apa accusingly for the rest of the day.

It was decided that we would have dinner with Omer and Uncle Shahid at their house, which was only fifteen minutes away from ours. Abbu told Dadi that it would mean a lot to all of us if she decided to come. If she changed her mind and decided to join us for dinner, he would come and pick her up. My grandmother remained firm in her resolve to have nothing to do with the matter. When the time came for all of us to get into the car and leave for Omer's house, she took her prayer beads and loudly prayed for our Shia souls.

'O Allah! Forgive them for they know not what they do! O Imam Hussain, turn not aside from them on the Day of Judgement when they implore your help to get to heaven! O Allah! Bear witness that I have been a good mother! I have told them about right and wrong and that is all I can do! O Allah, punish not my children because they wilfully choose the path of damnation! O Allah! Punish them not that they leave their aged mother alone at home while they go and eat without her! O Allah! Forgive my daughters for showing off their arms and shoulders to all kinds of na-mehram men! Forgive my son for listening to their wayward advice. Forgive his wife for not paying heed to the words of her mother-in-law!'

Her prayers became louder and more accusatory as we walked out the door.

It was strange going to visit Zeba Baji's prospective fiancé without Dadi. Under normal circumstances, they would have been coming to our house and not vice versa. I would have been ordered to dust the furniture, especially that of the drawing room. My efforts would have been checked by a fastidious grandparent who would put on her reading glasses to detect any minute particles of dirt that might have escaped my efforts. If any incriminating grime was detected, the dust cloth would be seized from my hands and the dust swished away with indignation, followed by a sharp admonition to not be careless and to clean the entire room once again. After that, Dadi's attention would be diverted to the kitchen, where she would dictate an appropriate menu for the occasion, not too grand so as to give the impression that we were desperate for proposals, but not too meagre so that people would think we couldn't afford to put forth a presentable trolley. The next step would be to select an outfit for my sister and to get her to promise to wear it, knowing well that it would not be kept. After that, I would be told to iron my own clothes and brush my hair and make myself presentable because who knew? I might attract a proposal in the process as well. Dadi was a firm believer in two-in-one deals. If a shop sold a detergent with a free dishcloth, it must be purchased. If arrangements could be made at home where two sisters were showcased in one visitation, all the better. As appalled as Dadi was at Amma Rizvi's offer for me, she was nevertheless proud that I had attracted a proposal at such a young age.

Dadi's absence was palpable as we drove to Omer's house. I kept looking at the front seat where Ammi was sitting next to Abbu and thought that that was where Dadi would have been if we hadn't been going to meet a man she thoroughly disapproved of. Our expressions resembled those of demoralized soldiers whose general was displeased with them.

Zeba Baji had selected a pink shalwar-kameez with full sleeves which she had taken to Dadi's room a few hours before and asked if she should wear it in a further attempt to appease my riled-up grandparent. Dadi had told her to wear black because according to her, Zeba was going to be damned. My sister probably remembered her words because when we neared Omer's house, she became increasingly jittery. Fati Phupps asked her what was bothering her.

'I don't know. It doesn't feel right. I mean it does feel right, but it doesn't. I cannot believe that we are actually going to meet Omer and Shahid Uncle! It feels like the time when I went bungee jumping in Thailand: horrible and exciting all at once.'

Fati Phupps shot her an amused look.

'My dear, you are the most adorable basket case I've seen! You're paving your own way to your future! It's exhilarating! Quite takes the breath away, like a rush of adrenalin! It's quite addictive! Better than smoking!'

I asked Fati Phupps how she knew. Fati Phupps said that she had felt the same way when she had moved out of her in-laws' house, put on her first sleeveless shalwar-kameez and applied for a job in a women's rights NGO. I asked her whether it wasn't even a tad bit scary, rebelling the way she had. She said she'd have been a nitwit if she hadn't been scared. Fear is a healthy emotion, to the extent that it tells us to be careful.

'But when one becomes so filled with fear that one cannot breathe the free air that God gave us without cringing about the consequences, then to hell with the consequences. I say inhale with all your might! Our sages are fond of telling us about the life of lions versus hyenas. Well, throw caution to the winds if it means you will be able to look back and say, "I lived my life my way, not according to some archaic formula drawn by a palsied old man with a frown on his face and a fatwa on his lips!"'

In the midst of this theatrical declaration so characteristic of my rebellious aunt, the car pulled up outside Omer's gate. Abbu turned off the ignition and looked at Ammi.

'Well, we're here.'

We sat in the car, unable to move, for five minutes. This was the defining moment, I thought. The minute we got out of the car and walked inside was the minute we would sever ties with tradition in a very big way. Who wanted to take the first step and get out?

The gate opened and Omer emerged, smiling.

Ammi looked helplessly at my stricken father. 'Oh my God, he's here!'

'Well, of course he's here, don't be daft! Now get out of the car, the poor chap is probably wondering what we're doing all huddled up together like this!' interjected Fati Phupps. 'Hussain, deactivate the child lock, please! What business you have keeping a child lock when all your children are grown up I will never understand!'

Zeba Baji was suddenly beset by a fit of frenzied giggling. She looked and sounded like she'd inhaled a tank of helium. She trembled with hysteria and kept on laughing until I grasped her shoulders and shook them, telling her to get a hold of herself. She responded that she was trying and she couldn't very well steady her nerves if I continued to shake her like a rattle. Presently, she sobered up, biting the insides of her cheeks to contain the ridiculous smile that threatened to form on her face. She got out from the car and beamed at Omer, who smiled back at her.

He was dressed in a white shirt and dark brown trousers. He opened the door for Ammi and said salaam and closed the door behind her. Ammi declared that he was quite the gentleman, and he blushed. Fati Phupps finally managed to slide out the car. She'd been taking all this time to put on her diamond earrings which she had hidden in her purse. Fati Phupps made it a point to never wear jewellery in the car because doing so made one a sitting target for all kinds of thieves and robbers. Omer said she looked ravishing. She announced that he had impeccable taste if he thought so.

Then it was my turn. He looked at me and made a slight bow and, with an amused smile, said, 'You must be Saleha!'

'Yes I am! Don't you remember, we met at the ice cream . . . ah . . . well, we've seen each other before but I don't think you remember because Dadi was screaming at you . . . ah . . . actually she wasn't screaming at you, she was angry at Zeba Baji because she was dating you in Moharram which you must know is very important to us because we're Shia and you're Sunni . . . ah . . . but of course you know that . . . not that I have anything against Sunnis, most of my friends are Sunni and I love the fact that you get to open your fast ten minutes before we do . . . ah . . . I'm pleased to meet you.'

To his credit, Omer didn't bat an eyelash as I made a fool of myself, even though his smile faltered a little bit. His expression remained amused as he said that he, too, was pleased to meet me and wouldn't we all come on inside? His father was eager to meet us.

Uncle Shahid, Omer's father, was a distinguished-looking man with a mane of snowy white hair that served as a sharp contrast to his moustache which looked like an ebony, upside-down crescent shielding his mouth. The lines on his temples crinkled up into folds as he nodded and smiled at me when Omer introduced us. He apologized for not receiving us outside, but the doctor had told him to rest his back, which routinely troubled him.

'Old age, you see, old age! And who is this ravishing young lady?' he said, looking at me. I liked him instantly and said it was very nice to meet him. He declared that I was very charming. Uncle Shahid asked Zeba Baji where our brother was. She said that Haroon Bhai and Saima Apa would be joining us later, after they had come home from work.

Fati Phupps took over Dadi's role as manipulator of conversation with admirable ease. She and Omer's father were soon engrossed in a heated debate about the role of non-governmental organizations in social development. Abbu and Omer discussed his plans for the future as to whether he was considering going into research or private practice, or whether he thought it better to just stick it out with a major hospital. I slipped in next to Ammi and asked her what she thought. She gave me a lopsided smile and said, 'Not bad.'

I noticed that Omer and Zeba Baji were trying valiantly not to give smitten glances to each other, but they failed miserably. Every time he looked around the room, his eyes rested on hers and she returned his gaze with a shy smile before looking away. Uncle Shahid too noticed this and beamed at his son. He turned to my father and said, 'Mr Bandian, I was immensely proud of my son for finding such a wonderful girl for himself. Today I'm even happier because he's introduced me to a lovely family like yours! Why, Zeba is like the daughter I never had! My late wife always wanted a second child. After Omer the doctor said that her body was too fragile to withstand another birth. I am missing her quite a bit today, because I know she would have approved of your daughter.'

There was an emotionally charged silence. A bearded servant entered with cold drinks and Omer reminded his father that he was to take Diet 7Up because the doctor had said so. Fati Phupps asked Uncle Shahid how he was feeling.

'Not bad at all, not bad at all! I'm as fit as a young schoolgirl playing hopscotch!'

We all laughed at the analogy and seated ourselves. Conversation flowed easily.

A trolley was rolled in and Zeba Baji got up to help serve. She was immediately intercepted by Omer who told her she didn't have to do that. Zeba insisted that she didn't mind.

'Arey sit down Beti! Today Omer is on display! Chalo Bhai, let's see how well you serve our guests! Make sure you don't spill anything!'

Ammi let out a laugh and asked Omer if his father teased him thus all the time.

'Auntie, you have no idea! When I was a year old, he made me wear a dress because I looked like a girl, and took a photograph. That picture has been circulated to my shame amongst my entire family! I had to hide it to prevent it from being shown to whoever came to our house!'

'Oh, that's unfair! I want to see what you look like in a dress!! What an adorable idea!' exclaimed Fati Phupps.

'Arey Bibi, my son thinks he's so clever! He hid the photograph in his writing desk. Upper-left drawer, as if I didn't know. And I took it out today.' Uncle Shahid put his hand in his pocket and took out a photograph with a victorious gleam in his eye. 'And here it is!'

Omer's eyes widened. 'Abba you didn't!'

Abba declared that he had indeed. Fati Phupps began rummaging frantically in her purse for her glasses. 'I'm blind as a bat without them, and this is one photograph I have to see!'

A public perusal of Omer's ignominy ensued, much to his exasperated amusement.

Haroon Bhai and Saima Apa walked in five minutes later and another round of introductions commenced. They apologized for being late. Abbu asked them if Dadi was okay and they said that she had gone to sleep. I was

disappointed to see them walk in alone. I had still nursed the
hope that Dadi would walk in with them, but she remained
conspicuously absent. Uncle Shahid asked Abbu how Dadi
was. Abbu looked embarrassed and said that she had been
tired of late. Omer's father seemed to realize intuitively that
this was not a subject Abbu was comfortable discussing and
so he said he was sorry to hear it.

Dinner was served. Omer's major-domo and cook, Akbar,
was an ex-navy chef who cooked up a mean nihari. I spread
gravy and onion over my plate and guzzled it down with
naan. Omer and Zeba sat next to each other, opposite us,
and I have to admit that they made a lovely couple. They
had an instinctual rapport between them and seemed
to communicate without having to speak. When Uncle
Shahid stopped in the middle of a story about how he was
once attacked by a wild boar while he was taking a walk in
Islamabad, Omer looked up, alarmed. Omer's apprehension
triggered Zeba's who also looked at Uncle Shahid and
immediately got up and went to the drawing room to retrieve
a cushion and put it behind her future father-in-law. Uncle
Shahid was embarrassed and pleased by her solicitousness
and explained to us that his back needed a lot of extra
support. Zeba Baji poured him some water and sat down
next to Omer and continued eating her nihari. Omer took
a wedge of lemon and squeezed it over her plate, telling her
that it would enhance the taste of the gravy.

Once dinner was over and green tea was served, Uncle
Shahid asked Abbu when he could come over to our house
to discuss some very important business. Abbu exchanged a

knowing glance with Ammi. 'Important business' meant an official proposal. He replied that any time that would suit Uncle Shahid would be fine.

Ammi was quick to interrupt. 'Hussain, I think next week is going to be slightly busy for us, you know, with Naureen's wedding coming up. Shahid Bhai, why not have dinner with us after that?'

'Splendid, splendid! But there is one condition that I have before I come to your house!'

'Of course, tell us what it is?'

'Zeba Beti must cook one dish!'

Zeba Baji laughed and declared that she would never be so cruel as to inflict her cooking on the people that she loved. But Uncle Shahid insisted, and she said very well, but she would also keep a bottle of Karmina on the side for any prospective digestive problems. 'And Omer will be there to save us all from food poisoning!'

On this note, Abbu took his leave. Uncle Shahid remained inside, apologizing that he could not see us off. Omer, however, accompanied us outside, opening the door for my mother and Fati Phupps. As we drove off, Fati Phupps nudged Zeba Baji and said, 'Not only a doctor but a gentleman at that. And no mother-in-law! I can't tell you how proud I am of you!'

Zeba Baji merely rolled her eyes and smiled.

Chapter Sixteen

How a Catfight Saved the Day

Dadi refused to discuss Omer with us. Abbu tried to tell her how delightful Uncle Shahid was but she merely replied that my father was soft in the head and that she didn't want to be a part of any of this, which meant she didn't want to know any details about visits made despite her disapproval. Besides, the various functions of Naureen's wedding served to distract us from her displeasure and they gave Dadi a way to busy herself.

The milad was a small affair and Dadi looked smug when she saw that Naureen's skin had broken out into angry pimples. But of course, she was the epitome of concern as she patted Naureen on her head and told her to put a paste of honey and turmeric on her face.

'It might make a difference. But what will you do on your wedding day? All your photographs will be spoilt! But not to worry my dear, the make-up they put on these days will hide all the blemishes. But what will you do on your wedding night when you have to wash off the make-up? Not to worry, I'm sure your face will be the least of your husband's preoccupations, if you know what I mean! But what will you do once that is done? Not to worry, I'm sure your skin problems will take care of themselves, you know, with things going in and things coming out, if you know what I mean!'

It was a matter of great bafflement to me that my normally prudish grandmother became downright lecherous in her humour whenever it came to a girl's wedding night. I asked Zeba Baji why all the women Dadi's age bandied bawdy jokes during weddings, and she said that it was because in Bhakuraj, these jokes were the only thing that constituted sex education for them. Fati Phupps told me that one of Dadi's cousins had no idea what was going to happen on her wedding night and ran out from her bedroom screaming bloody murder because she thought her husband was equipped with the tool of the devil. Therefore, to avoid such embarrassing moments, the women of Bhakuraj often assembled together and hinted to the unsuspecting bride what was in store for her.

Both Qurrat and Dadi giggled and covered their mouths with their hands while Naureen stared at them. Ammi told her not to pay attention to my grandmother, that the acne was hardly noticeable, which was a lie, and in another perjury said that she looked lovely.

Dadi's mood darkened, however, as Qurrat talked about how wonderful it felt to be relieved of all responsibilities, meaning granddaughters' marriages.

'Now I will not have a care in the world! You know what

I mean, Gulbahar Bibi . . . to be careful of what you say and do in front of people because who knows whether they have eligible sons interested in your daughters! Now I am free to do as I please! Very few women are lucky to see the day when all their daughters and granddaughters are happily married! I can rest in peace because I've fulfilled my duty to my family!'

'Yes,' replied my grandmother coyly, 'but luckier are those who arrange good matches for their sons. Good *Eastern* girls who don't have to change their names for the nikkah to be read.'

Both women looked at Qurrat's son and daughter-in-law, who had flown in from California for Naureen's wedding. Desiree looked uncomfortably out of place amidst the proceedings and clung to her husband. No one was making an effort to speak to her in a language she understood.

Qurrat Dadi excused herself and got up to distribute bangles to all the single girls assembled. Zeba was the first girl to get one. Dadi bristled, but remained quiet. I sat next to her through most of the milad and she undertook a thorough survey of the arrangements that had been made. She was happy to note that fewer people showed up for Naureen's milad than had for Haroon's and took it as a sign of the greater popularity of our family. 'Besides,' she said, 'people only want to attend functions of families who are loving and sincere, not petty and vindictive. Always remember that Saleha!' I asked Dadi if she thought the low attendance was because Naureen's milad was on a weeknight, while ours had been on the weekend. Dadi shrugged and said it was possible, but in that case she thought it revealed bad planning on Qurrat's part to keep an event on a weeknight. Men in other families went to work after all! I said that women go to work as well, to which she replied that good Eastern women lived their lives for their children and did not spend all day in an office with strange men staring at their bosoms. 'Always remember, Saleha, men will stare at your bumpies . . . those in front and those at the back! That's why girls from good families bother about dupattas.'

This sagacious advice was passed on to me periodically by my grandparent, who was obviously envious of her nemesis's position of having no more daughters to marry off.

Qurrat was clearly gloating. Their family had a small tradition of making the single girls sit with the bride-to-be so that her kismet could rub off on theirs and expedite their process of getting married. When the singing was done, Qurrat loudly announced that it was time for the 'baithak' or 'sit in' to begin. The first to be summoned was of course my sister, while Qurrat snuck a look at my grandmother for a response. Dadi kept her expression carefully bland, but inside she was livid.

'Look at how conceited she is: fat, hairy bear with a chimpanzee of a granddaughter! As if my fairy princess needs their help to get married!' she muttered to me.

Zeba Baji was reluctantly led to the wooden swing where Naureen was seated. She sat down and gingerly fed the future bride a gulab jamun, offered her felicitations and made to get up when once again Qurrat stopped her.

'Arey Zeba! Getting up so soon! No no, be seated for a

while longer. Who knows? Naureen's fate might be rubbing itself on yours as we speak!'

Zeba Baji looked embarrassed and attempted to joke her way into escape: 'Qurrat Dadi, I don't think it's decent to allow that much rubbing. Wouldn't you say?'

'Arey wah? And how would you know what too much rubbing is? Naureen might tell you after the wedding night, if you know what I mean!! Ha ha! No no, keep sitting! How eager you are to run away! Just wait and I'll tell the photographer to take a picture of you two! Keep sitting now, don't move! Smile! There you go! May Allah bless you with a husband as wonderful as Naureen's. Although I think that it would be difficult because Naureen is getting the best man in the world! But miracles have been known to happen! What do you think, Naureen?'

Naureen, who had slipped into the role of demure-mortified-bride-who-refuses-to-smile with natural ease, merely lifted her head, gave her grandmother a vacant look and then went back to staring at her lap. Zeba Baji got up and Qurrat Dadi zeroed in upon her next target—me.

'Oh ho, Gulbahar, you must forgive me. I forgot that you don't have one unmarried granddaughter with you, but two! Saleha Beti, come and sit next to your Naureen Baji, now that's a good girl!'

I protested and said that I was too young to get a husband, and that I was too preoccupied with my O Levels to bother about such things. Qurrat Dadi merely pooh-poohed and told me not to be shy. 'Shy girls don't get married. One must be bold, like a cheetah! What do you say, Naureen? Do you think there will be much growling and panting after you get married? He he!'

This lewd remark was followed by an admonition directed my way to not shuffle my feet and come sit next to Naureen. A photograph was taken and Qurrat proceeded to summon the various other unmarried women to come and partake in her granddaughter's good fortune. I could see that Dadi's patience was wearing thin—Qurrat had especially singled us out and Dadi was having a difficult time containing her anger.

Once all kismets had been intermingled in a well-choreographed orgy, Qurrat sat down next to Dadi and asked her if she wanted some paan. Dadi said she would like some, indeed. I sighed with relief, thinking the two were at least affecting a truce. I sat down next to Zeba Baji and Fati Phupps, the latter grinning widely. I asked her what she found so funny, and she said she was amused to see Dadi and her arch-rival catfighting in Bhakurajian style.

A Bhakurajian catfight differs from its physical counterpart in terms of subtlety. Since the assumption of all respectable Bhakurajian households is that they are superior to other families and therefore above the petty behaviour and argument that characterizes such feline contests, the women of Bhakuraj have devised their own form of battle which is conducted in a way that no non-Bhakurajian can detect as an argument. The paan-dan is an essential weapon of war: it establishes outward camaraderie but is really a signal between the two betel-leaf chewers that serious displeasure is being harboured in one or both breasts. Thereupon, pinching sentences are delivered as each betel leaf is masticated.

Comments are calculated to goad, hurt and antagonize. The first to shut the paan-dan and walk away from the verbal skirmish is deemed the loser.

Qurrat handed over a rolled betel leaf to Dadi, and the latter accepted it with good grace, folded it in half and took the entire leaf into her mouth. She chewed on it thoughtfully, gave her opponent the Kajolled Side Gaze that most effectively conveyed latent hostility, where the face points in one direction but the flashing pupils lodge themselves in the corner of the eyes to glare at the opponent without letting the latter find out. It is a look inspiring fear. The woman who sports the Side Gaze signals that she is about to deliver a lethal verbal blow.

'Desireé looks quite ravishing in that pink sari you made for her. She would look lovely if she lost some weight though. But what to do? Americans have such unhealthy eating habits. It's not her fault that she keeps expanding considering the rich diet they have over there. And what is the point, I wonder? She's already passed the genes on to your grandchildren. But who am I to say anything? I know that we grandmothers are only made to love our grandchildren. Even if the grandchildren have faces only a mother can love!'

Qurrat nodded in affirmation but her paan chewing paused for a second or two, an imperceptible pause to most but to Bhakurajian observers it was a significant sign that Dadi's words had had the desired effect of yanking Qurrat out of her smugness. The first strike had been delivered. It had been a strong one, but the retaliation was soon to come.

'*Mariam* does indeed look very pretty. After all, what

woman who has a husband does not? I say that a marriage lends a glow to a girl, and look at how my Naureen is radiant tonight! I hope that Zeba and Saleha, too, find someone to light up their lives! Waisay Gulbahar Bibi, you must not lose hope, even though Zeba is about to turn twenty-six next month. Times have changed. Why, in our era a girl was considered a rotting, overripe banana the minute she turned nineteen! But today girls should be educated. My Naureen spent most of her life studying medicine and is a doctor! I am telling her not to practise because she doesn't need to work since she's marrying a rich husband. She is lucky to be marrying a man who can support her. But education is also important: a well-educated girl will get the most proposals! Now your Zeba is a master's in English. That is good, I suppose, but perhaps you should encourage her to get a proper degree. You know what I mean? Perhaps then her fortune will change, and she will not look quite as forlorn as she seems while she sits next to your widowed daughter. How is Fatima these days? I often think in my mind that if only she had learnt to control her temper, she would have remarried! But sometimes women have demons inside them! At least she is working and distracting herself. That must be some consolation to you!'

Dadi shot Qurrat the Blazing Glare of the Disappearing Eyelid. The latter smiled sweetly and asked her if she wanted some choona for her paan. Dadi refused and made to get up. I sat up in alarm: my Dadi, Grand Champion of the Bhakurajian Catfight, was actually preparing to walk away and accept defeat!

She was stalled by Qurrat who placed one hand on her arm.

'Arey Gulbahar Bibi, don't go away just yet! I have been meaning to tell you something. I have invited a friend of my daughter's: Mrs Shabana Qamar-ul-Haq. She is a matchmaker, you know. Has nearly a hundred successful marriages under her belt and she's been in the business for many years. Very successful! Now you know I am not a selfish woman. Just because I'm free of my responsibilities towards my daughters does not mean I will forget women like you, who have two young girls sitting right under your nose! I want to introduce you to her!'

Dadi's face contorted with undiluted hostility as Qurrat summoned Mrs Shabana Qamar-ul-Haq. Mrs Qamar-ul-Haq was a singularly unattractive individual with no bosom to speak of. She did sport a sizeable paunch that would easily rival the midsections of most mid-career professionals and retired army officers. Her cheeks sagged and her eyes squinted behind thick glasses as she focused on my irate grandparent. Qurrat gave her a quick hug and invited her to sit between her and Dadi. She offered her a betel leaf, which was accepted.

Then Qurrat delivered her final blow.

'Mrs Qamar-ul-Haq, I've just been telling my sister here that you are an expert in matrimonial matters! It is such an honour for me to have you come to our house, even though I am not in the need of your services, but my sister here, sitting next to you, is!'

Qurrat went on to summon a few girls. Zeba Baji and I were also sent for, but we were unaware that it was our single status that was the reason for our being called; neither did we notice that Qurrat had assembled all unmarried, unattached girls in front of the Squinter, which is the name Fati Phupps had given Mrs Qamar-ul-Haq, who true to her sobriquet was peering at us with all the attractiveness of a bat exposed to sunlight. Qurrat beamed at all of us and declared:

'Mrs Qamar-ul-Haq, all these girls are ripe!'

Most of us let out a collective gasp. Fati Phupps looked horrified. One cousin, not known for being too bright, asked, 'Ripe for what?'

Qurrat merely smiled and looked askance at Dadi.

'To be plucked by whatever man should come your way! Now Mrs Qamar-ul-Haq, take a good look at all these girls! Most of them are young, below twenty in fact! Except for one or two . . . no, no, except for just one, most of them are just the right age to be engaged!'

Dadi surged up to her feet, clearly having had enough. This was the final straw, and she would stand Qurrat's taunts no more.

'Zeba! Go and sit down next to your aunt! Saleha—follow your sister! Qurrat, I was quiet but you've given me no choice! It is not appropriate for families like ours to solicit the help of matchmakers and matrimonial services to get our daughters married! That may be how you procured a proposal for your granddaughter, but it's not the route I took for any of *my* offspring and I'm certainly *not* going to start today!'

Qurrat gasped.

'Why Gulbahar Bibi, I was merely looking out for your daughters! They are like my own!'

'Well! It will please you to hear, in that case, that one of your own granddaughters, my Zeba, is also going to be engaged very soon! To a very reputable patheticologist!'

This announcement caused quite a stir and not just in the room. My heart turned a somersault and Zeba Baji turned pale and forgot to breathe. Fati Phupps jumped up from her seat and let out a whoop of joy, shock, surprise or all three together.

Qurrat, however, looked crestfallen. Dadi grinned victoriously as she watched her arch-rival lean down, shut the lid on the paan-dan and lead Mrs Qamar-ul-Haq away from the battleground-cum-sofa. Thereafter, Dadi took her seat with all the grace of a monarch assured of her reign. The Battle had been won and she remained Grand Champion.

I fled outside to tell Ammi and Saima Apa what had just occurred. Saima Apa went to relate the incident to Haroon Bhai, who told Abbu and we all followed my mother as she hurried inside to see what was going on. We saw Dadi proudly ensconced on the sofa as several women congratulated her on her Zeba's imminent betrothal. A dazed Zeba Baji stood still at the other end of the room, being hugged and kissed and asked all sorts of questions about her future husband. Qurrat tried to smile, but her face was a picture of dismay. Not only had Dadi defeated her in battle, but her announcement had also taken attention away from Naureen's function. When Mariam/Desireè congratulated her mother-in-law on the happy proceedings, she received a furious glare and quickly returned to the protection of her husband's side.

Upon seeing Ammi, several people surrounded her and

asked all sorts of questions. Who was the boy? What did he do? What was a patheticologist? Why didn't she tell them before? Did he live in Pakistan or abroad? In Karachi or elsewhere? When was the engagement? No wonder Zeba had been looking so lovely of late! Hadn't they said she was looking lovelier than usual? Of course they had! You cannot hide the happy glow of a girl affianced! How tall was he? How much did he earn? Was he fat or thin? Dark or fair? If fair, he and Zeba would have such beautiful children!

All Ammi could do was splutter out that she hadn't expected the engagement to be announced quite this soon. Dadi, surrounded by women asking her the same questions, merely smiled and said, 'Oh ho! Just wait! We hadn't planned on announcing it quite yet! Today was Naureen's big day but just look at me, I couldn't contain myself! But I'm very tired. There has been a lot of excitement for today! I think it's best if I go home!'

This sparked a wave of protests, much to Dadi's not-so-secret pleasure.

'Arey, don't leave us in suspense! Do tell us something before you go!'

'Be patient! I'm feeling faint and I need to get going. Hussain, help me up! Khuda Hafiz everyone! May God protect you. I will give you the details when we next meet on Naureen's mehndi. Right now I think I need my blood pressure medicine. My head is spinning!'

My grandmother made a strategic exit, avoiding questions for which she did not have a good response. We followed Abbu as he led Dadi out to his car. I got in with Zeba Baji in Haroon Bhai's and Saima Apa's car and drove home. My sister was silent, as if a big boulder had just fallen from the sky and hit her on the head. I asked her if she could believe what had happened.

'What *did* just happen? One minute we were all standing in line in front of that woman, and the next I was jumped at by screaming women congratulating me. Good Lord! Dadi almost announced my engagement to Omer!'

'Not almost!' I clarified. 'She went ahead and did it. Haroon Bhai, did you know we were made to stand in front of a matchmaker by Qurrat Dadi? Dadi exploded and then just announced that Zeba was indeed engaged!'

Haroon Bhai looked horrified. 'Don't tell me Dadi announced Zeba's engagement to spite Qurrat Dadi!'

'I think that is what happened,' replied Zeba Baji. 'Qurrat Dadi was on a roll, probably getting back at Dadi for all the times Dadi has one-upped her in the past. I mean she really laid it on thick, making me take a photograph with Naureen, calling me a rotting banana and then saying I was among those who were ripe.'

Haroon Bhai asked her what on earth she was talking about. I told him about the paan-dan catfight and he let out a loud laugh.

'If you think about it, Zeba owes Qurrat Dadi big time! For if there is one thing worse than letting your granddaughter marry a Sunni man for love, it's letting your arch-rival think she's got the better of you! Dadi must have been really riled up to be goaded into making a statement like that!'

'But I don't think it's time for us to celebrate just yet,'

interjected Saima Apa. 'Dadi Amma did announce your engagement but she avoided telling people what Omer's name was or about his sect. These two facts she won't want to share with the world, nor will she be able to hide them.'

'That's what I was thinking about, too,' said Zeba Baji. 'Knowing Dadi, she might try and browbeat Omer into changing his name or something like that, which he will not appreciate. That much I can assure you.'

We all sat in thoughtful silence. I considered Dadi's options. Dadi would have to answer many questions about Omer's religious affiliations, not just because ours was a conservative Shia family but Dadi was known to be the biggest and most vocal opponent of inter-sect marriages. I idly painted a scenario in my head of Dadi producing an actor to play the role of Omer the Shia Patheticologist. The more I thought about it, the more I realized that Dadi had landed herself in a real fix just to silence Qurrat in a dramatic sequence of events that would probably go down in the Bhakurajian Catfight Hall of Fame.

Chapter Seventeen

How Dadi Extracted a Proposal Just in Time

'That witch Qurrat goaded me into making that announcement! Telling a matchmaker to help my granddaughters indeed! Well, I showed her, didn't I? She'll think twice before she tries to ridicule me or my family again. What does she think? Just because she managed to get two daughters married into pool-owning families, she can flaunt her superiority to me? I had six daughters, no less! And I managed to get all of them married without the help of any fat, ugly marriage bureau person. The cheek of that woman, thinking she's got the better of me! But Zeba had to go choose a Sunni of all people! No, don't follow me into my room, Hussain, I have to undress and think about what I'm going to tell people. Where are my prayer beads? Good, hand them over to me! There, now leave my room and switch off the lights, I need to lie down. Hai hai, all this excitement is giving me a flutter in my chest!'

words. I remembered the time when I had gone behind Ammi's back and threaded my upper lip when I had been expressly forbidden to do so. The women of the Bandian family were famous for their lack of body hair. This was because the girl child was massaged with a mixture of flour and water during the first month of her life. I too had been marinated in this manner and therefore did not share the misfortune of hairiness that Qurrat's family suffered from. My mother and grandmother had told me not to remove hair from any part of my body as this would increase growth and texture, thereby complicating matters for myself. So whenever I wanted to rebel and get back at Dadi or Ammi, I shaved a different part of my anatomy. The first fight about orange in Moharram resulted in shaved arms. A second fight about going to the beach with friends resulted in shaved legs. I also managed to shave off my eyebrows when Ammi threatened to drag me to a milad that I didn't want to go to. To my mortification, I was dragged to the event anyway, brow shaved and browbeaten. When Haroon Bhai had thoughtlessly commented that I looked different I had exploded: 'Why? I haven't removed hair from *any* part of my anatomy!' My guilt, of course, drew attention to my crime, and I was chastised and grounded for a week.

Point being—had I not overreacted, I would not have been discovered. Perhaps a nonchalant attitude could keep the gossipmongers at bay. If we became too defensive, as I had back then, our family would have a field day and all sorts of incriminating charges would be laid on Zeba Baji's shoulders. No, we had to present a united, non-hysterical front.

After we were done discussing the exciting events of the night and Abbu let out a loud yawn to let us know that he was tired, we all retired to our respective bedrooms. I was too jittery to go to sleep that night, so I slipped into Dadi's room to find her busy praying. I slid into her bed and waited for her to finish but dozed off. I was jerked awake by my grandmother as she climbed into bed beside me.

'Dadi . . .' I murmured sleepily, 'what's the plan?'

'Stop being such an interfering little busy bee! Go back to sleep! Uff, move over a little bit, you've taken over the entire mattress.'

This response told me that Dadi still did not have the slightest idea about how to deal with a situation she had created. I rolled over to make room for her and when she settled down, wrapped my arms and legs around her, ignoring her protests that I was not a koala bear and she was most certainly not a eucalyptus branch. I drifted off to sleep listening to the sound of her breathing and the clicking of her prayer beads as she continued to pray.

Morning came and we convened at the breakfast table. Dadi remained silent as she thoughtfully spread her toast with her favourite guava jelly. Ammi poured her some tea and asked hesitantly, 'Amma Jan, you announced Zeba's engagement yesterday. So does this mean that you are agreeable to the match?'

'Arey, what difference does it make whether I am agreeable or not? But you tell me, how could I sit and let Qurrat ridicule me for having Naureen married before Zeba?'

Ammi became silent. Fati Phupps took over.

'But Ma, you do realize that now people will want to know more about Omer. You will have to tell the world that he's Sunni, that it is a love match. What have you thought about that?'

Dadi pondered the question carefully and sipped her tea. She turned to Zeba and asked, 'Would Omer consider changing his name?'

'Dadi! Of course not!'

'Hmm. I had thought not. Well, I do know of a few Shia men named Omer. It *is* possible although I don't know *what* their parents were thinking! You said his mother had passed away? We could just tell the world that his father is Shia but she was Sunni and that she wanted to name him thus.'

'Yes, except for the fact that Shahid Uncle is *not* Shia!' interposed Haroon Bhai.

'Arey Bhai, we don't have to tell people that! Use your common sense sometimes! Or did you leave it behind when you got married!'

'Amma, we are not going to lie to people!' exclaimed an outraged Fati Phupps.

'Why *not*? It is permitted to lie to save the honour of one's family.'

'For starters, it's morally wrong. And more importantly, what if we get caught? Then people will find out that we don't approve of Omer, and that will *really* give them something to talk about!'

'Oh ho! Zeba, tell Omer and his father not to tell our family that he's a Sunni. That will take care of that!'

'Will you listen to yourself? If Omer was a regular

Bhakurajian Shia boy you would never dream of asking him to take such a step!' cried Fati Phupps.

'If he was a regular Bhakurajian Shia boy I would not need to ask him to take any step at all. In fact, my temples would not be throbbing because I could not sleep, because how does one explain a Sunni love marriage in the Bandian household?' responded Dadi tartly.

'Well, I don't think Zeba should ask him to hide anything about himself. He is Sunni and that is that. When people ask, you just tell them matter-of-factly and unapologetically.'

'Wah wah! Listen to my daughter telling me how to do my business! I have more experience over things like this than you do! How do you think I survived when people asked me what my widowed daughter was up to, wearing saris and make-up and meeting all sorts of strangers instead of staying at home and observing her iddat? But I don't want to get into that right now. Zeba, call your Omer and tell him to bring his father this evening to our house and deliver a formal proposal. I can't have people thinking you are engaged if the boy hasn't even asked our permission for you to marry him! After that is done, we shall see how things proceed.'

'But Dadi . . .' protested my sister, as the cup in her hands shook so that she spilled some tea into the saucer.

'Do you want to marry this boy or not?' Dadi pointed the butter knife at Zeba.

'Erm . . . yes, I do.' She nodded eagerly, thereby spilling some more tea and staining Ammi's beloved snow-white tablecloth, the one that sported patterns of dainty women with kettles and kittens in their slender arms.

'Well, you better tell him to hurry up about his business. And get a wet cloth and wipe that spot so it doesn't stain. And learn to have your tea without spilling; I won't have your in-laws thinking that Bandian girls don't have any etiquette or hand–eye coordination! Bahu, whoever calls, tell them that I am unwell and that I do not want to entertain any visitors. If anyone starts asking questions about Zeba's betrothal, just say that you are busy taking care of me and will call them back. That will give us some time. But we *must* procure a proposal this evening!'

With that resolve, Dadi made a decisive incision in her omelette with her fork.

It was decided between my sister and her future fiancé that he would bring Uncle Shahid at eight o'clock that evening to deliver a formal proposal. Omer had been well aware of Dadi's opposition to their match and was only too eager to avail this unexpected opportunity of her sudden compliance and even impatience to get them officially engaged.

Meanwhile, the phone, according to Dadi's predictions, never stopped ringing. Qurrat alone called five times to find out details from my mother who apologized for being busy each time and promised that she would call as soon as Dadi was feeling better again. My grandmother was extremely satisfied with the effect of her announcement on her nemesis.

'See how many pins and needles are pricking into her brain! Just imagine, she has a granddaughter to get married off and she is still finding time to call me and ask me about Zeba. Bechari. She can't help it.'

Eventually we decided to keep the phone off the hook.

Ammi switched her cell phone off to avoid any more interference from inquisitive relatives but this resulted in a harassed Abbu calling Zeba Baji on her cell phone demanding to know why he was being disturbed by ridiculous calls while he was doing his rounds at the hospital. All in all, I discovered that refuge from a curious relative is seldom to be found.

The drawing room was dusted and trolley prepared. At seven o'clock, Uncle Shahid walked in, leaning heavily on his cane but sporting a huge grin as he declared what a pleasure it was to meet all of us again. He was followed by his son, who ushered in their major-domo, who buckled under the weight of a huge basket of fruits and sweetmeats to celebrate the Sealing of the Deal. We seated them in the drawing room and waited for my grandmother to make her appearance.

And what an appearance she made! Attired in a blue cotton gharara with a white dupatta, adorned with gold bangles and earrings and carrying her silver paan-dan, she made quite an impact. Omer shot to his feet, no doubt recalling the impact her forceful personality had made on him that fateful day at the ice cream parlour. He salaamed and she accepted his salutations with a slight bow of the head, like a queen acknowledging an awestruck subject. Uncle Shahid gave my father a wicked look and demanded to know why he had not told him that Dadi was such an incomparable beauty. This outrageous, blatantly sycophantic comment was delivered with great charm and Dadi, who was inordinately vain in any case, actually looked down and blushed like a little schoolgirl.

Desultory conversation ensued, followed by a dinner eaten silently. Only Uncle Shahid and Dadi spoke, exchanging notes about Partition as they both had witnessed horrible scenes of murder and displacement. Dadi, to whom no subject was exempt for discussion, asked Uncle Shahid why he had married so late. Uncle Shahid replied that he had fallen in love with Omer's mother when he was forty and she only eighteen. They had met in her older brother's garden, where she had spilled lemonade all over his suit while serving it to him.

'It was love at first sight. My suit was destroyed, but my life was made! Her parents were alarmed that she had chosen such an old man, but we were very happy until she passed away.'

Dadi offered her commiserations and asked Uncle Shahid if he knew that she and her husband also met in her garden. 'But he had the good sense to curb his passion and ask my father for permission to marry me. We come from a respectable family and our women have their matches arranged by their elders.' With a glare at Omer, she said, 'That is how it should be, instead of sneaking around behind people's backs in restaurants and ice cream parlours.'

Shahid Uncle remained prudently quiet and asked what Zeba Baji had cooked for him. She passed him the plate of biryani, which she had slaved over most of the morning, routinely yelling to Ammi for help every time she felt something had gone wrong. An awkward moment occurred when Zeba Baji tasted some herself and let out a mortified cry.

'Oh my God! There is no salt in it!'

There followed an embarrassed silence. Dadi glared at Zeba Baji for bringing this shame upon the family culinary honour. But Uncle Shahid was Grace personified when he took yet another helping, sprinkled some salt on it with the shaker and declared: 'There you go! Now it is scrumptious!'

I sensed Dadi getting more and more impatient as time passed. I knew she wanted Uncle Shahid to propose on Omer's behalf and be done with it. But Uncle Shahid was a leisurely eater and seemed more interested in enjoying our company than in the formality of the event. Green tea was served and we went to the drawing room once more. Dadi resorted to not-so-subtle hinting.

'Shahid Sahib, you do not know how happy it makes me to meet people who will in the future become a part of my family. They come, they give a rishta and then just like that, the bonds between us are cemented into something lasting. Isn't it miraculous?'

Shahid Uncle nodded and said, 'Indeed, it is truly a wonderful experience when two families come together.' He paused and looked at Dadi. Dadi returned his glance, leaning forward on the sofa in silent encouragement. Omer's father leaned back and asked Abbu how his practice was getting along.

Dadi blinked several times as if she had missed something. She prepared some paan for herself, asking Uncle Shahid if he would like some. He replied, 'No, thank you.' Dadi looked at Ammi helplessly. But still she valiantly persevered.

'You should not have brought such a huge basket of sweetmeats, Shahid Sahib. But it is very kind of you. I will have them distributed all over the neighbourhood to deliver the good news . . . once there is good news to deliver.'

Shahid Uncle merely smiled and looked uncomfortable. Seated where I was, I had a sudden epiphany. He had come to deliver a proposal, but he had no idea how to start. He shuffled in his seat and opened his mouth to say something. Dadi leaned forward expectantly once more.

A loud banging on the door prevented him from saying anything. Someone was outside!

Dadi threw her hands up in the air and looked at the ceiling, as if asking God what business he had in sending us a visitor at a time like this. Abbu opened the door to a highly flustered Qurrat who barged in and demanded to see her beloved cousin.

'All day I'm calling and people are telling me she is unwell, she has a headache! Not very good signs in a woman her age. I had to come and see for myself whether it isn't anything serious. There you are Gulbahar Bibi! You look fine to me. What was your daughter-in-law talking about? You're just a little pale, which is to be expected with all the excitement that has been taking place in your house, what with Zeba's engagement and all!'

Dadi's face had indeed taken on an ashen hue. Qurrat's untimely arrival and her blabbering on in front of Uncle Shahid before he had even offered a proposal was an embarrassment. Uncle Shahid blinked and threw a questioning look at Omer, as if asking him whether he knew about the engagement Qurrat was referring to.

Qurrat Dadi soon realized that she had barged into a meeting where she was most certainly not welcome. Therefore she took the average interloper's strategy and made herself right at home, becoming garrulously shrill by the minute to cover her embarrassment. Nodding a greeting to Uncle Shahid, she seated her bulky frame in between him and Dadi on the same sofa and asked what was so wrong with Dadi's health after she left in such a hurry after such an exciting announcement.

Uncle Shahid looked thoroughly embarrassed and perplexed and looked as if he wanted to make a hasty exit. He was prevented from doing so when Qurrat, ever the inclusive hostess even when she was in someone else's home, accosted this unknown gentleman in order that he may not feel neglected.

'I ask you,' exclaimed Qurrat, looking at Uncle Shahid, 'what am I, Gulbahar Bibi's closest living relative, supposed to think when she announces my Zeba's engagement, and that, too, when I'm preparing to introduce her to a matchmaker? And then she says she is dizzy and leaves so soon that I, too, am left behind and puzzled! Gulbahar Bibi, this is what happens when you keep secrets from your sister. No wonder you feel frail, keeping such a big announcement to yourself for all this time. But I wonder . . .' and Qurrat's eyes narrowed in suspicion 'what made you leave the dholki so soon? And why did you not tell anyone about the boy? After all, we are all well-wishers. We, too, want to know where our Zeba is betrothed. I'm calling and calling and your daughter-in-law keeps telling me you are ill, but you are fine! If you ask me . . .' Uncle Shahid was addressed once again, 'there is something fiiisshhyy goooinnggg oooonnnn!!'

Qurrat shook her head rhythmically to the melody of her

voiced suspicion. Dadi, whose head was probably throbbing for real this time, was dumbstruck. She could not announce Zeba's engagement because Uncle Shahid had not delivered a formal proposal. Yet Qurrat had managed to corner her in a manner so untimely that there was no getting out of this imbroglio without looking like a kitten cornered by a salivating wolf or a salivating bear.

A stricken silence prevailed. Zeba Baji looked like she wanted to throttle Qurrat. Omer's face was contorted with suppressed laughter. Uncle Shahid cleared his throat and Qurrat looked at him inquiringly.

'Arey, do forgive me, Bhai! Here I am barging in here unannounced without even introducing myself. My name is Qurrat and I am . . . well, you can call me Zeba's second grandmother, isn't that right, Zeba Beti?'

Zeba Baji bared her teeth and Qurrat apparently took it for a smile.

'And you are?' she asked the man cringing beside her on the sofa.

'My name is Shahid Khan and I'm . . .' he paused and took the cue from the vigorous nodding of Dadi's head: 'I . . . I'm Zeba's future father-in-law! Yes, yes, we are here to ask for Zeba's hand in marriage.'

Qurrat was dumbstruck. But then a thought occurred to her.

'But if you are here to give a proposal today, then how come Gulbahar Bibi announced the engagement yesterday?'

Shahid Uncle was taken aback. Dadi threw him a helpless look.

'Did I say I was here to ask for Zeba's hand in marriage? I meant to celebrate the engagement! Ha ha! Yes, today we are celebrating my son and Zeba's betrothal . . . and . . .' he looked at Dadi who nodded her head vigorously in encouragement, 'and we came here with sweetmeats!! Yes, sweetmeats! What a good idea! How about it Hussain? Let's distribute some sweets to celebrate this grand occasion! Qurrat Jee, you will partake of some laddoos, will you not?'

We were all galvanized into action. Saima Apa rushed into the kitchen to get a pair of scissors while Haroon Bhai tried in vain to make himself useful by tearing at the basket's plastic with his bare hands. When that failed, he yelled for a knife, not seeing that his wife was already handing him the scissors. He proceeded to slash away at the plastic to get at the boxes of laddoos. Then he opened one and opened his mouth to feed himself. Ammi scolded him and told him to feed his future brother-in-law first. Haroon Bhai seemed to recover his senses, let out an embarrassed laugh and proceeded to feed a laddoo to Omer, then Uncle Shahid, then Abbu and finally Dadi. When Ammi offered one to Qurrat, she declined.

'Gives me indigestion, you see,' she explained as she scanned Omer with razor-sharp eyes. 'Mashallah, what a handsome boy you've found for your granddaughter, Gulbahar Bibi! What is your name, Beta?'

We all became very still. What's in a name, you ask? Ah, for us conservative Shia Bandians, therein lay the rub!

'My name is . . .'

'Did I mention to you that he is a doctor? Trained in

patheticology in Amreeka!' interjected Dadi frantically.

'Yes Gulbahar Bibi, you did. But what is his name is what
I would like to know.'

'His name, Qurrat Khala, is Omer,' calmly declared Fati
Phupps, still seated across the room with her legs crossed
and her arm resting on the sofa's back.

Dadi let out a short gasp. The secret was out. The Breach
of Tradition had been exposed.

Qurrat couldn't seem to believe it. She repeated Omer's
name softly at first, as if her tongue was unused to the name.
Then a little loudly, seeking confirmation from Fati Phupps
if indeed, this was the name of Zeba's fiancé.

'Ahh . . . *Omer*,' as if the import of what this meant struck
her for the first time. 'I seeee . . . And how did you and Zeba
meet, my boy?'

Omer realized that he was treading on dangerous territory
and looked to Zeba Baji for help. She came to his rescue.

'We met in Islamabad at a conference.'

'Ooohhhh . . . at a confereeencee! I seeeee . . .'

Shahid Uncle looked perplexed, wondering what exactly
Qurrat saw. Dadi, however, attempted to put an immediate
end to this incriminating interrogation.

'Shahid Sahib, before we were so suddenly interrupted, I
was going to offer you my congratulations and best wishes
and express how happy I am that our two families have now
become one! I hope that Zeba makes you and Omer very
happy and you find in her a loving and caring daughter!'

Shahid Uncle looked slightly taken aback by the
suddenness of this passionate proclamation.

'Er . . . likewise, I too would like to congratulate you . . . um . . . ah . . . and Zeba upon this . . . engagement, which took place before yesterday . . .'

Dadi gave him a thankful look and glared at Qurrat who was observing Zeba and Omer speculatively.

Poor Uncle Shahid seemed quite perplexed because a lot seemed to have happened without anything being said. He seemed to sense tension between Qurrat and Dadi, but could not quite put his finger on what had caused this change between them. Of course, the rest of us could see perfectly well that the rising hostility came from the new status quo where Qurrat was beginning to gloat and Dadi's irritation was changing into silent rage at having her plan to secure a formal proposal sabotaged by Her Inquisitiveness, who, no doubt, could not wait to tell all and sundry about Omer and his Sunni ways and the non-arranged marriage of Zeba Bandian.

Dadi looked highly displeased but focused her ire on stuffing lots of chalia in a betel leaf and offering it to Qurrat with the intention of making her choke on the bitter stuff. Perhaps some of it could stick in her throat so she couldn't breathe so she could be hauled off to a hospital for some surgery where they would hopefully slit her throat? Unfortunately for Dadi, Qurrat declined the offer of the paan and continued to give Zeba and Omer the self-satisfied Smile of the Double Chin, revealing her not-so-secret malicious pleasure. Her chin almost touched her throat, rendering an impressive quadruple chin.

Omer, cowed down by Qurrat and overwhelmed by what

was not being said, signalled to his father that it was time they left. Uncle Shahid got up immediately. He was probably eager to get out and leave the awkwardness of this situation behind him.

Zeba Baji's future family was escorted out of the room by our entire family, barring myself, Qurrat and Dadi. We exchanged goodbyes and promises to meet again very soon. I opted to stay with Dadi in order to prevent her from launching a physical assault on Qurrat. I also wanted to see how she would handle the questions to be put her way by Qurrat.

'Wah wah, Gulbahar Bibi! Announcing the engagement but not announcing that it was a love marriage! And to a Sunni at that! No wonder all our questions made you dizzy.'

'No, you are right; we've never had a Sunni marry into our family before. African American Christian, yes, but no Sunni. Tell me, is Desireè Catholic or Protestant?'

Qurrat's eyes flashed with ire.

'Mariam has read the kalma! She is a Shia Muslim just like the rest of us.'

'Acha? Is that why she celebrates Christmas and eats pork?'

'She does not eat pork!'

'Arey Bhai, how am I to know? I merely asked your grandson what his favourite dish is and he said, "ham sandwich".'

Resentful silence. Followed by the counterstrike . . .

'But tell me, Gulbahar Bibi, how it is possible in *your* household that a girl goes behind your back to marry a Sunni boy for love! It goes against everything our elders have stood for! In my case, what was I supposed to do? My son was in the States when he met Mariam and married her. But here, in Karachi, right under your very nose! Maybe you should have spent more time paying attention to your granddaughters than your prayer beads, and this situation would have been averted!'

'What situation are you referring to, Qurrat Khala?' asked Fati Phupps as she returned to the drawing room, soon followed by the rest of the family with Zeba Baji at the end of the procession.

Qurrat looked warily at Fati Phupps and prudently chose not to elaborate. Zeba Baji, paying no heed whatsoever to Qurrat's presence, knelt down and enveloped Dadi in a great big bear hug and whispered: 'Thank you Dadi!' into her ear.

Dadi teared up and returned the hug with equal fervour, letting out a noise that sounded suspiciously like a sob. They remained in each other's arms for a while, overcome with emotion, their antagonism finally ended. Qurrat snorted her impatience and announced that she was leaving. She had had quite enough excitement for one night.

Ammi and Abbu offered to drive Qurrat back home, and she accepted. When they left, I launched into a bhangra in order to express my excitement at another upcoming wedding, especially as this time I would be the centre of attention as the bride-to-be's younger and only sister. Dadi shook her head and declared that I had lost mine. She turned to Fati Phupps and vented her ire at Qurrat.

'Daring to come to my house and taunting me about *my* granddaughter! I tell you, everyone is jealous of our family!

They see us happy and give us the evil eye! Which reminds me, Zeba, tell Omer to burn some spices around his head. I can't have him dying now that he is going to marry you!'

'How very kind of you Amma!' exclaimed Fati Phupps drily. 'No, I can't imagine why Qurrat would interfere like that in our concerns. Could it be because you interfered in hers when her son married Mariam?'

'Arey wah! What did *I* do? I merely offered a shoulder to cry on!'

'Amma, creating a hysterical scene in her house and offering your condolences for all her lost future generations is hardly offering a shoulder to cry on!'

'I do not recall doing anything of the kind!' said Dadi. 'Hai, Zeba, you *had* to go and choose a Sunni boy! Now what am I going to say to people? They find out about his sect and they will know it's a love marriage!'

'Well, dealing with Qurrat wasn't so bad was it, Dadi?' asked Zeba Baji.

'If that is the kind of reaction I will get from all my relatives, then I am going to have a heart attack before the week is out! No, no Baba, I cannot take all this tension. Fatima, you are here for another two weeks—you answer all the questions that are going to come our way once Qurrat has finished blabbering out her version to the world. Everyone is scared of you. They will not harass you!'

'Uff, Amma, they won't harass you either; just stop looking so ashamed when Omer's name is mentioned! The truth is that you have a very resourceful granddaughter who's found herself a loving man who promises to make her very happy. That's what you shall tell people!'

'Stop being so simplistic, for heaven's sake! They will ask how they met and I will say in Islamabad. Then they will assume that Zeba will have dated-shated and they would be right. And my head will bow down with shame! A Shia, Syed girl of Bandian ancestry dating! It's a scandal! Why, a woman only has two things in this society: her ability to bear sons and her reputation! Zeba's reputation will be what? She will be labelled "fast" and what will happen then? Qurrat's probably blabbering about it right now, telling everyone!'

'What nonsense, Amma! What is "fast"? And in any case, if such a category exists, I'd rather be labelled fast than slow! And, by the way, as I've learned in the fashion world, it's not a scandal if you don't act scandalized.'

Dadi thought about it for a moment. To treat this as a normal occurrence would be highly hypocritical of her, indeed. But being hypocritical was infinitely more preferable than being ashamed, or having people think that she was embarrassed by Zeba Baji's match. Pride made hypocrisy an acceptable option. But all these matters were too much for Dadi. Her granddaughter was engaged and that was that, and questions would be dealt with tomorrow. She needed to go and pray, she said, to thank God for Zeba's new affianced status and to fervently pray that Omer would change his name and convert to Shiaism.

Chapter Eighteen

How Things Came to Pass

Qurrat Dadi really did work fast. The news of Zeba's Sunni Suitor and fiancé filled her with a demonic frenzy that manifested itself into a frenetic storm of gossip and scandal. She went and told Momina Phuppi, who told Bano Auntie, who told Baji Naveeda's husband, who promptly printed the news in the *Bandian Gazette*—a newsletter started by Bhakurajians in Pakistan to let the extended community know about births, deaths and O and A Level results of other Bandian relatives. Of late it had increased its repertoire to include announcements of engagements, marriages and the acquisition of new jobs and positions achieved by the Bandian youth. The proclamation concerning Zeba was worded thus: 'Heartiest Felicitations to One Zeba Bandian, upon her engagement to pathologist Omer Khan, whom she met at a hotel in Islamabad not long ago. May she have the utmost happiness and bring pride to her parents and grandparents.' We later heard rumours that this notice had been dictated to Baji Naveeda's husband by Qurrat herself.

With such an announcement, it was to be expected that our house would be besieged by well-wishers wanting in on the scoop. Most had been informed by Qurrat that Zeba and Omer had dated and even lived together at a hotel in Islamabad before getting engaged. They were also aware that he was unadulterated Sunni, not a drop of Shia blood to redeem him. Apa Kulsoom, an avid reader of the *Gazette*, came with balooshahis and tried to get a rise out of Dadi by asking all kinds of questions, but saw that my grandmother was quite unamused; thus they desisted from any further attempts to extract some more juice out of this opportunity.

Apa Kulsoom was followed by a myriad of relatives, all bearing glistening silver boxes of Sony Sweets. They descended upon our drawing room in hordes. Included in the visitors was Phuppo Falaq—whose daughters were insipid looking and therefore she had had considerable difficulty in securing good matches for them. Even though they were happily married, Phuppo Falaq bore a permanent grudge against all good-looking girls who, unlike her daughters, had proposals fall in their laps like ripe mangoes. The chip on her shoulder made itself especially heavy whenever Phuppo Falaq encountered my sister's good looks. She was therefore unwilling to let this opportunity, to grill my grandmother about her wayward granddaughter, go without a try.

So in walked the aforementioned relative, her resolve firm and her nose snubbed and her belly wobbling like jelly as she plunked herself on our sofa. Her limp hair was worn in

a loose bun with a middle parting that had slowly expanded
to colonize the entire top of her head, so that she was nearly
bald on top and looked like a Karate sensei, and she had a
thin moustache to boot. Underneath the facial hair was a pair
of lips permanently pursed in faint disapproval at the world
and God for not distributing favours where her daughters
were concerned. Her crane-like neck, which supported her
bowling ball of a head, swooped down at Dadi as she offered
her congratulations.

'A thousand good wishes to you, Gulbahar Khala! What
good fortune to have a grandson and granddaughter married
off within the space of a year! What good kismet you have!'

Dadi was quick to accept the wishes and took the
conversation by the wheel to steer it towards waters that
were not so choppy.

'Thank you, Falaq Beti. So kind of you to come. Would
you like some potato cutlets? No? Ulcers you say? What is
this ulcer-shulcer business in you young people? Look at me,
I am so old and I have never had an ulcer, not even after
bearing nine children, not even after losing two of them,
may Allah rest theirs and their father's souls!'

But Phuppo Falaq was not to be diverted with talk of
ulcus pepticum.

'No, no, I am fine! Just have to rest the stomach for a few
moments, have just had pao bhaji and halwa for lunch. In
fact, if you don't mind, I think I shall have a cigarette: helps
loosen up the bowels, you know,' and she reached into her
bosom from her neckline, took out a packet of Goldsmith
from her bra and asked for a lighter. Dadi, who was quite

used to smoking as it was very common for the women of Bhakuraj to give their husbands company (as, very often, cigarettes were the *only* thing husbands had in common with their wives), offered her a matchbox without blinking an eye.

Swirls of smoke framed her face in gentle curls and Phuppo Falaq's beady eyes zeroed in on Dadi as she began the interrogation.

'But Gulbahar Khala, how did all this happen?'

'Arey, Allah smiled on us the day Zeba Beti went to Islamabad. You know these teachers nowadays are just like businessmen, they have their workshops waghaira as well. So there they met, of course, and it just sort of happened from there.'

But Phuppo Falaq was not satisfied.

'Yes but *how* did it happen is what I would like to know! Respectable Bandian girls exchanging numbers with strangers in hotels in foreign cities . . . it doesn't really happen in our family. And what meetings too! Much must have happened for them to continue talking even when they returned to Karachi!'

Dadi should have smacked the mustachioed grin that was forming on Phuppo Falaq's pompous face but, in their generation, there existed a tacit understanding that it was perfectly permissible for one relative to intrude shamelessly into the affairs of the other. After all, Dadi herself had done it a countless number of times. The law of survival was to endure the questioning with as much insouciance as one could feign. So Dadi endured this violation of privacy and decency as she continued with her Oscar-worthy performance of blithe composure.

'Arey Falaq, you do not know how many young men chase after pretty girls. It is not an experience you have had, I understand, so I think you should let me explain to you what it is like to be the grandmother of such beautiful young women. And Omer has such good taste! You should see their house—one does not expect that a home without a woman would be decorated so well! And the engagement ring he has given to my Zeba! Mashallah, mashallah, may Allah protect her from the evil eye, it is the biggest diamond I've ever seen! Almost as big as a potato!'

And then began Dadi's Introduction to Omer which ran like a mantra since she had had so much practice repeating the same words to whoever came to 'wish us well'.

'So handsome he is! And so tall! And he makes close to 5,00,000 a month! And that is just his beginning salary; he has a long way to go, if Allah permits! My Zeba will live like a queen. Owns his own house too, none of that rent-shent business. No mother whatsoever to speak of; very sad but very convenient for Zeba, wouldn't you say?'

But of course, even a skilled conversationalist like my grandmother who knew the art of diverting discourse in whatever direction she liked could not evade questions about what motivated her to accept such a controversial match. Falaq Phuppo was also not to be deterred as she said, 'But Khala, a Sunni!'

However, after careful reflection and a few sleepless nights Dadi had managed to come up with a justification.

'Oh ho! He's a poor motherless boy. He's coming into a staunch Shia family. Who knows, maybe he will convert in the future? I'm telling Zeba to take him to all the family majalis in Moharram. Bas, in my heart I'm sure that eventually, he will want to be a part of our sect. It has been known to happen. And because Zeba will be the only female influence in that house, she will determine how her children will be brought up, what they will believe in. In a way, I'm doing a good deed, spreading the truth of the message of our Shiaism into a house where no one has even heard of the story of Imam Hussain! Imagine how many sawabs Zeba will earn once she convinces Omer to start praying with his hands on his sides rather than folded on his navel. I have no doubt it will happen: a woman's influence is not to be undermined. Now if his mother had been alive, it would have been another matter. But she is not. So that is that!'

But what about the love-shove part of it? Phuppo desperately grilled. Had Zeba really dated-shated?

'A couple of meetings in crowded places! Hardly qualifying as a date you know! Hai hai, I just read in the paper the other day that a boy and a girl had been apprehended in the parking lot of a hospital, doing, you know, *things* in his car! Her blouse was unbuttoned when the police intervened! The Day of Judgement is approaching fast, I tell you! If that is the kind of thing people do on dates nowadays, then certainly, my Zeba did *not* date at all!'

'But Qurrat said that they knew each other from a hotel in Islamabad,' countered the indefatigable Falaq.

'Arey, bechari Qurrat! She's still smarting from the blow her son delivered to her when he told her he was marrying that Desireè. Now I ask you, how many hotels would *they* have visited, if you know what I mean? Can you blame her for thinking that *all* children do what her son did to her? It isn't her fault. I tell you, my heart bleeds for her. She's so fair and her grandchildren are so dark! My mother, Allah bless her soul, used to tell me that Qurrat was snow-white when she was born and her mother used to bathe her in pure cow's milk till she was six months old! What is the point of such fair skin when your grandchildren are going to be black as sin, just tell me that?'

At this point, Phuppo Falaq gave up and Dadi successfully directed the conversation on to her daughters and their husbands and how many offspring they had managed to produce; a topic that, of course, was delved into deeply and eagerly by Madam Inquisition. Zeba Baji was soon forgotten.

As Fati Phupps had predicted, such open support to the match resulted in a general loss of interest. Several relatives came in with the Smile of the Double Chin, only to leave with the Bored Look of the Spaced Eye because they could not detect in Dadi's attitude even an iota of embarrassment or outrage. In fact, Dadi was so stellar in her performance of the proud, beaming grandmother that no one really wanted to ask her about her previous condemnation of any subversive deviations from the Arranged Way of Life.

The performance that Dadi gave day after day for over a month after the grand announcement at Naureen's dholki took its toll on her. Pretending that she was happy with the Sunni that Zeba had chosen for herself violated her most basic principles of life and left her exhausted. In public, she praised her future grandson-in-law to the skies. In private, she lamented that the Bhakurajian Bandian code of conduct had been brutally breached by none other than her own cherished granddaughter right under her very nose. She often expressed to me how glad she was that her mother and grandmother were not alive to see how she had been tricked by an evil, malicious, envious opponent into sanctioning a match that was not only not traditional but religiously condemnable as well. I often walked into her room to find her praying fervently on her prayer beads, praying for Omer's immediate conversion to Shiaism to vindicate some of her actions in the eyes of her deceased ancestors. She had a photograph of my great-grandmother beside her bed and Dadi made a regular practice of asking God to bless her soul before going to bed and her mother for forgiveness for having gone against the sacred dictates of Arrangedness and Shiaism, which henceforth would no longer be considered inviolable. One exemption from the rule ensured that the possibility of other love marriages had become real. I was continuously lectured about the merits of modesty, of marrying a maatham-ing husband whom my parents had chosen for me. Ordinarily I would have rebelled by shaving some part of my anatomy but since I knew it was Dadi's way of reassuring herself that all was not lost and that I presented some hope of the Reassertion of the Bandian Order if the Correct Way of Life was reiterated to me, I forbore with considerable fortitude and teeth permanently gnashed.

If Omer had hoped that Dadi would warm to him, he was sorely mistaken. She was never rude to him; he was a future son-in-law and that role merited respect to protect the future of Zeba's marital life. Dadi was not one to put Zeba's relationship with her future husband in jeopardy. She treated him with cool reserve. He was the jackdaw that had stolen her prime jewel from under her very nose. She felt tricked, duped, bitterly bamboozled. She returned his greeting with a dignified nod and wished him a long life, but her countenance assumed a faraway dreamy pose, as if his presence did not concern her. Omer was not offered a single betel leaf from Dadi's paan-dan. She treated all of us to orange ice lollies . . . after Omer had left for his house. She treated Uncle Shahid with the greatest courtesy because of his face-saving tactics when Qurrat had gatecrashed the eve of the proposal. But Omer was ignored as politely as possible.

As far as brothers-in-law went, Omer Bhai was pretty great. He treated me with amused affection and won me over to his side when he championed my cause and convinced Abbu to let me choose business-related subjects in A Levels instead of the three sciences. My father was disappointed that neither Haroon Bhai nor Zeba Baji had shown the slightest interest in becoming a doctor and had pinned his hopes on me. He had been browbeating me into becoming a doctor, a skin specialist in particular, and had appealed to Omer to reason with me.

'Tell her Omer, tell her how much money skin specialists make! Their patients are never cured, neither do they die; and they have a steady flow of desperate clientele! And she's a girl! She will get married and have a house of her own one day. A dermatologist can keep office hours and still make a decent living *and* manage a family. Tell her!'

Omer Bhai suggested that I should do whatever I chose because medicine was not something one should be pushed into if one was reluctant. My hero! Abbu was disappointed that his son-in-law-to-be had not championed his cause, but got over it soon enough once Omer Bhai convinced him that commerce, too, had a lucrative side with convenient hours, should I get married.

Haroon Bhai, generally affable and easy-going, liked Omer well enough. Ammi grew very fond of him and to my mother he fast became the son that she had lost to Saima Apa.

It was decided that Omer should be introduced to the family in a formal engagement when rumours that we were ashamed of Omer were being spread by a certain jealous relative—how we thought Zeba had brought Shame upon the Family Honour which was why there was no formal function; how all the proceedings had taken place in such a hush-hush manner. Dadi was appalled at how correctly Qurrat had interpreted her actions and therefore took immediate steps to create the opposite impression. On the eve of the engagement, no one was more doting, loving, proud and gushing than my grandmother who waved hundred-rupee notes (another strategy of bribing the evil eye to go and affect some other hapless individual) round the heads of Zeba and Omer and kissed her granddaughter and patted her future grandson-in-law on the back in front of all and sundry, posing several times for photographs while she was at it. Qurrat sulked through the entire function, smiling only when Naureen made her glittering entrance as the new bride, resplendent in diamonds and expensive shalwar-kameez provided by her wealthy new husband.

Shahid Uncle expressed his wish of getting Omer and Zeba married as soon as humanly possible. He wasn't getting any younger and the couple didn't have any work or academic obligations to delay the marriage. Abbu and Ammi were of the same opinion, but Dadi was taken aback by this particular development. She complained that she needed more time; she was only getting used to the idea of Zeba's love-engagement, she wasn't ready for a love-wedding, for God's sake! But Ammi, in deference to Uncle Shahid's (and Zeba's and Omer's) wishes, convinced her not to delay the Event. It would take three months to prepare for the wedding, what with clothes and furniture and all; that would give Dadi enough time to get used to the idea.

Dadi was rebellious but could not say no to Uncle Shahid, which is what Abbu suggested she would have to do since he had already given his word to Omer's father. She complained bitterly about no one caring for her feelings even though she had worked so hard to salvage the family honour by valiantly giving one performance after the next about how she considered this match to be the most brilliant one in the world. As the weeks flew past and preparations for Zeba's wedding hurtled along at supersonic speed, she assumed the role of the poor mother whose son and granddaughter had been appropriated by evil love-mongering Sunnis and how she would never get any of them back.

Dadi had a peculiar custom of lighting a candle on the day of Fareed Chaccha's death and placing it at her window. She used to say that he was not dead; rather he was trying to find his way back to her after having realized the error of his ways and the unsuitability of the scarlet-lipped Sunni who had entrapped him. But this year, when his death anniversary approached, no candle was lit. I asked her whether she'd forgotten that this was the day he had disappeared. Dadi merely said, 'He's dead. He died in the '71 war. Don't mention it again.' After which she burst out crying, her frail body heaving with heart-wrenching sobs. Zeba Baji hugged her and Dadi clung on to her, telling my sister not to leave her like her Fareed had.

Dadi grieved for the remainder of the two months that were left for Zeba's wedding, but that was not to say she remained uninvolved in the wedding preparations. She insisted that Ammi provide bedroom furniture to her daughter—it was the Way of the Bandians. She reminded us of the Mishap of the Floor Mat and advised us to prepare against any similar calamities from befalling my beloved sister. This mishap occurred when the unfortunate Banoji, daughter of the austere Hajjan Baba, was betrothed to Nawaz Mian of the adjacent Najpur village. Her mother had planned the grandest dowry that Bhakuraj had ever seen, included in which was a grand bed whose legs were made of solid gold. Nawaz Mian's family got wind of the proposed ornate furnishings and stripped his room of everything except a floor mat to make room for the grand new additions. However, it so happened that Banoji's ultra-religious father deemed all the preparations frivolous and forbade them. Banoji was sent to her in-laws with nothing but the clothes on her back. Her in-laws were outraged at having been short-changed in this

manner and declared that she should share her husband's
floor mat. Banoji, who had been accustomed to the softest of
mattresses for her slumber, spent an uncomfortable fortnight
on the floor with her unaffected husband who thought it
was completely natural to mount his bride repeatedly on the
hard floor. She bore it as well as she could, then fled to her
mother's home, pregnant and sore backed, vowing never to
return. Nawaz Mian, who found it a blessing to be free of
his wife's constant complaining, readily accepted and even
encouraged the new arrangement, visiting his wife every
month to perform his husbandly duties and then returning to
Najpur to manage his affairs, both business and extramarital.

Dadi was determined to save Zeba from a fate similar to her
unfortunate ancestor. She also stitched two ghararas for my
sister with her own hands, lovingly folded them in the finest
silk and put them in Zeba's suitcase, ordering her to wear
them in the first week of her marriage as befitted a new bride.
Despite the fact that Uncle Shahid loudly protested against
any dowry, Dadi made Abbu buy a flat-screen television, an
air conditioner, a microwave, a fridge, freezer, pots and pans,
crockery, cutlery, dinner set, tea set, linen and God knows
what else to give to my sister. When Abbu objected, Dadi
said, in front of Saima Apa, that this was how respectable
girls got married if they wanted to hold their heads up high
in front of their in-laws. Uncle Shahid was reported to have
thrown a fit when two Suzukis filled with Zeba's dowry
unloaded carton upon carton on his front lawn. What was
he supposed to do with all the things he already had? He
couldn't very well throw away his own air conditioners now,

could he? He called Ammi and said that he was returning everything, but Dadi intervened and begged him to accept this 'small' contribution that they were making for their daughter. In the end, a compromise was reached whereby the larger electronic equipment, for which there was no space in the house, was returned to us and the rest of the cartons were locked away in a store room for Zeba Baji's future use.

The time came to recruit a Shia cleric to read the nikkah. Dadi approached the family maulana and asked him if he was ready to marry Zeba to an 'O.S. Khan'. He said he would be happy to, but would need the boy's full name. Dadi stalled for several days, pretending to forget what it was. She asked him to do an istikhara for her, based on his initials and his height and age. He insisted it was not possible to do one without the full name but she coaxed him into it, telling him that she was sure he could manage with his spiritual prowess. He called back to say that he had had a dream with positive connotations. A triumphant Dadi thereby told him Omer's full name in a bid to convince him to read the nikkah without objecting to the groom's Sunni status. This revelation was met with much irritation on the part of the maulana who declared that the meaning of the istikhara only applied to an exclusively Shia couple and was now to be considered null and void in the case of Omer and Zeba. Dadi was beside herself with grief. The maulana consoled her and asked her if the boy would become Shia. Then the marriage could be blessed. Dadi said that in her heart of hearts, she was convinced that he would see the error of his ways once he had been around our Shia-ness for a few years.

With that, the maulana was reluctantly persuaded to agree to conduct the ceremony.

Once again, relatives arrived en masse to attend the wedding, barring Haseena Phuppo who was still convinced that she would be the victim of a target shooting the minute she set foot outside Jinnah Airport. She was represented once again by Hassan Bhai who took a week off from work to attend his favourite cousin's wedding. Zainab Phuppo also arrived, this time without her sons and coldly congratulated Zeba Baji and privately asked Ammi if Omer was the reason Zeba had repeatedly rejected her darling son. Ammi lied and said she had no idea and hugged her peeved sister-in-law and suggested that she let bygones be bygones.

Rania Phuppo arrived without Robs and Maw, thankfully; they were too busy with exams and internships to spare time to come to Pakistan and their mother felt wretched that they had to be left behind. Naima arrived and we were delighted not to have two overdressed, overdeveloped cousins to be compared to.

Zeba Baji's clothes formed the familial highlight of the summer season. No less than thirty relatives came to see what had been stitched for my sister the night before we were to shift her belongings to Omer's house. Dadi proudly displayed the customary fifty-five outfits to gaping onlookers. Old Indian saris, made of the finest silk and Banarasi zari, had been lovingly packed in glittering silver boxes. Designer shoes and bags were packed in five separate containers, but Dadi insisted on unpacking them on public request so that they could be shown off. Each Phuppo and one Khala had provided an expensive gold jewellery set as wedding present to Zeba Baji and these too were put on display, each one grander than the next. Almost all the stones were represented: sapphires, rubies, opals and amethysts, but no diamonds. Dadi, who had gone perverted in public again, declared that Zeba would have to earn herself a diamond set after her wedding night, if you knew what she meant. Sakina Phuppo was rather miffed that the set that she had purchased was smaller than Malaika Phuppo's even though it had been more expensive. Malaika Phuppo suggested that she had been cheated by the jeweller and Sakina Phuppo all but made to march off with it to Sadar to demand a refund. She was advised to do no such thing by my mother who indicated that she would not be humoured and that her set was solid gold while Malaika's was hollow, Indian style. That explanation assuaged Sakina Phuppo's ruffled sensibilities.

Each item of clothing was waved about by Dadi for general perusal by all who inhabited the living room in a display of extravagance which did much to raise our esteem in the family's eyes. Naima and I were made to carry each jora for close inspection to each onlooker, much to my mortification. As soon as we got up to comply with Dadi's dictum that I had better oblige or face disownment, the women burst into a wail-like song to the effect of:

'The hoors from heaven descend with beautiful clothes for the bride!'

This sparked off a jealous interjection from my a-tad-bit-competitive Rania Phuppo who said that the real hoors were too busy studying for their exams in Bombay, but oh well, these hoors would have to do.

The wedding functions that followed were nothing more than a display of wealth, so necessary for the maintenance of the girl's respectability in the eyes of her in-laws. There was a painful milad, followed by a festive mehndi and a tearful nikkah. Dadi clasped Zeba Baji's shoulders and prevented her from saying 'I do' the first and second times as befitted her modest upbringing. She was thoroughly ruffled when, on the third question, Zeba Baji let out a loud and clear 'Yes!' instead of a faint whisper, and thwacked her on the head in admonishment, after which she clasped her granddaughter and wailed inconsolably.

Zeba Baji went to a famous make-up artist, accompanied by Fati Phupps and me for moral support. This person was an extremely loud and aggressive individual who seemed to suffer from an attention deficit disorder, so distracted was she because her receptionist had managed to book five brides in the space of one hour. Zeba Baji was lined up with four other dazed-looking individuals, all hoping that their face would not suffer from this mistake of mass production.

She came home looking like a drag queen, complete with dramatic green eyes, orange cheeks and red lips and her hair mounted high, resembling the structure of the Sydney Opera House. She took one look at herself in the mirror—she had not been allowed to do so at the salon—salon policy she had been told—and promptly burst into tears. She washed off her face, which by the way, had cost her about Rs 30,000 to put on, and did her own make-up and looked far lovelier. Dadi sobbed like a baby when we left home for the hotel where the wedding reception was to take place, knowing that she would return without Zeba Baji.

The rest of the family was far too preoccupied to be saddened; there were too many things to be taken care of. Abbu growled that we were horribly late and that it was very rude for guests to arrive at the function before the hosts. When we got there, Zeba was carted away for a photography session where a thin-mustachioed, paunch-bellied, bleach-haired photographer made her assume all kinds of ridiculous poses. He asked her to put her hand on her forehead in a kind of salute and look far into the distance, as if she were waiting for her heart's desire to come and rescue her. Then he wanted her to look adoringly at an empty chair and hold it with both her hands, as if she were holding her beloved. She was made to stand with her back to the camera but turn her head to look at it, then he sat her down and made her look up at the camera, after which he lay down on the floor and made her look up at him. He did this in all earnestness, inspiring Zeba Baji by commenting that she looked like a mix between Madhuri Dixit and Rani Mukherjee. She might have looked nice had she not started laughing hysterically at him and he was quite upset that she was not cooperating. Fati Phupps didn't help matters by pretending to be Omer and locking Zeba in one passionate embrace after another for the photographer's benefit. He was *not* amused and almost stomped off in a fury. He was placated by Haroon Bhai who convinced him not to take the 'standard' poses which were 'in demand' these days but to focus on conventional poses where people just stood and smiled at the camera. The photographer was highly unimpressed by our lack of adventure in this regard but complied nevertheless.

The time came for Zeba Baji to leave with Omer for her new house and it struck me that my sister was going away for good. She would spend her nights somewhere else. Her room next to mine would be permanently empty. She would visit our house and live somewhere else. It didn't feel right. As she got up from the stage, under the shelter of the Quran that Haroon Bhai carried over her head, I couldn't control my tears. Naima saw me and started making fun of me, telling me I was a sissy. Five minutes later, she burst out crying as well. Hassan Bhai trailed behind us, telling us to get a hold of ourselves and not to be stupid, but I heard his voice thicken with emotion and realized he too was not as unaffected as he was pretending to be.

Omer's car was adorned with roses and floral decorations. Zeba Baji paused before she got in and hugged all of us, crying softly. She clasped Ammi hard and her shoulders heaved with emotion. But it was Dadi who stole the show, holding on to my sister for dear life and refusing to let her go as Zeba Baji bid her final goodbye. Two, three, five minutes passed and Uncle Shahid tapped his cane impatiently and looked at his watch. A sombre Abbu tried to detach Dadi from Zeba Baji but to no avail. Dadi held on and wailed loudly. Things were becoming painfully uncomfortable, what with Zeba Baji trying to detach herself from her emotional grandparent without revealing the struggle to the outside world. Fati Phupps bent into Dadi's ear and whispered something into her ear and Dadi let go immediately and all but shoved Zeba Baji in. The car drove away, taking Omer, Zeba and Uncle Shahid with it and leaving all of us sobbing in grief. It was a horrible experience and I hugged Saima Apa fiercely, finally understanding what she had gone through when she had left *her* home. At least Zeba Baji was going to an uncomplicated family with no women; Saima Apa had been coming into ours, with Dadi and Ammi and me! How she did it, I would never know.

As we reached home with a heavy heart, feeling horribly incomplete without our sister, I asked Fati Phupps what she had said to Dadi to make her let go of Zeba. Fati Phupps shrugged and said she had conveyed to Dadi what she had heard: Qurrat telling Naureen that Dadi didn't have the heart to let Zeba go to the infidels just yet.

~

It is infinitely easier, emotionally speaking of course, to say goodbye to a sister than to say hello to a sister-in-law. It is infinitely strange to be invited to a dinner party and have your sister arrive on her own and leave with someone else in another car. It is infinitely bizarre for her to say, a month into the wedding, that she wanted to go 'home' when we wanted her to spend the night. I felt betrayed, abandoned. She'd switched camps with the insinuating ease with which a snake sheds its skin.

I felt Zeba Baji's absence keenly. The day after the wedding was a depressing one, not just because Zeba Baji was not present but because Sakina Phuppo and Rania Phuppo got into a monstrous fight about the latter's inappropriate sense of dress at the wedding. Resplendent in a glittering, diamantes-studded bikini blouse with a see-through chiffon sari, Rania Phuppo had created quite a stir in the hearts and groins of men. Rania Phuppo retaliated by accusing her older sister of being a prude. Sakina Phuppo retorted that it was better to be a prude than a slut. The conflict remains unresolved to this day.

That Zeba Baji was deliriously happy with Omer was a fact that offered the rest of the family some consolation but not to me. Seeing her happily gallivanting all over town with her husband was like salt to my tender wound of separation. As a sister, I was struck with the ease of her transition and felt it my duty to show her, through some sulking, that one must show *some* sense of loyalty at least. Zeba Baji would laugh and hug me and kiss me when she arrived, dressed in her bari clothes, which had been lovingly hand-picked by Omer and Uncle Shahid. She was touched that two men who knew nothing whatsoever about clothes had actually gone through the trouble of venturing out into unknown territory, aka a women's clothing store, armed with the knowledge that Zeba Baji's favourite colour was blue. With the result that Zeba Baji had a dozen gorgeous outfits; all of them different shades of blue as father and son thought it best not to experiment too much in the realm of colour.

Two days after the valima, he flew her to Nairobi for a honeymoon. When I asked him why Nairobi, he said he wanted to watch the migration of the animals. I thought that it was highly unromantic, but Zeba Baji thought it was adorably unconventional. Haroon Bhai merely rolled his eyes and said Timbuktu was more unconventional than Nairobi. Zeba Baji declared there was always next year.

Back in Karachi, she visited extensively, every day in fact. Each day Dadi complained that she was forgetting what she looked like, so seldom did she see her. She attempted to persuade her to spend at least a few nights at our house. Zeba Baji would smile, hug her and then merrily return home with her husband in the evening. I shared Dadi's complaint for the first few months of the marriage, but Omer Bhai often took me out to have ice cream with them and I found some consolation in visiting Zeba's 'home' whenever our house began to seem too empty.

Events took an exciting turn when Saima Apa and Zeba Baji discovered that they both were pregnant within a week of each other. Saima Apa was first to get the news and Dadi responded with an 'It's about time!' When Zeba Baji discovered that she too would hear the pitter-patter of little feet eight months later, Dadi let out a horrified exclamation: 'So soon?!' In Dadi's estimation, a good, respectable girl waits for about three months to get knocked up; anything less is downright immodest! She promptly took up her prayer beads and wondered what speculations Qurrat would put forth *this* time, especially if the baby was born prematurely. As for the rest of us, we were ecstatic. I was going to become an aunt twice!

It was Saima Apa who went into premature labour and gave birth to a beautiful baby boy, named Fareed, who promptly became Dadi's reason for living. Zeba Baji became a mommy to a baby girl, perfectly formed, with light brown hair and blue eyes. Omer wanted to name his daughter Ayesha, but because Dadi almost had a heart attack at that suggestion, he decided to call her Sheherbano, after his deceased mother, instead. Dadi made plans to arrange a marriage between her great-grandchildren, to appropriate the Sunni entry back into the Shia stronghold where she belonged.

Life seemed perfect for a while. Dadi was extremely contented to coddle her grand- and great-grandchildren to her heart's desire. Her ice lolly funds came dangerously close to bankruptcy—even Omer was included once or twice, though her disappointment at his refusal to convert still persisted. But she could not contain her happiness at having her dearest progeny near her and often boasted to Qurrat about how she had no time to spare because she was thronged with family.

Several proposals came my way and many trolleys were wheeled in and out, but to no avail. Dadi remains present and continues to lecture me whenever I reject a suitor and console me when I get rejected. She has pinned her hopes on me to reassert the Way Of the Bandian after Zeba's dismantling of it.

After Zeba Baji's breach of tradition, five couples married outside the family for love. My sister is her generation's heroine and the previous generation's nightmare. Several cousins called Ammi accusingly when their daughters decided to marry men of their choice, some suitable, others unsuitable, on the pretext that if a conservative Bandian girl like Zeba was allowed to marry of her own accord, then why weren't *they*? Ammi often lent a sympathetic and apologetic ear and then advised them not to force their daughters to marry men they didn't like; it wasn't worth it.

Thus ended with Zeba Baji that unadulterated saga of marriages arranged and pre-planned. Whether I live up to Dadi's hope of re-establishing the time-honoured tradition, I do not know. I am still trying to find The One, while Dadi hopes that The One's mother succeeds in finding me. In the meanwhile, I sit with her in her room, giving her a massage and having her complain about how hard my hands are, as she continues to regale me with stories from Bhakuraj—about Chandni Jan, Banoji, Achan Mian, unfortunate Lallan and all those ancestors of mine who managed to get married Bandian style: correctly and modestly, living their lives the Arranged Way.

~

Acknowledgements

This book would not have been possible without the people who supported me through the entire process of writing it. My heartfelt thanks to Sameer Khan, my first reader and co-conspirator; to Musharraf Ali Farooqi who encouraged a total stranger and became her friend, mentor and inspiration; to my wonderful editor Robert Wyatt for his endless patience and encouragement; to my friend, neighbour and walking partner Afia Aslam for her keen eye for detail; to Somak Ghoshal and Chiki Sarkar and the team at Penguin India for their enthusiasm for my book; to Fatima Quraishi, Mahrukh Akram and Yusra Naqvi, my earliest readers and critics; to my brother and sisters for the laughter and the love and the teasing. Finally, my eternal gratitude to God for giving me my mother, the love of my life and my greatest inspiration.